SPI

Yolonda Brown did not think about begging. Begging never got her anywhere in all of her fourteen years. She begged when her father died seven years ago, and begged again when two years later her grandmother toppled over from heart failure into a sink full of dishes. Begging brought only a beating. Or worse—silence.

When he slapped her so hard blood squirted from her left eye, she knew she would die. And hers was not going to be an easy death. She fell against a wooden two-by-four in the half-finished house at Rudger's housing development on the edge of a small Mississippi town called Haven.

Through a veil of blood, she saw two white hands grab her shoulders. Her head snapped back and forth as the man shook her with the force of a crazed animal. Yolonda, affectionately known as Peachy Girl, bit back the hysterical urge to laugh, and she thought maybe this would be it—a fierce shaking and she would be allowed to wake up in the morning.

"This will teach you to threaten me!" he hollered.

"I didn't mean to . . ." she gurgled through blood and sobs.

He drew back his hand, slapped her again. Peachy Girl brought her hands to her face to wash away some of the blood, but only ended up smearing it into a crimson mask. So much blood she couldn't see, but she could taste and smell her own blood. She struggled into a crawling position, but the man kicked her until she fell onto her back. She passed out before the man reached down and slit her throat with a red Swiss army knife.

SPIRAL OF GUILT

Faye Snowden

Pinnacle Books
Kensington Publishing Corp.
http://www.pinnaclebooks.com

PINNACLE BOOKS are published by

Kensington Publishing Corp.
850 Third Avenue
New York, NY 10022

Pinnacle and the P logo Reg. U.S. Pat. & TM Off.

First Printing: October, 1999
10 9 8 7 6 5 4 3 2 1

Printed in the United States of America

Prologue

Peachy Girl did not think about begging. Begging never got her anywhere in all of her fourteen years. She begged when her father died seven years ago, and begged again when two years later her grandmother toppled over from heart failure into a sink full of dishes. Begging brought only a beating. Or worse: silence.

When he slapped her so hard that blood squirted from her left eye, she knew she would die. And hers was not going to be an easy death. She fell against a wooden two-by—four in the half–finished house at Rudger's housing development on the edge of a small Mississippi town called Haven. The pain in her head and eye didn't allow her the luxury of fainting—at least not yet. She staggered to her feet, and realized the sobbing she heard belonged to her.

Through a veil of blood, she saw two white hands grab her shoulders. Her head snapped back and forth as the man shook her with the force of a crazed animal. Peachy Girl bit back the hysterical urge to laugh, and she thought

maybe this would be it—a fierce shaking and she would
be allowed to wake up in the morning.

"This will teach you to threaten me!" he hollered.

"I didn't mean to . . ." she gurgled through blood and
sobs.

He drew back his hand, slapped her again. Her muddled
brain screamed *run* through the pain. She took what she
thought was a sure step backward, but the three–inch heels
she bought at the Payless in Vicksburg hampered her prog-
ress. She felt cool cement on her ankle, adding to the
chorus of pain. The man placed his palms on both of her
shoulders and pulled her up, forcing her to stand upright.

"Hurts, doesn't it?" he taunted.

Peachy Girl brought her hands to her face to wash away
some of the blood, but only ended up smearing it into a
crimson mask. So much blood she couldn't see, but she
could smell and taste her own blood and remember her
grandmother's stainless steel scissors.

Her grandmother kept those scissors in a black velvet
pouch. Before the woman died, Peachy Girl would take
the scissors out of the pouch, and touch them with the tip
of her tongue. She loved the metallic taste then, but she
hated it now. Blood must have been on those scissors, she
thought stupidly.

The man pushed Peachy Girl with all of his might. She
fell backwards, landing on her butt. She skidded across
the gutless room and slammed into beams which separated
the would–be family room from the bathroom.

She struggled into a crawling position, but the man
kicked her until she fell onto her back. Through the blood,
she imagined she saw midnight stars raining through the
frame of what would someday be a roof. When she noticed
the moon, fat and full in the velvet sky, she considered
her tombstone as an icy calm settled over her.

Her mother would only let Mr. Malcom carve it. He had

been carving tombstones for the folks in the Bottoms of Haven, Mississippi for over fifty years. She and her cousins would sometimes go to watch his fluid but knurled hands chisel names into the marble.

But this time, moonlight and blood revealed her own name flowing from Mr. Malcom's chisel: Yolonda Brown, Born June 5th, 1981, died August 6th, 1995. She passed out before the man reached down and slit her throat with a red Swiss army knife.

Chapter 1

While Yolonda Brown lay dying on cool cement in a gutless house in Haven, Mississippi, Sidney Adamson Mc-Calaster and her husband Julian walked into their Crystal City condo in Virginia. Sidney's heels sank into the white carpet as she stepped off the tile entryway. Julian followed as she continued through the living room. He whistled the same song the blues singer had sung at the Farrington's dinner party, "Too Much Sugar for a Dime."

Sidney walked up the dark, metal staircase which spiraled into their loft bedroom. Looking over her left shoulder, she saw Julian take off his tuxedo jacket and throw it on the curving cream sofa. The white shirt molded his upper torso as if it were made for him—and it should have, because it was. He ran his fingers through his curly hair, and walked behind the bar. He took a bottle of expensive scotch from the glass shelves, then paused, returning her gaze. When their eyes met, he smiled beautifully, and winked.

Sidney would have felt special if she had not seen him flash that same straight–toothed smile and wink at a half dozen women tonight. She continued up the stairs, the hem of her white backless dress grazing the dark metal steps.

In the bedroom, Sidney tugged at the back of her neck until the metallic silver collar gave way. She pulled the dress halfway down to her waist. She studied her reflection in the frameless mirror on the dresser designed by a woman who called her furniture 'pieces' and charged outrageous prices. She paused as she stared at her own reflection as if looking into the face of a stranger. Her creamy brown skin told the story of a mixed heritage. In her case, a black mother and a white father. She found her eyes in the mirror. When she was little she used to pretend they were brown. But in reality, they were gray, and very large in her small, square face. She ran her index finger along the bridge of her nose. She had always thought it was too short and too straight for her face. She considered her lips to be her best feature. Although they were large and full, they were cleanly curved. At least she had a mouth like her mother's. *Stop taking inventory, Sidney,* she thought to herself, *it's not your fault your husband can't stay out of bed with half the women in Washington.*

She tugged the pins from her hair until it fell in waves of glossy black layers around her shoulders. After removing her diamond earrings, she let them fall one by one on the black marble dresser. The two–carat diamonds made a clinking sound as they bounced on the cold marble.

Julian started singing in earnest now, his loud, strong voice preceding him up the stairs. His voice belied his wheat–colored skin, and reminded Sidney of another hot August day in her hometown of Haven, Mississippi.

*   *   *

Sidney stood at the door of her mother's room in the only house with arches that close to the Bottoms in Haven, Mississippi. It was August 1975, and Sidney Adamson was ten years old. Peachy Girl had not been born, and Sidney had never heard of Julian McCalaster.

The French doors leading to the patio were thrown wide open. The syrupy smell of honeysuckle slid into the room on rays of unrelenting sunlight. Sidney looked past her mother and saw the last drops of dew drying in the face of the sun on the gray brick patio. When her eyes found her mother again, she knew Covina was suffering another one of her spells.

"Damn birds!" Covina ran over to the French doors and pulled at the gold handles until the doors slammed shut. "I hate those damn birds. And you know what, Sidney?"

"No, what?" Sidney straightened up in surprise. She didn't know her mother knew she was standing there.

"Now that your Daddy's dead, the first thing I'm going to do is chop down those magnolia trees back there. I hate those magnolia trees almost as much as I hate those stupid birds."

Covina walked back toward the center of the room and stood trying to remember what she had been doing in the first place. She flashed Sidney a look.

"Don't know why God would put flowers like that on a tree anyway," she finished.

Covina had managed to shut out the birds' singing, but not the sunlight. Sidney shaded her eyes as she walked into the room.

Covina's glistening black skin ate up the sunlight. She was sweating so profusely, it looked as if she had wiped herself down with baby oil. Her white eighteen–hour bra glowed fluorescent against her dark skin. The sweatpants she wore barely managed to stay above her slim hips as Covina flew around the room in an aimless circle.

The bedroom she had shared with Carl Haven, Sidney's father, was in complete disarray. Three of Carl's Armani suits had been pulled from the closet and thrown carelessly beside the four–poster mahogany bed.

Sidney watched her mother pull open one of the dresser drawers. Covina threw out a silk bra and a matching pair of panties. They landed on the pile of Armani suits. Next came the potpourri packages, and the scent of dead dried roses competed with the honey-suckled sun for attention. The smell reminded Sidney that her father's funeral was today.

"What are you doing, Mamma?" She picked up a tube of topless Max Factor lipstick by the bed. Burgundy raisin, the label proclaimed.

"I've got to find it, you understand. I've got to," Covina answered her.

Covina pulled open another drawer, this one filled with papers. She lifted the drawer in the air and turned it over. Unopened bills, coupons her mother saved to use but never did, and several of Sidney's baby pictures floated to the green shag carpet.

"Find what?" Sidney stepped out of Covina's way. She bent down and started sifting through the papers.

"Do you know what's going on here, Sidney?" Covina turned her black eyes toward her daughter. They were hard as marbles, the surrounding skin tight and shiny.

"Of course I know what's going on here Mamma." Sidney plopped on the bed. "The bastard's dead."

"You never had any respect," Covina said, then sat down beside her. "Even though he was white and didn't take too much time with you girls, he was still your daddy."

"*Too* much time, *humph,*" Sidney snorted, "how about no time at all?"

Sidney walked around the room. She had to navigate between piles of clothing, books, and even a few broken perfume bottles. She only recognized White Linen mixed in with the smell of the dead roses when she saw the bottle. She sat down again, next to her mother on the bed. She put her arm around her, trying not to wince. Covina's skin was sticky and hot.

"What are you looking for, Mamma?" she asked her again.

"The paper! The paper! The paper!" Covina shrieked and pounded her fist into her lap.

"Mamma, please," Sidney urged, her voice a loud whisper, "you are going to wake up Marion."

Although Sidney's sister Marion could sleep through almost anything, she did not want to risk the seven–year–old walking in when her mother was such a mess. The last time this happened, Marion was afraid to be in the same room as Covina for days afterwards.

"Now," Sidney said, her voice as calm as water as she kept one arm planted firmly around her mother's shoulder, "tell me about this paper."

Covina swallowed and turned to face her daughter. "A long time ago, your daddy gave me a paper on this house and the acre of land around it. It said if he died, I get the house, what's in it, and the land including those damn birds and magnolia trees."

She folded her hands in her lap. "I made him, you see; it was for you girls and for me, just in case something happened to him. And I was right. It did. He's dead." Covina unfolded her hands and covered her face.

"So what, he's dead?" Sidney still did not understand.

Covina looked up, the adult once again. "Girl, just when I think I didn't raise no fools, you go and say something

downright ignorant. Your daddy is dead. Do you know
what that means?''

Sidney shook her head slowly, and Covina sighed in
relief at the healthy fear in her daughter's light gray eyes.

"Well, it means," Covina said, then stood up, "it means
no more of those weekends you and your sister have to
stay in your rooms while I'm entertaining. And it means
you don't have to think of answers to his stupid questions
'cause the angel on his shoulder told him to talk to you.''
She put her hands on her hips. "But most of all, it means
that his family, the family who don't appreciate him having
a black mistress and two bastard black children is going
to be coming around. They gon' want this house. And they
gon' want this land.'' Covina sat down, the wind knocked
out of her. "It means if we don't find that paper, we gon'
be out on the streets.''

This time, it was Sidney's turn to sigh in relief. Now that
she knew what the problem was, she knew how to fix it.
She looked around the room and knew her mother had
not been thinking straight again. She had been looking
in closets and underwear drawers, Sidney thought. Even
the laundry hamper had been turned upside down.

"Mamma," Sidney said, "remember Aunt Margo?''

"Sidney, what in Jesus's name has Aunt Margo got to
do with this situation happening here?''

"Remember Aunt Margo before she drunk up death?''

"You mean drunk herself to death, Sidney," Covina said
tiredly.

"She had that record cut, remember? You said the only
reason that record made it into the top one hundred was
because Aunt Margo sent it to everyone she ever even
farted at.''

"Yes, I remember," Covina said.

"Even so, you were so proud, Mamma. You played that
record over and over. And when you found it in the trash

because Carl threw it away, you had one of your spells and you hid it. You said you hid it good, where nobody could ever find it. Where is it, Mamma?''

Covina stood up, clenched her fist, and screamed. Deftly dodging the debris on the bedroom floor, she ran to the big walk-in closet. Sidney followed, and saw her poking at a panel in the closet's ceiling with a broom. When it gave way, a black duffel bag fell to the floor. Covina carried it back to the room and dumped it on the bed. There was her daughter's birth certificate with the father's name marked 'unknown', a Polaroid snapshot of Carl and his two daughters, and Aunt Margo's record. Covina tore open the jacket and discarded the record impatiently. She felt inside until she pulled out a single white sheet of paper.

She unfolded it and started reading it aloud. "I, Carl Haven, being of sound mind . . ." she stopped, refolded the paper, brought it to her lips and kissed it soundly.

"Thank God!" she said, and smiled. "Thank God I found it!"

Sidney didn't respond. Instead, she examined an intricately carved gavel made of mahogany. The handle was a small sculpture of the blindfolded lady of justice. The carving was so detailed, Sidney could see the bend and fold of the lady's dress and hair.

"What's this?" she asked Covina.

"Don't know. Carl brought it over once," she said, distracted as she began putting the papers back into the duffel bag.

"Why did he bring it over here?"

"Don't know if he knew he had it. I found it while I was going through his briefcase. I took it 'cause it looked like it was worth something. You know, ol' an' stuff.''

"Can I have it?" Sidney asked.

"Take it. Don't need it now. We," Covina said, waving

the folded paper through the air, "we be home owners now."

Sidney stood up to leave the room. When she got to the door, her mother's voice stopped her.

"You know what Sidney?" Covina asked, clutching the folded paper to her chest. "I'm glad he's dead; now I'm free."

Sidney saw Julian's hands through the loft opening of their bedroom. He had a drink in one, and snapped in time to his own music with the other. He had removed his tie, and his tuxedo shirt hung open, revealing acres of his broad hairless chest. When he saw her standing in front of the mirror with her hair spread out around her shoulders and her dress pulled down to her waist, he walked over to her and kissed her on the neck.

"Oh, baby," he said, "you shouldn't have."

"I didn't," she said pushing him away. "And you are drunk."

Julian laughed and plumped down on the round, king-size bed made by the same designer who made the dresser. The headboard, black marble, angled crazily against the wall. The bedroom itself was shaped in a semi-circle, the curved wall opposite the bed made entirely of three long windows stretching from floor to ceiling. The many lights from the Washington, D.C. skyline glittered through them like jewels.

Inside the room, skylights were nestled in the vaulted ceiling. Besides the round bed, and the dressing table where Sidney sat looking at Julian, the only other place in the room to sit was on a straight-backed chair next to the bed. Thick white carpet covered the floor. There were no pictures of Julian or Sidney to personalize the room, only an abstract black and white painting hanging above the bed. It almost had the look of a hotel.

"So what? I'm drunk," he laughed, and fell backward on the white lace comforter. Scotch spilled over his glass.

"God damn, Julian," Sidney said, and walked over and took the drink from her husband's hand. She sat it on the marble night stand.

"That was some party tonight, huh baby?" he asked.

"They are always 'some party,' " she answered as she stepped out of her dress.

She glided over to the closet still wearing the strappy sandals with the thick heels she bought from Nordstorm's. She pulled a blue robe out of the closet and shrugged into it. Julian sat up on his elbows.

"Now that's sexy, baby," he said.

Sidney ignored him and tied the terry cloth sash around her waist, tight. She sat down on the bed and peeled the sandals from her feet. He placed his hand on the small of her back.

"And that woman," he whistled, "she may have been fat, but she sure could sing."

"Oh?" Sidney turned to look at him. "I didn't think you noticed the singing, you were so busy looking at everything in a skirt tonight."

Julian groaned as he rolled away from her. "Not again, babe." He covered his face with his hands. "Not tonight."

Sidney sat still as a statue on the bed. The room was so quiet, she imagined she could hear the seconds tick away on Julian's Rolex.

"I'm not crazy, Julian," she replied.

"I never said you were," he said while his hands still covered his face.

"Which one was she?"

"Sidney."

"The whore in the red dress?" she accused him.

"She's not a whore," Julian breathed, too drunk to care anymore.

Sidney breathed in slowly. And let it out. She blinked one, two, three times, waiting for tears that never came. Her eyes were as dry as the desert. She stood up and walked to the long windows serving as one entire wall for their bedroom. She looked out into the sky; the glimmering stars seemed so close. She reached out trying to touch one, but only felt cool glass.

"I won't put up with these women," she said, this time meaning it.

Julian didn't answer her. He could have been dead for all she knew. She looked hard over the skyline trying to find the White House. When she spotted it, she looked to the south and imagined she saw the Anacostia neighborhood where she and Julian lived after they both graduated from law school.

She remembered a long–ago day in 1989, when she first told him she was leaving the ACLU to join the law firm of Fosters and Fosters. She felt then as she felt now: resolved. She looked out into the night again, wondering why so many old ghosts were chasing her, calling out. She saw the apartment they shared on the bottom floor of the Lincoln Apartment Complex, and she remembered the first and only day she had ever defied him.

Julian and Sidney's one–bedroom apartment was barely six blocks from the White House. A fierce snow storm had piled snow so high that day, it covered half of the bedroom window.

Sidney, dressed in two pairs of sweatpants, gloves and a knit cap, alternately paced and looked at Julian, who stared at her with his fists balled at his sides. Despite the cold apartment, he wore nothing but a pair of Guess jeans. The heat had stopped working two hours ago. He had been in the midst of changing into his suit when his wife–to–be blurted out to him that she was leaving the ACLU for the prestigious law firm of Fosters and Fosters. When she saw the look in his green eyes, she immediately retreated to the living room, hoping for a small reprieve while he continued dressing. She did not anticipate him following her.

"What do you mean Fosters and Fosters?" he asked.

"They are one of the biggest law firms in the country," she said, and blew into her gloved hands for lack of anything better to do.

"Didn't we just beat the pants off of them in the Ambersen's case? Didn't we just annihilate them, Sid? Even though they tried everything in and out of the book to beat us?"

Sidney banged on the radiator, hoping to get the heat started again. "Yes, but we won," she told him.

Julian threw both of his arms above his head. "What's the matter, Sid?" he asked. "KPIX sticking a microphone in your face every five minutes make you want more? You like hearing your quips played over and over again so much you are willing to leave the best law organization in the country for a little fame?"

Sidney sat down on the couch they had bought from the Salvation Army. She smoothed the afghan her sister Marion had crocheted to hide the bare patches on the old couch. She remembered when her little sister had come to visit her—six months after Sidney joined the ACLU. How Marion stared at the couch, beige not from color, but from grime. She ran her soft, brown hands over the chip in the yellow 1960ish Formica table with the mismatched chairs. And no, Marion didn't think the hardwood floors were trendy. She looked at them the same way she looked at the thugs hanging out on the corner in front of the liquor store. Her sister, barely out of college herself, was never one to say what was on her mind, but ten minutes after they arrived at the apartment from the bus station, she asked, *Aren't you a lawyer, Sid? Can't they pay you more so you can live someplace decent?*

Sidney just shrugged and told her she didn't care where she lived as long as she could help people in need. She had to admit it was fun at first, but now it was just old.

"I'm not thinking about fame, Julian," she told him. "I'm thinking about money. I'm sick of this rat hole."

"Then we'll move!" Julian yelled so loud the crack addict living next door pounded on the walls.

"With what, Julian?" she asked. "How much did we make together from the ACLU and the pro bono cases we took last year? Forty thousand? And how much of that did you give away or invest in the brothers at the halfway house, as you like to put it? How much did you waste away at the football games or spend on lattes at three–fifty a cup? We are in debt up to our eyeballs, Julian."

Julian's light brown skin tightened around his mouth. The Big Ben clock sitting on the yellow Formica table ticked like a time bomb in the silence.

"I can't believe you are talking to me like this," Julian said to the young woman he had ferreted off to Washington, D.C. after they both graduated from Old Miss..

During the three years they had been together, Sidney did as he told her. He said join the ACLU, and she did without a murmur of dissent. Then the Ambersen case came along. It was the sweetest little illegal immigrants against the big, bad textile companies case to come along in a long time. The directors at the ACLU did not want to take it, saying it was impossible to win. But Julian talked them into it, just as he talked Sidney into it. And now, enter Fosters and Fosters, dangling a fat salary and an office with a view in her face.

"You are not joining that firm," he folded his arms across his bare chest.

"I already did," Sidney said matter-of-factly.

"What?" Julian arms fell to his side. He felt all control slipping away.

"It's a done deal, Julian," she told him. "Live with it."

"Don't think they are hiring you because you are any good," he said. "They are hiring you because they want to kill two quota birds with one stone—female and black."

Sidney studied Julian. Three years and she'd done what he said just because she was so lost after law school. Just like the mindless gesture of blowing into her hands earlier, she'd followed his advice for the lack of anything better to do.

"Julian," she said. "I love you. I want to marry you. But you can't run the rest of my life. Now it's my turn. I'm going to the firm, like it or not."

Sidney began shedding her clothes, letting them drop to the floor. The heat had finally been fixed, and she was sweating. She balled up the extra clothes to take them to the bedroom. But Julian got there before her, and slammed the door in her face.

When he emerged, he wore the same tight jeans and a sweater from Macy's Sidney knew cost more than a hundred and fifty dollars. She knew he could have only put the sweater on their only credit card. The last time she checked, they were within two hundred dollars of their limit. *Now fifty, if that,* she thought wryly, thinking about how much he had probably paid for the sweater. She turned away as Julian slammed out of the apartment.

She stayed with Fosters and Fosters, winning one case after another. She became the only partner at the firm to be slapped with the label 'bleeding heart liberal'. Julian stayed with the ACLU, winning some cases and losing others. The fact that his career never took off as his wife's did not seem to bother him. He sank right into the vacations in Hawaii and the Caribbean, their plush Crystal City condo and the dinner parties, two or three times a week.

The smell of whisky and scotch from Julian's breath on the back of her neck brought her back to reality. He was so close, she knew if she turned away from the window she would be forced into his arms.

"Get away from me, Julian." She leaned her forehead against the glass. The coolness steadied her. Julian raised his arms to touch her, then changed his mind. She left the window and sat in the straight–backed chair, tucking her feet beneath her. It was hard and uncomfortable.

"I quit Fosters and Fosters last month," she told him.

"I know," he said, and let out a sharp laugh. "They've been calling, asking me to talk some sense into you."

"And why haven't you tried?" she asked.

He looked at her then, a sadness in his green eyes. "We don't seem to talk that much anymore, even about simple things like the weather. How am I supposed to talk to you about that?" he challenged.

"I want a divorce," she said. That should have made her cry too, but it didn't.

"I know," he said.

"I don't want it to be ugly," she said.

He rubbed the back of his neck for what seemed like a long time. "It won't," he said finally. "Do you want me to leave?"

She walked over to him and put her arms around him, wanting to think they could still be friends. After all, they had been together a long time, for almost ten years.

"No," she said, "they've asked me to teach a semester at the University of Mississippi. I have a flight out on Delta at ten o'clock in the morning. This will give me a chance to get an early start."

Julian didn't return her embrace.

"It's the women, Julian." She laid her head on his chest. He reached up and pulled her arms from him. He lifted up her chin, forcing her to look into his face.

"No, Sidney," he said, "it's not the women."

He took a pillow and comforter from the bed. And when his head disappeared through the loft opening, she realized he would probably be the one crying tonight.

Chapter 2

As Sidney's plane pushed away from Gate Dll at Dallus International Airport, Haven's Sheriff—Jacob Conrad—drove his 1966 cherry red Mustang onto the gravel that would someday be the driveway of 1686 Easterbrook Drive in Haven. He banged the door of his Mustang on a police cruiser parked next to him, leaving a single red dot on the cruiser's white paint.

"Goddammit." Jacob slammed the Mustang's door shut. He looked at it until he was satisfied that his own door was free of any white paint.

"Sorry, Sheriff," Deputy Barney Grange said as he stepped from the doorway of the house. He tiptoed over the gravel, holding the belt of his khaki pants as if to keep them from falling to his knees. His belly swung over his belt buckle with each step he took.

"Didn't hurt it, did you?" he asked when he reached Jacob.

"No," Jacob said. "It'll live."

He put his hands on his hips and looked toward the house. He then looked over at Grange, who was sadly shaking his head and also looking toward the house. Jacob realized that Grange wasn't wearing his hat. He always wore that hat, even indoors. *Even to the bathroom.* Jacob knew this because he had worked in the same small office with Grange for years. The hat was like a part of Grange's body.

"What happened to your hat, Grange?" Jacob asked him.

"Oh, ahhhh, I must have left it in the police cruiser," Grange lied.

He didn't want to tell him he lost it while running like a scared rabbit from the first murdered body he'd ever seen—the body of Yolonda Brown.

"That Robinson?" Jacob pointed in the direction of the black preacher standing near a wheelbarrow filled with cement. The man looked toward the sky, holding a cross in his hands while mouthing a silent prayer.

"Now who else is that gonna be, Sheriff?" Grange asked him. "He's the only black preacher in Haven. If you got to church a little bit more, you'd know that."

Jacob stared at Grange until the man looked away. Grange was glad he couldn't see the look in Jacob's eyes behind the black lenses of his sunglasses.

"He found the body," he said. It sounded more like a statement.

"Yes." Grange bit his bottom lip to keep from saying more. He had pink, fat cheeks, like a baby's. "Yessir, he did."

Jacob, in no hurry to go inside the house, strolled over to Robinson. It was already hot and humid on this early August day. Jacob felt the sweat pour down the back of his neck into the collar of his shirt. He took a handkerchief out of his pocket and wiped at his face. He strolled over to Robinson, slowly, thinking of the murdered young girl inside. *A murder in Haven,* he thought as he stuffed the handkerchief back into his pocket. It reminded him of his years in New York as a homicide detective. But that was a long time ago, another lifetime.

When he reached Reverend Robinson, the man still prayed, his eyes on the blue heavens above. Jacob waited patiently until he finished, an uncomfortable knot in the pit of his stomach. Though Jacob himself was raised Catholic, he liked to think of himself as an atheist. But this didn't stop him from feeling embarrassed in the presence of such faith—a faith his mother had always lived by.

"Did you find the body?" he asked after the reverend looked down and crossed himself.

"Chief, I done tol' you . . ." Grange started.

"Shut up, Grange," Jacob said without even looking at him.

Robinson sat down heavily on the edge of the wheelbarrow. It tipped slightly from his weight, and Jacob resisted an urge to put out a hand to steady it.

"Praise be to the Lord, I did," the reverend replied.

Jacob stared at the empty lots around the house, and the thicket of trees behind them.

"And just what were you doing way out here?" He stuffed a piece of Juicy Fruit in his mouth. "I don't see any churches around here," he finished.

Robinson stood up. His cross fell to the ground.

"You ain't 'cusing me . . ." he started.

"I just asked you a question, Rev," Jacob took off his glasses and wiped them with the now damp handkerchief. "Don't get all riled up."

". . . 'Cause I couldn't do to a dog what was done to that girl," Robinson continued as if Jacob hadn't spoken.

"I'm waiting, Reverend Robinson." He stared at him.

Robinson narrowed his eyes at Jacob. "How long you lived here, son? Five, six years?"

Grange kicked at the gravel beneath his feet as Jacob Conrad and Reverend Robinson regarded each other. He adjusted his gun belt and looked toward the house.

"None of your business," Jacob put his glasses back on his face and waited.

"Because in all that time, I ain't seen you in church."

"I'm an atheist," Jacob stated matter-of-factly. He ignored the image flashing in his mind, the image of his mother forcing him to stand beside her as she kneeled and prayed in the Holy Mother of Jesus Catholic church in New York. He remembered her head bowed so low, it looked almost as if she didn't have one.

"I ain't seen you at Rollie's either. Or at the diner, or at the bar. I ain't even seen you in Johnson's Grocers. Do you even eat, son?" Reverend Robinson had a talent for not listening.

Jacob put one foot on the wheelbarrow and looked past Robinson, waiting for him to finish.

"What I'm trying to say, son," the preacher continued, "is that you don't even try to fit in. Not with the black folks, not with the white folks either. And you have the nerve to stand here and 'cuse me of sumpthin'."

"Now hold on, Reverend," Grange said, wanting to interrupt his tirade, "the Sheriff just tryin' to do his job."

Jacob took a deep breath. He felt his temper gather in his throat. "Come on, Reverend. I don't have all day. You can either tell me here what you were doing out in the middle of nowhere to find that girl's body. Or you can tell me in town."

"I camp sometimes in the woods," Reverend Robinson said, and waved his hand toward the trees, "to write my sermons. It's quiet out here. I feel closer to God."

"Oh, and tell me," Jacob said, folding his arms, "do

you feel closer to God in the middle of a construction site?''

"Now, Sheriff," Grange tried again.

"Shut up, Grange," he repeated.

"My dog is usually with me," Robinson stiffened. "This morning, he run off barking. And I chased him to the house. And when I went in, I found . . ." he started to sob.

Jacob took a deep breath, the tears reminding him how tragic this situation was. He gave him the wet handkerchief he had used earlier, and waited while the reverend blew his nose. It sounded like a trumpet.

"And that was when?" Jacob said quietly when the reverend finished.

"About an hour ago," Robinson breathed heavily. "He had been whimpering all night, but I thought he was after a rabbit or sumpthin'. This morning, I guess he couldn't stand it no more. And he ran off. I found him in there." He pointed to the framed house.

"Did you hear anything in the night?"

"No."

"Did you touch the body?" Jacob quizzed.

"No, I just ran out." The reverend lifted up his left foot. The sole of his shoe was darker in some places than in others. "I think I may have stepped in some blood, though."

"Oh, shit." Jacob threw his hands over his head before he could stop himself, his temper flaring once again.

"Whatsa matter?" Robinson asked, confused.

"You may have disturbed some evidence," Grange told him solemnly.

Reverend Robinson sat back down on the wheelbarrow. Jacob walked back to the house and leaned in the doorway.

"Grange, get over here, please," he called.

Grange did the same tippy–toe dance over the gravel until he reached Jacob.

"Doc on his way?"

"Yep, so is Grayson," Grange said, smiling proudly.

"Who the hell is Grayson?" Jacob asked.

"He's the town reporter. You know, the *Haven Crier?* He did that whole spread on Annette Haven's wedding not three months ago."

"Okay, okay," Jacob laughed as he stepped in the house. The two–by–fours of the wooden frame cut up the sunlight streaming through the roof.

He felt the coolness from the diminished sunlight touch his skin. He smelled the blood and heard the flies buzz before he actually saw the body. When he did see it, he felt as if someone had sucker–punched him.

The body lay in the doorway of the would–be kitchen. The head tilted as if in question, and one eye was gone. Blood formed a halo around the girl's neck and shoulder. Flies danced around the gaping neck wound and missing eye. *New York wasn't that far from Haven after all,* he thought.

"Grange!" he hollered. "What are you waiting on? A written invitation? Get in here!" He heard Grange's shuffling feet and heavy breathing behind him.

"I want this whole place sectioned off." Jacob stood up and backed away carefully. "I want you to call up Vicksburg, see if they can send a forensic team down here. See if we can borrow their coroner, too," he continued. "Get the camera out of the cruiser, and bring me some latex gloves."

"Yessir," Grange said, turning toward the door.

"Oh, and Grange?" Jacob looked up at him. "Don't forget your hat." He pointed toward the front doorway.

"Oh, thank you sir." A furnace burned in Grange's face.

When he left, Jacob studied the girl and noticed the bruises on her cheek, the swollen lip. He stood up and looked around. A completely distinct splatter of blood stained the cement about fifteen feet from where she lay.

Obviously, whoever did this had beaten her before cutting her throat.

Grange came back in and began snapping photos of the girl's body.

"Did you call Vicksburg?" Jacob asked him.

"Yep, sure did," Grange answered him from behind the camera.

"And you sectioned off the house already?"

"Nope. The Reverend is doing that."

"What?!" Jacob exploded.

"Now, Sheriff." Grange snapped away at the body. "It's only me and you. He just sittin' there on that wheelbarrow doing nothing."

"Okay. Okay," Jacob shook his head, giving up.

"This ain't New York," Grange said, still not looking at him.

"Not yet, anyway," Jacob answered him. "Where are the latex gloves?"

This time, Grange stopped snapping pictures to look at him.

"Couldn't find 'em," he said.

"You couldn't *what?*" Jacob asked, disgusted.

"Sheriff, I couldn't find 'em!" Grange rarely yelled back, but taking pictures of Yolonda Brown's grinning neck began to take its toll. "The last time there was a murder in this town was six years ago. And you wasn't even Sheriff!"

"Okay. Okay, Grange."

Jacob walked out of the house to the Mustang. He opened the trunk and rummaged until he found some latex gloves and paper bags for evidence. Robinson was nowhere to be seen, but he saw the yellow tape staked to the ground with sticks. The tape itself was barely high as his ankles. Anyone could simply step over it.

As he walked over the gravel, he heard the sound of a car. Looking up, he saw a hearse. The black doors swung open. A gray—haired man wearing a white coat got out on one side; a man with horn—rimmed glasses got out on the other.

"Sheriff," the town doctor said.

He must be a hundred, Jacob thought as he watched the doctor step over the police tape, without causing it to so much as flutter.

"You're too early," Jacob said, but shook the old man's hand. It was like sticking his hand into a vice.

"This here is Grayson, if you don't know it." Doctor Max, as he was called, jabbed a wrinkled thumb at the man standing beside him.

"Very pleased to meet you, sir." Grayson had a high—pitched voice like a woman's. His eyes looked like they were trying to escape his face. When Jacob reached out to shake his hand, Grayson grabbed his fingers and wagged them back and forth a few times.

"You're early," Jacob said again.

"What do you mean early?" Doctor Max asked. "Grange said the girl was dead."

"I still got a couple of things to do here," Jacob answered. "And I don't want you cutting that girl. I've got a coroner coming up from Vicksburg."

"Now just wait a dangblasted minute!" Doctor Max's face grew florid. "I'm the Coroner around here."

"You are the town's doctor," Jacob contradicted.

"Yeah, but when the body's dead, I'm the Goddamned Coroner!"

"When was the last time you did an autopsy on a murder victim?"

"You know damn well when," Doctor Max said hoarsely. "Six years ago, on that black bastard that brought your fancy New York ass here."

"I rest my case, " Jacob said, and spread his arms out to his side.

"Okay, Okay, I get your point," Doctor Max gave up. "Let's go see what we have."

They both started toward the house with Grayson hopping behind them.

"Hold it. Hold it," Jacob said, stopping in mid-step, "he's not going in there with us."

"But," Grayson squeaked, "I need to, the story."

"I'll vouch for the man," Dr. Max told Jacob.

"Now that makes me feel tons better," he replied. "Come on. But don't touch anything."

"I won't. I won't," Grayson said. He sounded like a fifteen–year–old who'd been told he could go see an R–rated movie.

Grange had finished his pictures and stood just inside the doorway to greet them. When Doctor Max saw the body, he stood still for a long time. He looked at Jacob.

"When did you call Vicksburg?" he asked him.

Jacob could have sworn he saw gratitude in the old man's eyes. "About thirty minutes ago," he answered.

"Good." Doctor Max licked his lips. "Good."

"Can I see?" Grayson forced a space between them to get a look at the body. Jacob's own stomach turned over when he saw the man's face.

"Get him out of here . . ." he started, but before anyone could react, Grayson threw up all over Yolonda Brown's shoes. He turned away, still spewing vomit. It sounded like heavy rain against the cement floor.

"Shit!" Jacob yelled. "Get him out of here, Grange, now! Shit!" he said again.

"I'm soooooory," Grayson sobbed. "I'll clean it up." He reached for a handkerchief in the pocket of his linen jacket.

"Don't touch it!" Jacob grabbed the man's wrist. Grayson howled in pain. "Don't touch it. Just get out of here."

"I'll handle it, Jacob," Doctor Max said, pushing Jacob away. "Let go 'fore you twist the man's wrist off."

When they left, Grange looked at Jacob and shook his head sadly. He held his hat—his prized possession—in his hands, twisting it mercilessly.

"This ain't New York," he said, his soft voice piercing the silence.

"Tell me about it," Jacob sighed, running the palm of his hand over his hair. Sick of the metallic smell of blood and vomit rolling around in his mouth, he went out to join the others.

Chapter 3

Sidney noticed the man the moment he walked into the Oxford Law School lecture hall where she lectured about eighty students who had decided to give up the summer for her course on ethics in law. He was a bald man, as small and neat as a new silver safety pin. His silk Armani neck tie was so tight, it seemed to be choking him.

Annoyed, Sidney ignored him. With only ten minutes of class left and a broken air conditioner, her students had a hard enough time concentrating on this hot, August day. Sidney imagined she could actually see the heat sliding off the walls, collecting on the window sills, and pooling around her bare feet. She had abandoned her black pumps halfway through the lecture to cope with the stifling heat.

And to make matters worse, a student in the third row with Barbie doll–blond hair must have taken a bath in White Linen perfume. The smell was so obtrusive, the student behind her kept coughing and sputtering through most of the lecture. Someone's watch beeped, and it was all over. Sidney had to yell out the homework assignment over the sound of slamming books and zipping book bags as the students scrambled from the room. Another class had ended. It had only been a few days since she left Julian, but it seemed like a lifetime.

Still leaning against the back of her desk, Sidney watched the man step toward her. She folded her arms across her chest as he approached. She didn't smile. When he reached her, he extended his left hand. Sidney looked down at it, her arms still folded.

"Well," he said, "I guess you remember me."

"Yes," Sidney answered.

His name was Rupert Englestorm and he was the Haven lawyer. Carl's lawyer. Sidney met him two times in her life, once in her mother's living room, shortly after her father died. He stood in their Haven home the entire forty–five minutes he was there, as though he was too good to sit. He droned out instructions, handed her mother a check, and left.

She met him again when she was fourteen. He stood in the same spot in the living room and told Covina that her children—Carl's children—were beginning to become somewhat of an embarrassment to the Havens. He handed her mother another check, glanced at Sidney's chest, and mumbled something about boarding school.

Without a word, Covina took the check from his trembling fingers. The next day, she and the girls went to Vicksburg and bought a 1979 red Buick with velvet red interior that reminded Sidney of a hearse.

"We're both adults," he told her now. "We can at least be civil to one another. After all," he said and stuck out his hand again, "we are both in the same profession."

Sidney hesitated, then pressed his palm briefly . "What do you want?" she asked, then turned her back to him and walked behind her desk. She picked up the tattered leather book bag she had carried since law school.

Rupert placed his fingertips lightly on the top of her desk. "I'm afraid there has been a bit of a family problem," he said.

Sidney stood up, forgetting that the book bag was in her lap. It fell to the floor, and her checkbook, lipstick, and her father's gavel which she always carried with her, spilled to the floor.

"Is my mother . . . " she began.

"Your mother's fine." He held up his hands, effectively putting a stop to her panic.

Sidney bent down and picked up her book bag, scooping the contents into it quickly. She was glad Rupert didn't offer to help, and that he didn't notice the gavel. She stood up.

"Then what problem are you talking about?" The room temperature dropped ten degrees from the ice in her voice.

"I'd rather not talk about it here. Are you free for coffee tonight?"

"Are you asking me for a date after all these years Mr. Englestorm?" Sidney laughed.

"No, I'm certainly not." He stood up straight. "This is a business meeting."

"I have no business with you or any family whose problems you happen to be associated with, Mr. Englestorm," Sidney said in the same icy tone.

She put the strap of the book bag over her shoulder and started walking past him. He stepped in her path and looked as threatening as a little man could look.

"I'm afraid this is your problem," he said. "You see, it indirectly involves your mother, and her well-being . . ." he made his voice so soft she had to strain to hear it. He reached into his coat pocket and pulled out a business card. "Meet me here at eight o'clock tonight."

Sidney snatched the card from him and looked him in the eyes. Watching him, she balled the card up in her fingers. Holding her hand high in the air, she let the card fall to the floor. He caught it before it hit the ground, and smoothed it out. He put it on her desk, smiling at her.

"I know you are smart enough to know what's good for you and your mother," he said. "I'll see you there." He turned away and left the room without saying good-bye.

Sidney stood in the silence for a moment, then headed toward the door. When she reached Miss Barbie's desk, she smelled the faint lingering of White Linen perfume. She stopped again, and walked back to where the card lay crumpled on the desk. She picked it up, and without bothering to look at it, dropped it into her book bag.

The address on the business card was of a coffee shop near the University. It was trendy—hardwood floors, exposed brick here and there in the wall—and blessedly empty, except for Rupert, who sat at one of the little round wooden tables with his legs crossed. When he saw her standing in the doorway, he stood up and waved her over to him.

"Please, sit," he motioned toward the wooden chair next to him. "Would you like some coffee?" he said as he took a sip out of his own coffee cup. It looked like a soup bowl with a handle.

"I don't like repeating myself, Mr. Englestorm," she answered.

"Ah, yes. What do I want?" he said absently. Coffee sloshed over the edge of the cup as he set it down on the table. "I thought we could be pleasant about this."

He pulled a white linen handkerchief out of his pocket and wiped at his fingers. Sidney sighed. Sighed and waited.

"Well," he said as he stuffed the handkerchief back into

his pocket, "as I was telling you before, there has been a bit of *family* trouble." He picked up his coffee cup and took another long sip.

"What family, Mr. Englestorm?" Sidney asked impatiently.

"The Havens, I'm afraid." Rupert set the cup down, carefully this time.

"And what does that have to do with me?" Sidney's gray eyes became hard as jade.

"Under normal circumstances, nothing. Under these circumstances, everything," he answered.

"Mr. Englestorm," Sidney said as she stood up to leave, "I'm getting tired of these games."

"Okay, okay. I'll get straight to the point." He waited until she sat down again. "There's been a murder."

"In Haven?" Sidney laughed. "There hasn't been a murder there in what. . . ?"

"Six years. That murder," he said, pointing at her, "as you recall, brought in some unwelcome guests, and one of them decided to stick around."

"I think my mother told me about that. Some investigators from New York when that boy got . . . "

"Got himself killed, Sidney. He grew up in Haven. He should have known better. No one to blame but himself. And we're paying for it. The Havens are paying for it."

"But that was six years ago. What's that got to do with why you are here? Hundreds of miles away from Haven?"

"Nothing. Everything," Rupert said. He leaned back as a waitress with spiked hair and an earring in her nose poured more coffee into his soup bowl-turned-coffee cup. He waited until she left before continuing.

"The one who decided to stay behind, a Jacob Conrad, has been nothing but trouble ever since. Do you know he's Sheriff now?"

"I think I heard my mother talking about him. She even voted for him," Sidney answered.

"All of the black folks voted for him; that's how he won. But still," Rupert said, leaning across the table toward Sidney. "He just doesn't fit in, Sidney," he finished in a conspiratorial tone.

A young couple walked into the coffee shop hanging onto each other and giggling.

"He's always had it in for the Havens. Tried to tie Samuel, of all people, to that boy's murder. Never had any proof, thank God."

"And was there any proof to be had?" Sidney asked.

Rupert's mouth worked. "Of course not!" he said as if she had asked him what color underwear he was wearing. "And I don't want to go over ancient history with you."

"You brought it up," Sidney shrugged.

"I brought it up because of the family trouble we are having." He took out the coffee–stained handkerchief and wiped his forehead. "Some colored girl got herself killed. And Sheriff Conrad has arrested Dex."

Sidney sat up in her chair. "Dexter Haven?" she asked.

"The same." Rupert put his handkerchief back into his pocket.

The silence in the café was interrupted by faint sounds of laughter. Sidney could not think of Dexter Haven as her brother, no matter how hard she tried. He was one of her father's legitimate children. He and his sister Annette got to stand in plain view as their father's casket was lowered into the ground, while she and her sister had to watch from the bushes. Hearing that Dexter Haven was in trouble only put a slight distaste in her mouth, like hearing about the misfortunes of a stranger. She ran her fingers through her hair.

"What has that got to do with me?" she asked.

Rupert took another sip of his coffee. *It must be cold by now,* Sidney thought as she waited for him to answer.

"We've tracked your career, Sidney," he replied. "Your career at the ACLU, your partnership with Fosters and Fosters. And I must say, I've read every one of your books." He ignored her raised eyebrow.

"Get to the point," she said, unimpressed.

"And the town—" he continued, "you've quite a reputation. You are very well respected."

He waited, expecting to hear a response, and when she remained silent, he went on. "We need you to represent Dexter Haven in this, uh," he stopped, then waved his left hand like he was batting away a fly, "this unfortunate manner."

Sidney looked at him long and hard. In his eyes, she saw her half brother and sister at their father's graveside. Dexter even had reached out a hand and touched the shiny casket.

"No," she told Rupert now, simply, as if he had just asked her if the sun rose in the west.

"You will," he responded.

"They must have a hell of a lot of evidence for you to be here, huh?" Sidney lowered her voice. "I may like lost causes, but they will be holding the Winter Olympics in Hell before I would waste one breath defending a Haven."

Rupert reached in his coat pocket and pulled out a folded piece of paper. He handed it to Sidney.

"Take it," he said.

She snatched it from him, and read it quickly. Color drained from her face.

"It's a fake," she told him.

"Yes, it is." This time, he answered simply. "But just think how much fun you will have trying to prove it." He paused and looked at the ceiling. "I've already decided how I will present my case. I will say that Carl Haven was overcome with conscience for cheating on his poor wife. So overcome, even though he was coerced into deeding his property to his mistress, he tucked away another will, hoping it would be found after his death." He smiled angelically. "And thankfully, his wife found it in a knothole while she was refinishing his old roll–top desk."

"You can't get away with this," she told him, angrily.

"Your mother would have to testify, and she's ill, isn't she? Some say not quite right, is it?"

"Ill or not, I won't be seen in the same courtroom as one of those bastards."

Rupert leaned back in his chair and crossed his arms across his chest.

"Remind me again, Sidney. How did Carl die?"

"You are a sonofabitch," Sidney said between her teeth.

"I'll take that as a yes," he said. "You need to be in Haven by Wednesday. I've scheduled a meeting between you and your client at two PM." He started to walk away and then turned to look at her. "And Sidney," he said almost as an afterthought, "don't be late."

The morning after he left her, Sidney went to the administration at Oxford Law School to tell them she could not continue teaching the course. At first, they balked. She was their star, their draw for this summer school course. But she insisted on a leave of absence, telling them there was a family emergency involving her *brother*—the word so foreign in her mouth it took her almost a full minute to choke it out.

Remind me again, Sidney, how your father died. Rupert's words reverberated through Sidney's head as she boarded the 727 on the way to Vicksburg, Mississippi. She hadn't thought of the day her father died in almost twenty years. But it only took one man to mention those words in an empty coffee shop for those memories to overwhelm her. She gave in to them as the plane escaped into the sky.

* * *

In 1975, she lived with her mother and her sister Marion. Carl Haven built a small house near the poorest neighborhood in Haven called the Bottoms so he could be comfortable when he visited his mistress. He never dreamed he would die there on one clear night that same year.

Even though Sidney was only ten years old, she knew Covina fascinated Carl. She could tell by the way he stared at her mother when she whirled through the house, as unpredictable and temperamental as a black funnel cloud.

And Rupert was correct when he said Covina was 'not quite right'. Sometimes, Sidney thought her mother used that to her advantage, because at times, the woman seemed sane as daylight. But at others, she would lock herself in her room for days drinking Black Velvet and smoking unfiltered Camels.

She would do things too, some of them as irrevocable and lasting as the names of her children. Covina named Sidney after Carl Haven's father, and she named Sidney's sister Marion after Carl's wife. Sidney knew Covina did it out of spite more than she did madness.

The night her father died, she heard her mother screaming from the room she shared with Carl. She banged on the door for at least thirty seconds before picking the lock with one of her sister's red bobby pins. Her mother was crouched near the headboard of the mahogany four-poster bed, clutching the covers to her chest. Carl—butt naked except for his black dress socks—lay face down on the bed at an angle. His hands were sprawled over his head, and his feet dangled off the bed.

"Mamma, what . . . ?" Sidney asked as she watched the moonlight streaming through the French doors play on Carl's naked white butt.

"He's dead, Sidney. I think I killed him," Covina sobbed.

Sidney sighed. Not again, she thought. Please don't be having a spell when I have a math test tomorrow.

"Sidney!" Covina said, not moving from her crouching position. "The bastard's dead. Look at him, he ain't moving."

Sidney looked at the moonlight dancing on Carl's butt.

"Do you think if he wasn't dead he would be lettin' you stare at his naked ass?" Covina asked her.

Sidney licked her lips. "Maybe he just fainted?" she ventured.

"Well, go and check," Covina said, and waved a black hand toward Carl.

"Why me?" Sidney asked.

"Girl, I'm naked as the day I was born!" Covina replied.

"Mamma, so is he!" Sidney wailed.

"Sidney, please!" Covina begged, sobbing.

"Okay." Sidney walked over to Carl. She felt her stomach jump into her throat and prayed to God she wouldn't throw up. She never realized how fat and meaty Carl was. Rings of fat circled his torso, and his thighs were like molted cottage cheese.

"Mamma, how could you . . ." Sidney began in disgust.

"Sidney, stop stalling and go see if your daddy is dead!"

"Okay," Sidney replied and walked toward Carl. She touched him. His skin felt as cold as a dead sun.

"Mamma, what happened?" Sidney asked fearfully.

Covina dropped her head into her hands.

"We was, you know we was . . ."

"Mamma."

"Okay," Covina drew in a deep breath. "And he grunted, like he was done, and fell on me. I thought he was sleeping." She wiped her mouth hard with her fingertips. "I must have nodded off. And when I woke up, I felt something pressing down on me. It was like sleeping under a slab of ice."

"How could you fall asleep with that thing laying on top of you?" Sidney motioned toward Carl.

" 'Cause I was tired," Covina sobbed again. "I been up all day helping you study for that damned math test and gettin' ready for this bastard."

Covina sat down and crawled into a tangle of covers to the opposite side of the bed. "I guess we should call the police," she said sadly.

"What? Police? No way, Mamma!"

Covina stared at Sidney, still in a confused daze. "But . . ." she began.

"Mamma, you call the police, and the Havens will have a fit!"

"Then what in the name of Jesus do you think we should do, girl?" Covina looked at Sidney as if she had just walked off the moon.

"I don't know, call what's-his-name." Sidney waved her hands in the air. "Mr. Carl's brother."

"You mean Samuel?" Covina asked.

"Mamma, you didn't . . ." she began as her mother walked to the phone and dialed Samuel Haven's number by heart.

"Of course, I didn't," Covina replied as she cupped her free hand over the speaker. "What do you think I am, some kind of slut? Now get to bed, I'll take care of the rest of this," she finished.

Sidney went to bed, and closed the door behind her. The next morning, she read in the paper that Carl Haven died peacefully in his sleep of a stroke, at the Haven's mansion. Memorial Services were to be held at the First Baptist Church with graveside services at the Haven Family Plot on August 15, 1975.

A jolt of turbulence obliterated the memories of that day and brought Sidney back to the present. Suddenly, she realized the reason she was on her way to Haven: to

defend a brother she had never met. No matter how much
those memories might fade over the years, she knew she
would never forget the feel of her father's icy body on her
fingertips.

Chapter 4

Jacob slumped on his couch in his narrow brick house on Everson Street in Haven. He balanced a bottle of Coors on his flat stomach, enjoying the icy coolness against his bare skin. Every light in the house burned, and the artificial brightness only intensified the darkness outside. The voice of a Baptist preacher blared from a radio upstairs, reminding him that he had forgotten to turn it off.

Nagging thoughts in the back of his mind told him to turn off the lights, turn off the radio, and go to bed. But those thoughts could not stop him from thinking about Dexter Haven's arrest. He turned it over and over in his mind, like a book he had read a thousand times. He kept telling himself that the arrest was just, not revenge for never proving Samuel Haven murdered that young boy— CD Heater—six years ago. He had plenty of evidence— witnesses to testify that they saw Dexter arguing at Rollie's Juke Joint with Yolonda Brown the night she was murdered, and semen with his blood type in her vagina.

He took another sip of beer, and it was warm. He stood up and stretched. In the kitchen, he poured the beer down the sink. But instead of seeing the beer disappear, he saw Grange's face when he told him on Tuesday that they were going to arrest Dexter Haven.

When Jacob arrived at Haven's police station with an arrest warrant crumpled in his front shirt pocket, Grange opened his pink lips in surprise.

"But Sheriff," he said, the mustard from the turkey sandwich he clutched still on the side of his pink face, "it's six at night. I got only thirty minutes left before it's time to go home. Can't this wait until morning?"

Jacob looked at him, then shook his head.

"I know this isn't New York, Grange," he told him. "But I don't want that sick bastard on the street longer than he has to be."

"It ain't like he gon' do nothing between now and the morning, Sheriff," Grange protested.

The Haven police station was not open twenty-four hours. When people needed help at night, the phones automatically forwarded to Grange or Jacob's house. The last call they had received in the middle of the night was from Mrs. Dustin, who thought the cat fight in her ally was someone trying to get into her side window.

"Let's go get him in the morning," Grange pleaded. "That way, I won't have to stay here all night watching him."

Jacob ignored Grange and walked into his office. He reached into his desk drawer and pulled out the keys to the jail cell. He inserted the key into the lock, clicking it smoothly into place.

"Sheriff," Grange started again.

"Get your holster on," Jacob cut in. "I want to get this taken care of now."

Grange realized he could say nothing to convince Jacob to arrest Dexter Haven in the morning. They drove over to the Haven's mansion in separate cars. Grange drove in Haven's only police cruiser, and Jacob used his Mustang.

The Haven mansion glowed white in the approaching darkness. Both Grange and Jacob stepped out of their separate cars at the same time. Jacob walked up to the double mahogany doors while Grange followed a step or two behind. He pressed the doorbell two times in a row, then pounded on the heavy door with his fist. Finally Jason, the Haven's butler, opened it. Jacob didn't speak, but brushed past Jason as if he were a black ghost standing by a long–empty grave.

Jason stuttered, "Sir, Sir, you can't," his cloudy eyes gazed at Jacob, then at Grange.

Jacob ignored him and continued walking through the black and white tiled foyer. His shoes tapped loudly, almost drowning out the sound of laughter and tinkling glass coming from the dining room. He stepped boldly into the room as if he were an invited guest arriving shamelessly late. He scanned the table, quickly looking for Dexter.

All of the Havens were there, including a European relative he did not know, and that snake Englestorm he didn't care to know, but unfortunately did. Jacob spotted Dexter sitting next to his mother, Marion. She was the first one to notice him and the first one to speak. The room fell silent when she gasped.

"What are you doing here?" she asked him, so white she competed with the light from the chandelier above their heads.

Without speaking, he walked around the table. He pulled the cuffs from the holder on his belt.

"Dexter Haven," he made his voice routine, trying to

ignore the tinge of excitement rushing through him, "you are under arrest . . ."

Marion dropped her Waterford Crystal goblet. It shattered into a thousand diamond pieces on the table top. Samuel Haven stood up so quickly, his chair fell backward. It thudded on the thick carpet, sounding almost like a body hitting the floor.

"Please keep calm," Deputy Grange said crisply, in the most official voice he could muster.

Marion began to cry, softly.

"You can't do this . . ." Samuel Haven sputtered.

And Englestorm, that snake who doubled as the Haven's lawyer, stood up and approached Dexter and Jacob.

"Excuse me, Sheriff," he said, placing a hand on Jacob's muscled forearm, "can I see the warrant?"

Jacob looked at the man's white hand as if it were a garden snake that had crawled carelessly into the path of a python. Rupert drew back as if he had been hit. Jacob removed the warrant from his coat pocket. He thrust it at Rupert Englestorm, who read it with the poker face he used to be famous for in the courtroom.

"All right," he said, folding the paper, "so it's a warrant. You could have called. My client would have surrendered himself quite willingly."

Jacob did not respond. He twirled Dexter around and splayed his arms against the silk wall covering of roses twisting under green leaves.

"You are under arrest," he began again, "for the murder of Yolonda Brown. You have the right to remain silent, you have the right to an attorney . . ." He began frisking Dexter as he continued the Miranda rights.

"Are you carrying any concealed weapons?" he asked finally.

"Of course not!" Dexter screamed in pain as Jacob clicked the cuffs around his bony wrists.

"Do you understand these rights?" Jacob asked him.

"What?" Dexter asked, disoriented by the pinch of pain against his wrists.

"I said . . ." Jacob began again.

"Yes, I do. Of course. But I don't know what you are talking about. I don't know any Yolonda Brown."

"Tell it to the judge," Jacob said, realizing this was only the second time he had uttered that phrase since coming to Haven. The first time was for the arrest of Samuel Haven. But instead of being in jail, the man stood here with a look of outrage on his face as Jacob arrested his nephew.

Jacob grabbed Dexter by the arm and yanked him through the foyer to the front door. Deputy Grange did a fast tippy–toe ahead of him, and opened the back door of the police cruiser. After Jacob guided Dexter into the cruiser, he glanced at the front door.

Samuel Haven walked slowly down the walk, never taking his eyes from Jacob. *The man could snatch the stars from the sky and put them around his wife's neck,* Jacob thought to himself, *but today was probably only the second time in his long evil life the old man was at a loss for what to do.*

Jacob heard an AMEN coming from the radio upstairs. And in an instant, he was shirtless, back in his kitchen, the memories of the other night gone. Grange told him that after the arrest, Samuel Haven had packed up almost the entire family and sent them to Vicksburg. He only allowed Marion, Dexter's mother, to stay with him at the Haven mansion.

Jacob knew why he had all the lights on in the house. He knew why he played his radio so loud he could hear it in his kitchen, even though it played upstairs from his night table.

He wanted the light to kill the memories of the other

night, and he wanted the noise of the radio to drive out the tinge of guilt he felt for enjoying the arrest of Dexter Haven. For enjoying it, and questioning himself as to whether it was the right thing to do.

Chapter 5

Sidney's plane arrived in Vicksburg, Wednesday morning, August 16th. Yolanda Brown would be buried on Thursday, a full ten days after her murder. Sidney rented an Easter egg–blue Ford Taurus at the Hertz counter in Vicksburg for the one hundred and fifty mile drive north to Haven. She decided not to take the train because she wanted to think on the drive. And besides, there were not any car rental places in Haven, and she would be damned if she would be seen driving around town in her mother's hellfire red Buick.

Haven rested between the Yazoo and Big Black rivers. The drive was a lonely one through a one hundred fifty mile stretch of dense forest. It had been founded by Samuel Haven of Vicksburg—one year before the Civil War ended. He was the first Samuel Haven, and the great–grandfather of the man people now knew in Haven as Samuel Haven the third.

Samuel Haven the first, sensing the South's defeat, sent

three of his best slaves, his foreman, his wife, and two sons to an area he bought from the government four years earlier. He built a small, modest house in what was then a wilderness. He sent the fortune he made in the shipping industry to Spain—just in case the worst happened. And before he knew it, it did.

Grant marched on Vicksburg in 1865, imprisoned Samuel and seized the remainder of his fortune. If it had not been for a pimply–faced Union soldier, Samuel would have wasted away in prison for the rest of his life.

But instead, he was able to bribe the sixteen–year–old guard with the promise of three thousand dollars when he reached his destination. The boy, who happened to be the only surviving male member of his own family, gambled and lost by letting Samuel out. The last he ever saw of Samuel was his back as he walked out of prison, and the last he ever heard from him was the crunch of his boots against the gravel as he ran.

For two months, Samuel made his way to his family, existing on dandelion greens and leaves when he wasn't lucky enough to catch small opossums. Legends still abound in Haven today about how he crossed the Big Black River in his bare feet, wearing nothing but the ragged velvet pantaloons he had on when he was captured by the Union army. But the truth was that he had help from sympathizers along the way.

After he arrived at the house he had built several years earlier, they lived in relative contentment in the area Samuel carved out of the wilderness. Anna, his wife, had a small vegetable garden and both he and his foreman had always been good hunters. His slaves provided the life of ease they were accustomed to.

Two years after he arrived, Samuel noticed his surroundings. He was right near a river and smack dab in the middle of the most beautiful hickory, elm and pecan trees he had ever seen. So many trees occupied the place, Samuel imagined the sun playing through the leaves—chunks of gold falling from the sky. And he thought of one word— timber. Soon, with the help of relatives and some of his slaves, they cleared much of the forest surrounding the house and sold it for timber.

At first, they used the river to carry the timber from Haven to Vicksburg, but then Samuel built a small railroad between the two towns. Although the railroad still operates today, it is mostly a passenger train, as the Haven family use trucks to carry the timber, cotton and soybean crops to market.

As Sidney drove through the forest on her way home, she imagined she saw the first Samuel Haven running through the trees to get to his family. She wondered if he felt any empathy with the runaway slaves who had also escaped to freedom.

She remembered the Haven of her childhood. It was mostly a caste system divided between the wealthy Havens and those who worked for them. Almost every white citizen of the town claimed to be related to the founders, and most were, as were most of the blacks descendants of for- mer slaves who joined Samuel in his adventures.

They were not much bothered by the outside world, and had become so lost and proud in their isolation, they separated themselves on two levels. First, one was either White or Black. Second and most of all, they were either a Haven—born and raised in the town—or an outsider. They may differ in race, but in the end, they were all from the same beginnings.

The Civil Rights movement was but a gentle, firm wave in their otherwise peaceful existence. The law of the land was decreed, and the town's governing bodies followed it to the letter. They took one look at the rest of Mississippi's businesses being destroyed by sit-ins and boycotts, and integrated. As well as money, Samuel passed down the all–motivating factor of greed to his descendants.

It was in late 1987, two years after they started carrying passengers on the railroad, when the outside world intruded—historians fascinated by the town's history, and developers smelling money.

If you asked anybody in Haven about that time, they would tell you the worst part was they had been betrayed by one of their own natives. Although he was of a different race, white people of Haven believed it was C.D. Heater who betrayed them for attempting to unionize the mills. He was born and raised in Haven, and his first loyalty should have been to its citizens. He shouldn't have brought the outside world to the town as he did.

Oddly enough, Black people believed Samuel Haven the third betrayed them for selling them out. He didn't give a damn about what happened to them in the mills. They believed he forced them to turn to the outside world for help. His one loyalty, they said, was to his all–encompassing greed.

Sidney knew of C.D. when she was a girl, but she hadn't seen him since she was ten years old. He started making trouble about the fact that those working in the mills didn't have health care benefits of any kind. Most of them hadn't even heard of the word 'union' and if they did, they felt it was in no way connected to them.

The boy was found dead on his twenty–second birthday. If the present Samuel Haven—Samuel Haven III—had kept his mouth shut, no more would have been said. The Heater death would have been just another blip in the town's strange history. But sitting in his study with an historian from Harvard, thinking the curl of smoke from his Cuban cigar made him invincible, Samuel said casually, as if he were discussing the weather, "In my Grandfather's time, we would have skinned that nigger and hung him out for the animals. He got off easy, don't you think?"

The historian wrote an article called "Haven, the Forgotten Town," citing the comment, and Civil Rights activists from all over the country demanded an investigation. The government assembled some of the best investigators in the country, including Jacob Conrad, a homicide detective from New York. The investigation went on for six months without any success. Everyone in town knew Samuel Haven III killed that boy, but no one, not even the federal government could prove it. After the investigation ended, Jacob pressed on, soon quitting his job to stay in Haven to find the killer. C.D.'s death was a rallying cry for the blacks of Haven, and when Jacob Conrad ran for Sheriff a year after the murder, they elected him hands down.

And now he is going to be a thorn in my side, Sidney thought as she slowed down to negotiate a curve in the two–lane highway. She only had time to do a brief history on Jacob Conrad before coming to Haven. She knew he had spent eleven years in New York as a homicide detective and had as many disciplinary actions against him as he had accommodations. And now, because of this man, she was driving back to a place she despised because he had the raw nerve to arrest a Haven in a town by that name. A Haven who happened to be the brother she never knew.

Sidney pressed the gas to pick up speed as the curve gave way to straight road. A robin, its feathered breast blazing blue, arched daringly in front of her windshield before bounding upward and disappearing into the unclouded sky. It reminded Sidney of what Covina would tell her when she asked that awkward question: *Mamma, what color am I?* Covina would just laugh, saying in a voice so musical it sounded like singing, *blue bird, black bird, it don't matter 'cause they all part of the same sky.*

Same sky my eye, Sidney thought now as she recognized

several shacks along the side of the road. Haven was getting
closer. Growing up, the black people of Haven treated her
as one of their own for the most part. There were rare
occasions, though, when some would remind her of where
she came from. She remembered the snickers and smirking
glances at the corner grocery store when she bought her
mother's Camel cigarettes, or the times at school when
she couldn't find anyone to sit with at the lunch table.

But she had managed to get through it still being a
part of her mother's people. She couldn't remember ever
having to mention her father's name. Now, coming back
to defend her white brother, she had a nasty knot in the
pit of her stomach. She felt as if she were finally throwing
down the gauntlet and admitting, after all, who her father
was. The thought made her want to vomit.

Soon, instead of only one or two shacks along the road,
there were many. Then there were houses, and wide tree-
lined streets. And in the distance, as Sidney drove toward
town, she could see the pointed roof of the courthouse
pictured against the sky almost as if it were waiting for her.

There was a small moment of uncertainty when she
thought she didn't remember the way to the jail. But almost
automatically, she made a left here and a right there until
she found herself outside a squat, square building which
served as Haven's jailhouse.

She parked the Taurus outside the Haven jail, a small
two-room building made of white wood. Bars covered both
windows on either side of the door. When the first Samuel
Haven built the jail, he wanted something simple to house
the workers who became a little rowdy on Saturday night.
He started building the jail in 1872, four days after complet-
ing the town's first bar.

Grange was the first person Sidney saw when she walked
through the door. He sat in a black swivel chair with his
hat cocked back on his head; and his feet propped on the

desk. When he heard the door slam, he looked up from his newspaper and scrambled to his feet.

"You need some help, darling?" he asked, and Sidney knew for sure she was home. But then, maybe that was a little unfair. In her Levi jeans and Redskins T-shirt, she probably looked younger than her thirty years. She wiped sweat from her forehead with her fingertips, and smoothed back the curly tendrils of hair on her forehead.

"Yes, I need a police report for a prisoner you had here," she answered.

Grange switched the toothpick he chewed to the other side of his mouth.

"Cooter? You mean Cooter?" Grange asked. "Why he ain't here. We sobered him up and sent him home a couple of days ago. Maybe if you come back next week, he'll . . ."

"No," she answered and walked through the swivel gate separating the square patch of floor by the door from the rest of the station. "Dexter Haven," she explained.

Grange cheeks turned pink. "You a reporter?" he asked. " 'Cause if you a reporter, I can't get you nothing. Specially no outta town newspaper reporter."

"I'm not a reporter," she sighed. "I'm his lawyer, Sidney McCalaster."

"He has a lawyer," a voice said, flat as stone.

Both Sidney and Grange turned to look at Jacob, who had just walked in from the small office at the back of the jailhouse. Sidney walked back to the desk where Grange stood, and opened her tattered book bag. She pulled out a folded piece of paper and handed it to Jacob. After he read the retainer agreement, he folded his arms across his chest. He gazed down at Sidney's navy blue Keds and let his eyes wander upward over her Levi's and T-shirt. He stopped at her face, which gleamed from the heat. He looked her boldly in the eyes.

"So," he said, "you're his lawyer. So what?"

Sidney thanked God she wasn't the blushing type. The man annoyed her more than she ever thought he would. But even though annoyed, she was still captivated by his smooth, dark skin and the sharp planes of his face. He seeemed to make the room stand still just by being in it.

"Look, Sheriff," she said, then threw a look at Grange, "can we talk?"

He stared at her a moment longer and then turned toward his office without a word. Shaking her head, Sidney followed him.

Once inside, they faced each other over a small, wooden table. Jacob stood with his arms still folded. Sidney wished she had not closed the door behind her. She avoided the gray metal chair and stood against the wall by the door. Jacob stood next to a picture of the present Samuel Haven, the founder's great-grandson and presently mayor of this sleepy town. Sidney wished he was standing in front of that picture instead. Facing a smiling Samuel Haven and a frowning Jacob made Sidney nervous.

The heat made the room seem even smaller than it was, and although only ten seconds had passed since Sidney shut the door, it seemed eons longer. She could feel the hair curl on the nape of her neck from the sweat dripping down her back. She couldn't remember Mississippi ever being so hot, not even when she was a little girl living in the Bottoms. She could see the heat also affected Jacob, but in a disturbing way. It caused his short sleeve white shirt to hug his broad chest, and his own Levi's to mold attractively to his muscular thighs.

Sidney guessed him to be in his late thirties. Jacob was a very tall man, well over six feet, and broad-shouldered. His eyes looked like black oil set in his angular face. Except for an almost imperceptible scar near his chiseled mouth, his skin was very smooth, the color of dark sable. His black hair was cut so low, Sidney could see his scalp in places.

"What can I do for you?" he asked, smiling.

She noticed, when he smiled he tilted one corner of his mouth upward, never quite letting it touch his eyes.

"Sheriff Conrad," Sidney could tell he didn't take her seriously. She felt as if the man was laughing at her.

"Call me Jacob," he interrupted her, his arms still folded.

"All right. Jacob," she answered. "I know you arrested my client last Tuesday . . ."

While she spoke, Jacob grabbed one of the silver chairs by the back rail and pulled it from the wooden table. He sat in it and propped his feet carelessly on the wooden desk. *Annoying,* Sidney thought.

"Please," he said, "sit." He motioned his large black hand to a chair on the opposite side of the table.

"I'd rather stand," she said. "I need the police report on my client. I'd also like to see the police report on the victim. Yolonda Brown? Was that her name?" Sidney saw him stiffen. The man did have a temper.

"Your client?" he asked. "You mean Dexter Haven?"

"You know damn well who I mean," Sidney said. She had lost her patience.

"Oh, him," he continued. "You mean Dexter Haven? The man who raped and cut up a fourteen-year-old girl, whose name you can't remember?" Jacob took his feet off the table. He sat upright without taking his eyes from Sidney. "I don't have to give you a damn thing," He finished.

"You know you do," she said, amazed.

"The prosecutor will give you everything you need." Jacob stood up, ready to end the conversation.

"He's out of town. Vacation or something," Sidney answered.

"Then you can wait until he gets back."

Sidney walked closer to the table. "Sheriff Conrad,"

she said, "I have a meeting with my client at two in the afternoon. Today."

"Good. Then get it from him," he said smiling broadly. "Or don't you trust him?"

Sidney sat down, and stared at Jacob without blinking. While she looked at him, she came to the realization that he really didn't know who she was. It didn't surprise her. Despite what Rupert Englestorm said, she was little known outside of law circles, and still ran across the law enforcement person every now and then who didn't know of her reputation as one of the hottest lawyers in the country. She knew the way she was dressed made her appear young, and in it was a definite disadvantage.

"Mr. Conrad," she said, her voice rigid. "By law, I have the right to understand why you arrested my client. He still has some rights left, and he isn't yours yet. No court has convicted him."

"Yet," Jacob answered.

It was Sidney's turn to laugh. "Not if I have anything to do with it. Now, about those reports . . ." she started again.

"No," Jacob said, still insisting on being stubborn.

Sidney sighed and reached into her book bag. She pulled out a small steno pad.

"Do I have to get your . . ." she flipped through a couple of pages of the notebook, "Judge Harold to issue a subpoena for those documents, Jacob?" she asked.

"And if I say yes?"

"Then I say you are not only being ridiculous, Sheriff, I'd say you're being hysterical." Sidney tossed the steno pad back into the open mouth of her backpack.

Jacob stood up and took a step near her. She ignored him as she hoisted the strap of her backpack over her shoulder.

"Further," she continued, "I'll get the ACLU involved and make it my business to have them crawl up your butt so far with a microscope, the good citizens of Haven will start mistaking you for Madame Curie instead of the long arm of the law."

Sidney had to bend her neck back to look up at Jacob, he stood so close. She hid a little sigh of relief as the door swung open, and Grange stuck his head inside.

"Hey, Sheriff," he said, "I've got your food out here. Your lunch is getting cold." Obviously Grange was not aware of the tension in the tiny room.

"Grange," Jacob said, not taking his eyes from Sidney, "Get the Haven police reports for the Counselor."

"But, Sheriff," Grange protested.

"Now, Grange. We seem to have a little trouble on our hands."

After Grange left, Sidney started for the door. "I assume our business here is finished?" she asked.

"It's just beginning," Jacob answered smoothly.

Sidney sighed, "I suppose you are right. I probably will be seeing you and your deputy Barney Fife in court."

Jacob ignored the barb. When Sidney walked outside, the Mississippi heat covered her like a blanket.

"Damn," she said aloud to no one in particular, "damn, it's hot."

She quickly checked her watch, and thought about meeting her half brother, Dexter Haven, for the first time. As she drove through the town, past the courthouse, and the park with a gray–green statue of the first Samuel Haven, she tried to tell herself she was more curious than nervous. She could count on her hand the number of times she had actually seen Dexter Haven up close. Though they lived in the same town, she had only seen him from a distance. Now, she wondered if he was at all like her.

Sidney stopped her rented Taurus across the street from the Haven mansion one hour before her scheduled meeting. She could hear a dog barking and a child laughing in the silence.

The Haven Mansion had always appealed to her, and she noticed how she had instinctively parked the car near the willow she used to hide behind as a child. She would imagine herself running along the long front porch, or climbing the ancient willows and magnolia trees dotting the front lawn. Now she would have a chance to do what she never could as a child, to go inside and meet the rest of the family.

She reached into the back seat and pulled her book bag to the front. She grabbed the papers and photographs Grange had handed to her right before she left the Haven police station. He had given her everything—even a brief biography of the victim, Yolonda Brown. The girl was fourteen when she died, and lived with her mother, Wilma Brown, on 21st Avenue in the Bottoms, the poorest section in Haven. They lived three blocks north of MLK Avenue, where Sidney grew up. Wilma Brown nicknamed her daughter Peachy Girl because of her yellow skin and green eyes. Sidney knew the family, and had even attended high school with Wilma Brown. Covina, Sidney's mother, had told her that the grandmother passed two years ago.

And there were pictures, too. Pictures of Yolonda Brown in a pool of blood and a hole in her face where her left eye should have been. Could Dexter Haven have done this? Just then, she saw a little girl in a blue dress and blond curls chase a pink ball in front of her car. She stopped when she noticed Sidney in the front seat, and stood staring while clutching the ball to her chest. A breathless uniformed maid grabbed the girl by the arm and led her back onto the wide green lawn. Sidney turned to look at the Haven mansion again, thinking how close she had come to growing up in a place like this. A place so silent.

She looked at her watch again. It had just turned two

o'clock. She stuffed the papers back into her book bag and left the car. When she arrived at the same door that Jacob pounded on Tuesday night, she paused, then took a deep breath before ringing the doorbell.

Jason, the butler, answered the door. His tone was as formal as his black bow tie and white jacket. "Yes, Madam, may I help you?" he said.

"I have an appointment with Dexter Haven," Sidney answered.

Jason didn't move, but looked her up and down. Sidney could feel her jeans, sticky from the heat, cling to her thighs. She knew she was sweaty and in bad need of a shower. But she was annoyed at Jason. He knew damned well who she was, even baby-sat her and her sister when they were kids. But then, Carl Haven—Sidney's father and Jason's boss—had forced that duty upon him.

Sidney remembered her mother telling her that after Carl died, the man would turn up his nose as if he caught a whiff of bad wind when he passed her on the street. And now, he looked at Sidney like she was a wet kitten who had just crawled onto his doorstep.

"I'm his lawyer," she said flatly. "He's expecting me."

"Oh, yes," he said.

He poked his head out of the doorway, and Sidney had to step back or he would have hit her in the chest with the top of his shiny, bald head.

"The servant's entrance is . . ." he said as he pointed toward the side of the house.

"I'm sure Mr. Englestorm doesn't use the servant's entrance," Sidney interrupted. "Just tell him I'm here." She brushed past him into the house, almost knocking him over.

"Well. I guess it's okay," he said as he shut the door. "Please wait here, and I'll tell Mr. Haven you have arrived."

He turned to walk away, then turned back to her. "And please, wipe your feet," he finished.

Sidney ignored him, and followed him into the black and white tiled foyer. They turned left into a wide hallway carpeted with a red Persian rug. Portraits of past male Havens dotted the wall. Each one had a little light with a gold nameplate. They reached two mahogany double doors. Jason knocked briefly, then opened them before waiting for an answer.

"Mr. Haven," he said as he poked his head inside the door, "Mr. Dexter's lawyer has . . ."

Sidney brushed past him for the second time that day. This time, Jason so seriously lost his balance he had to catch the door handle to keep from falling.

"That will be all, Jason, thank you," Samuel Haven said as he reclined behind a wide mahogany desk, smoking a cigar.

Sidney knew they were Cuban, and very expensive, because Julian sometimes smoked them. After Jason closed the double doors to the study, Samuel waved toward one of the winged-back chairs.

"Please, be seated," he said.

Sidney sat down, and put her book bag on the floor. A floor to ceiling window looked out onto the garden behind Samuel Haven. A woman in a blue silk dress and white straw hat knelt beside a basket of roses. Their heads hung out of the baskets like blood drops. The entire scene reminded Sidney of a watercolor painting.

"Yes, that's Marion, Carl's wife." Samuel leaned forward to watch her expression. "Lovely, isn't she."

"She looks as cold as I've heard," Sidney said casually as if she were discussing the peculiarities of the weather.

Samuel laughed softly, "Carl always said you didn't have any respect." He puffed on his cigar. "Now I can see for myself that it's true."

"Where's my client?" Sidney asked. "I don't have all day."

Samuel Haven stood up and walked past Sidney to the bar. "He will be along shortly," he replied. "Can I get you something to drink? You look thirsty as hell."

"Yes, lemonade, please," she replied. "Where is he?"

Samuel poured lemonade into a crystal goblet. "He's meeting with Rupert," he answered, handing the glass to her.

She put the glass to her forehead and absorbed the coolness. "Since when do you meet with your lawyer to meet with your lawyer?"

Samuel laughed again. "These aren't exactly normal circumstances." He sat back behind the desk. "Rupert told me your hesitation in defending Dexter."

"Oh," Sidney said as she arched an eyebrow, "did he tell you he had to blackmail me to get me to do it?"

Samuel ignored the comment as he stabbed the cigar out into an ashtray on the desk. Sidney took a long drink of her lemonade. It tasted sweet, the texture pulpy.

"I guess you are wondering why I didn't let Rupert do this," he said in what sounded to Sidney like a deliberate effort to be casual. "Defend Dexter that is," he finished.

Sidney watched him as he twirled the crystal ashtray on the desk with his fat pink-tipped fingers.

"The thought did cross my mind," she finally answered. "But what was it that Rupert told me?" she said just as casually. "Because I'm well respected in this town?"

Samuel gurgled a laugh that lasted so long, he began to cough. He dragged a handkerchief roughly across his mouth. "Not quite," he finally said. "It's just that Rupert doesn't have the balls for this." He ignored Sidney's raised eyebrow. Samuel stood up and walked around the desk.

"During that whole Heater business, when that boy got murdered," Samuel continued, "he went around red—

faced all the time. I thought the man was going to have a heart attack.''

"And why is that?'' Sidney asked.

Samuel continued as if she hadn't spoken. "You believe he actually cared—I mean really cared—about that boy's dying? Talked all the time about finding the *real* murderer. It took all my strength to make him keep his damn mouth shut,'' he said in a rough voice. Then incredibly, he laughed again, almost doubling over.

"Probably about the same amount of strength it took for you to keep a straight face,'' Sidney said dryly. She felt sickened all of a sudden.

"Besides, the town never really trusted him after that,'' Samuel continued. "We all lost a lot of credibility over that one, that's for sure.''

"And why is that?'' she asked again, sarcastically.

Samuel waved his hand. "That's all water under the bridge, now. All that counts is that you are here. And Rupert's right. This town does think a lot of you, however misguided . . .'' he finished weakly.

"Mr. Haven,'' Jason said as he poked his head through the door, "Mr. Englestorm and Mr. Dexter . . .''

"Yes, yes Jason. We know the way.'' Rupert pushed him aside as he walked in. Dexter followed, and if Sidney had not been watching closely, she would have missed him. He slid past Rupert silently, and sat in a chair by a bookcase that reached all the way to the ceiling. He crossed his thin legs and laced his fingers in his lap. Sidney could not see his face because of the shadows cast by the bookcase. Rupert went straight to the bar.

"Blast it, Samuel,'' he said. "Where is the whiskey?''

"Where it has always been, Rupert,'' Samuel answered.

"Oh.'' Rupert reached under the bar and brought up a bottle of Jack Daniel's. "I thought you would have had it out by now." He untwisted the cap, and nodded toward Sidney in acknowledgment.

"Now, about the boy's defense . . ." he said as he sank into the brown leather sofa.

"How can we talk about the boy's defense when I haven't even met the boy?" Sidney asked.

"Oh. Oh . . . *eh–hem*, yes." Rupert sat his drink on the table and reached down to his shoes to brush away some wished–for dirt.

"Dexter, come over here, and get out of the damned shadows," Samuel said.

Dexter stood up and walked into the light. His faded blue jeans hugged his thin waist snugly and stopped just above his bony ankles. He wore a white collarless shirt and his blond curly hair spilled around his head like a melting halo.

"Hello," he mumbled.

Sidney noticed his eyes were the same faded blue as his jeans. Instead of responding to him, she stood up and looked into his face. The man was tall, at least six feet, but thin. She took one of his bony hands. She studied it for a moment, and then reached for the other one. When she was satisfied, she let it drop. His hands were soft, his nails clean. There were no faded scratches or bruises.

"Was he examined by a doctor?" she asked.

"A what?" Rupert asked, confused.

"A doctor," she said. "You know, the people who wear the white coats and funny necklaces?"

"You don't have to talk about me like I'm not in the room," Dexter said, sounding surprised by the resentment in her voice.

"Don't worry about whether or not a doctor saw him," Rupert piped in. "I'm driving this defense."

"Okay, fine." Sidney reached for her book bag. "Drive it." She fished for her car keys and started for the door.

"Wait just a minute," Samuel Haven said. "I thought we had a deal!"

"You can threaten me all you want," Sidney answered. "But I don't fight battles unless I can choose the weapons." She looked at Rupert before continuing, "And I don't want be pushed around by some petty little lawyer who hasn't litigated a case since 1970."

Rupert choked on his whiskey. He set his glass on the coffee table and stood up to answer. But Samuel Haven held up his hands to stop him.

"She's right," he said. "We chose her as his lawyer. We can't do this half-assed."

Dexter winced. "Uncle, do you have to curse?"

"Whatever you want, Samuel." Rupert sat down and crossed his legs. "Go ahead Sidney," he said, his smile small and fake.

"Okay," she said, and took another sip of her lemonade. "Were you examined by a doctor after the murder?" She looked straight at Dexter.

"No." He rubbed at his wrists, remembering the pinch of the handcuffs.

Sidney scribbled something in her notepad. "Did you know the victim?" she asked.

"No," he answered, not meeting her eyes.

Sidney waited, watching Dexter. He walked to the window and touched the glass. Only the sound of ice tinkling could be heard in the silence.

"Of course he didn't know her," Samuel answered for his nephew, the boy who had become like a son to him since Samuel's brother Carl had died. "Why would he?"

"Isn't that the blue dress I gave Mother for Christmas?" Dexter asked, pointing toward his mother in the garden.

"What's your blood type, Dexter?" Sidney asked.

"O positive, I think," he stopped. "O positive," he said again.

Sidney rifled through the police report. "They found semen on the girl," she said casually. "It came from a man with O positive blood." She looked up from the papers at Rupert and Samuel for confirmation. "That's a pretty rare blood type, isn't it?" she asked.

"DNA's not back yet," Rupert said dryly, and sipped his whiskey. "Just because it's the same blood type doesn't mean it belongs to Dexter."

"Did you know the victim?" Sidney asked again.

"No. Yes." Dexter leaned his head against the window. "Yes. I knew her."

Samuel sighed in disgust. "Just like your father," he breathed. "Now look at this mess."

"Did you see her the night she was killed?"

Rupert jumped up. "He's already been asked these questions, and if you read the police report, which I think you have, you'd know he didn't see her!"

"I know what he told Sheriff Conrad," Sidney replied. "But you can't lie to me. I have to know if there are any surprises."

"I saw her," Dexter said, turning to Sidney, "but I didn't kill her."

Sidney looked into his faded blue eyes.

"You don't believe me, do you?" he asked.

"It doesn't matter what I believe."

"Just like your damned father!" Samuel stood up and blustered around the room. "Couldn't leave the damn black girls alone."

"Did you have a sexual relationship with the victim?" Sidney asked, ignoring Samuel.

"No." Dexter leaned one shoulder against the long window facing the garden. He folded his arms. "No. I didn't. And that's the truth."

"Just so flashy and full of himself." Samuel waved his arms. His diamond pinkie ring caught the light and flung it around the room. "And what happened to him?" He looked at Rupert. He looked at Dexter. Then he fixed his gaze on Sidney. "I'll tell you what happened," he said solemnly, "he died in a whore's bed."

Sidney stared back at him as if the man had just peed on himself. Then she turned back to the police report.

"Samuel," Rupert said, his face turning red, "no sense raking up the past."

"What was your relationship with the victim?" she asked Dexter.

"Just a friend," he answered. "I got her into Rollie's bar. We hung out together." He bowed his head. "She was my friend."

"A fourteen–year–old in a bar?" Sidney asked in disbelief.

"She looked twenty," Dexter answered.

"Don't they all!" Samuel threw up his hands.

"Samuel. Stop it," Rupert warned.

"Do I have to talk about this anymore?" Dexter looked beseechingly at Rupert.

Both Rupert and Sidney answered No and Yes at the same time. They looked at each other for almost a minute.

"This isn't getting us anywhere," Samuel said in a tone indicating a decision. "We should finish this later."

"Fine," Sidney agreed. She was tired and wanted to get to her mother's house and get some sleep. Thank God Covina was visiting Marion, Sidney's sister, in Vicksburg. Marion was pregnant with her first child. With Covina away, Sidney knew she wouldn't be faced with her endless questions. At least, not yet.

Marion, Sidney thought and shook her head. She looked outside the shimmering window to see the other Marion, Carl Haven's widow, rearranging the red roses in the curved wicker basket hanging from her arm. *How does it feel to know that you were the namesake for your dead husband's illegitimate child?* Sidney thought.

"Your arraignment is next week, Wednesday. I take it you want to plead not guilty?" Sidney asked Dexter.

"I didn't kill that girl," Dexter said.

"Okay, not guilty it is," Sidney shrugged tiredly.

"I'll have Jason show you out," Samuel told her.

"No. No," Rupert said, standing up, "I'll see Ms. McCalaster to her car."

Rupert took her by the arm, but Sidney jerked away. He showed his teeth in a mockery of a smile and followed her out of the study. On the fluid marble steps of the Haven mansion, he stopped and turned to her.

"Dexter didn't kill Yolonda Brown," he said. "Surely, you could see that boy couldn't hurt a fly."

"Do you know how many times I've heard that song, Englestorm?" she asked him.

He smiled. "You've been away from Haven too long, Sidney." It was the first time he'd used her first name.

The wind blew briefly. Sidney breathed in the scent of honeysuckle it brought with it before turning to Rupert.

"No," she said, and shook her head, "no, I haven't."

As she drove away, she looked in her rear–view mirror to see Rupert standing on the marble steps, and she couldn't tell if he frowned or smiled.

Chapter 6

The boy was excited. He was going to sing! Granted, it was a funeral, but if he were lucky, about a hundred and fifty people would hear his high, clear voice. He would sing a good song for Peachy Girl. And he decided it would be "How Great thou Art," no matter what Peachy Girl's mother said. Miss Wilma wanted him to sing "He Walks with Me," but Yolonda deserved "How Great thou Art." He would sing that song for Yolonda Brown, for Jesus, and yes, for himself.

He looked at his mother walking him up the aisle like she did in the wedding he was in when he was four. He was too scared to walk up the aisle by himself. And even though he was now six, he was still afraid. Because instead of a bride and groom standing at the other end, there was a shiny brown casket. It shined so much he could see his face in it. And Peachy Girl slept inside, his mother told him. Yes, he repeated to himself, she only slept.

They reached the front of the church, and his mother

turned him to face all the people. She licked her fingers, and wiped the sides of his mouth. She straightened his bow tie while he stared at the black veil triangles dangling around her big hat. She kissed him, then sat down heavily in the front row where he could still see her.

He opened his mouth and his voice became a living thing that got away from him. As he started with "How Great thou Art," it flew out of his mouth and curled around his head like smoke from the sun. It floated into the congregation, put tears in the eyes of old women wearing big black hats. A tortured cry came from the back of the room. He thought it sounded like Johnny, Peachy Girl's uncle. He couldn't see the face of Peachy Girl's mother because a black veil covered it. But he saw her touch a white handkerchief to her eyes. So alive was his voice, he was sure it could give breath to the dead. He looked back at the casket tilted so Peachy Girl's face could be visible in the pews. She still slept, but he could have sworn he saw a peaceful smile on her face.

Sidney watched the boy sing. His eyes were big pools of liquid oil in his chocolate brown face. She saw his fuzzy head turn toward the casket to stare at Peachy Girl. *Mr. Macolm done right by her,* she could almost hear Covina's voice in her head. Mr. Macolm, the man who had carved tombstones for as long as Sidney could remember, also prepared bodies. He combed Peachy Girl's thick black hair over her hollow eye and piled pancake makeup over her bruises and swollen lips. He hid her open neck with an innocent white lace collar. If Sidney had not seen the crime scene photographs, she would not have believed the story of Peachy Girl's violent end.

The boy couldn't have been more than six, but he could sing. The old woman sitting next to Sidney clasped her hands together and shook her head slowly. At one point she leaned over to Sidney and said, "That child sure can sing. He has the voice of an angel." Her voice was low and sweet, like molasses. Sidney had to move her head aside to keep from being poked in the eye by the brim of the old woman's hat.

"His name is Arnold. Thelma's boy. You remember Thelma, don't you chil'?" the old woman asked her.

"Yes Ma'am, I remember Thelma," Sidney lied, and looked around the room to avoid the woman's whispered conversation. She could barely hear her over the open sobs in the tiny church. She would have expected sobs from Peachy Girl's mother, Wilma. But instead, the woman remained silent. Sidney could tell by the set of the woman's shoulders that she was angry.

All of a sudden, she felt eyes on her. She turned around and her eyes collided with the sight of Jacob, who sat one row behind her in an aisle seat on the opposite side of the church. He smiled at her, wryly. She turned to the boy, then back again to where Jacob sat, expecting him to look away. But instead, his eyes remained on her, his face full of stone. For the rest of "How Great thou Art," Sidney felt the back of her head burn.

When the song finished, Reverend Robinson rose and stood at the pulpit. He bowed his head to lead the congregation in prayer. Amid the bowed heads and closed eyes, Sidney left the church, purposely avoiding Jacob's gaze.

She didn't realize how dark the church was until she stood outside, the sunlight sliding beneath her eyelids. She ran the palms of her hands over her forearms. Even though the short black dress she wore was sleeveless, she was still sweating shamelessly. *Damn, I hate the heat,* she thought.

She looked in her purse and grabbed the package of Newports she had found at her mother's house. Although she had quit smoking almost eight years ago, the impending divorce and meeting her biological family made her crave a cigarette. When she noticed the cigarettes on the hall table before she left for the funeral, she scooped them into her handbag without a second thought.

She leaned against the Taurus and stuck the cigarette to her lips. She reached into her purse for a lighter before realizing she hadn't had a lighter in her purse since she quit smoking.

"Light?" a voice asked.

She looked up and saw Jacob looking at her with a green Bic lighter in his hands.

"Yes, thank you," she said, and reached for his hand to steady the flames, and their eyes caught and held. She sensed power emanating from his inky eyes. In them, she saw a man sure of what was right, and sure of what was wrong. The smooth planes of his face told of a man who was as sure of himself as the sun. For a brief second, she envied him.

"That's a filthy habit," he told her, breaking the connection.

She leaned against the car, taking a long drag from the cigarette. "Then why do you do it?" she asked.

"I don't," he waved the smoke away from his face.

She laughed. "So you just carry lighters around for people who do?" she asked.

He didn't smile. "Something like that." He positioned himself beside her against the rental car. "Lighters come in handy sometimes. Like now."

They stood in silence while Sidney smoked, trying not to move. He stood so close to her, she could feel the damp sleeve of his white shirt touching her bare shoulder.

"Dangerous, don't you think?" he asked suddenly.

"What?"

"The steeple." He pointed to the sharp white steeple on top of the church. It jutted toward the sky like a weapon. "Kind of a dangerous thing to put on top of a church. Why do you think people do that?"

"Do what?" Sidney asked, annoyed.

"Put steeples on churches," he answered.

"I take it you don't agree?" she asked him.

"With the steeple or the church?" he countered.

"Either," she answered.

He shrugged his shoulders. "No, not really. I'm an atheist."

Sidney laughed. "A black atheist," she said. "You must fit in really well around here, Sheriff."

"I fit in well enough to know my business."

Sidney took another long drag of the cigarette. "And what business is that?" she asked casually.

"To know who killed that girl lying in that casket." He pointed toward the white, wooden church.

Sidney dropped her cigarette to the ground, and crushed it with the heel of a black patent leather pump. "What you know and what you can prove are two different things," she said dryly.

"Unfortunately, it happens that way sometimes."

"It seems to happen with you a lot." Sidney let out another small laugh.

Jacob turned toward her. She expected to see anger in his eyes, but he made it clear he was going to ignore the bait.

"You mean the Heater murder?" he asked.

"Yes, I mean the Heater murder," she said, returning his frank gaze.

He shrugged. "I couldn't prove the Havens had anything to do with that one. But this one, this one is different," he said and smiled into her eyes. "We have plenty of evidence."

"It must be pretty boring to be right all the time. What makes you so sure of yourself?"

"I know people," he answered. "And I know enough to believe my own eyes."

"Your evidence is circumstantial at best," she said.

"Is that what your client told you yesterday?"

Sidney stood away from the car, and folded her arms. "So that's what this is all about? You think with a big smile you can wheedle out of me what I discussed with Dexter Haven yesterday?"

He cocked his head slightly. "Are you usually so suspicious?" he asked.

"Only when it's warranted," she spat back.

Just then, the doors of the church opened and mourners swelled out on a sea of organ music. Reverend Robinson held onto Wilma's arm as they walked down the steps of the church. When they reached the bottom, the hugging began. Everyone went to Wilma, kissed her cheek, pressed her upper arm. Reverend Robinson stood shaking hands while looking appropriately solemn. When he saw Sidney and Jacob standing by the car, he hurried over to them.

"What are you doing here, Sheriff?" he asked.

Jacob put his hands in his pockets before answering. "What do you think I'm doing here, Robinson? I'm mourning."

"What I think you doin' is conductin' business over that girl's dead body," he answered Jacob indignantly. Then he turned to Sidney.

"I remember you," he said. "You one of Covina's girls."

Sidney smiled tightly. "Yes. I am," she said.

"Some fancy lawyer now, ain't you? I hear you defending the boy what done it."

"My," Jacob said sarcastically, "news travels fast around here."

"And I'm sure you had nothing to do with the traveling?" she asked him dryly.

Jacob shook his head. "Suspicious," he repeated.

Reverend Robinson took out a handkerchief and wiped

sweat and Care-Free-Curl juice from his face. "Listen," he said, "I don't want you two disruptin' this funeral."

"You kicking us out, Robinson?" Jacob asked.

"I'm asking you to show some respect," Reverend Robinson's voice was so loud, a couple of mourners turned to stare. "It's bad enough the girl was killed in that way without having you show up and make a mockery out of her funeral."

"Don't get all dramatic on me, Reverend," Jacob sighed in disgust. "I'm leaving."

And without even casting a glance in Sidney's direction, he walked over to Wilma. When he reached her, he bent his head to speak into her ear, and put his hand on her shoulders. Sidney saw him clasp Wilma to him for a few seconds and hold her tightly. When he let her go, he looked in Sidney's direction. She swallowed as he turned and walked toward his red Mustang.

"He somethin', ain't he?" the Reverend said, watching her.

"Something else," she murmured.

"Go pay your respects to Wilma, and get on," he told her. "Like I said, I don't want no disruptions."

Sidney studied the man for a while, then shrugged her shoulders. She walked over to Wilma, and was glad the woman chose to be the first to speak. But only for a brief instant.

"I just have one question," Wilma said, and lifted her tear-streaked face upward. Sidney noticed that Wilma had started crying when she began walking toward her, as if seeing her reminded her of who took her daughter away. Wilma's eyes were green like her daughter's.

"I'm sorry about Yolonda, Wilma," Sidney said.

"I don't need your sorries," Wilma answered. "I need my girl back."

"Wilma . . ." Sidney begin.

Wilma held up her hands. "No, let me talk. My daughter is dead. I should be allowed to talk."

Sidney remained silent.

"Remember high school, Sidney? I was always on your side. Remember?"

"Yes, I do," she replied.

"When no one wanted you to sit at the lunch table, I would clear out a spot for you. I let you sit right beside me."

"I know you did, Wilma."

"I thought we were friends," she said.

"I'm not the one saying we are not," Sidney countered.

Wilma laughed, bitterly. "You always did have an easy tongue, Sidney. But if it weren't for the Havens dragging you here, would you have come to my daughter's funeral today?"

"No one is forcing me to be here, Wilma. I've just come to say I'm sorry."

"But not sorry enough to help put your brother into jail, where he belongs for killing my girl."

Sidney felt a knot in her stomach. In all of her life, no one had ever talked so openly about her being part of the Haven family. And she didn't like it.

"I'm doing a job," she told Wilma.

"Did your brother murder my daughter?" Wilma asked her frankly.

"I don't know," Sidney answered.

Wilma laughed that same bitter laugh. "Chil'," she said, "you can't even lie when the time calls for it."

Sidney said nothing.

"If you find out he did," Wilma continued, "whose side will you be on, Sidney?"

"I'm doing a job," Sidney repeated. "I can't choose sides."

"Not even the side of right?" Wilma asked.

Sidney again said nothing, and the silence around her rang in her ears. Everyone had stopped to listen to them.

"I guess you're more Haven than Adamson after all," Wilma said referring to Sidney's maiden name, and then turned her back. Sidney looked into the faces around her, but they too turned away as if she had just disappeared into thin air.

Chapter 7

Sidney drove to the murder scene on the next Thursday morning, the day after Dexter Haven's arraignment. As expected, he pled not guilty in Judge Harold's chamber with Rupert Englestorm and his uncle looking on. The Judge allowed the arraignment to take place in his chambers over both Jacob's and the prosecutor's protests. He claimed he didn't want to play into a media circus.

But the only media was Mr. Grayson of the *Haven Crier* with a twenty-five dollar tape recorder strapped to his shoulder. The outside media could care one iota about a small town murder in the middle of nowhere.

Jacob sat through the entire arraignment staring at Dexter, who kept casting nervous glances at him while rubbing his wrists. As the judge read the charges against him, Dexter shifted his gaze to Sidney as if expecting her to save him.

"How do you plead?" Judge Harold asked Dexter after the charges were read.

"How in the hell do you think he pleads, Harry?" Samuel said, twisting in his chair, "not fucking guilty!"

Judge George Harold turned red as he looked from Sidney to Jacob. Clearly embarrassed, he pointed his gavel at Samuel.

"Mr. Haven," he said, "just because you let me win at golf two days ago, don't think I won't throw you in jail for contempt. Now pipe down, and let the boy speak."

"He's hardly a boy," Jacob interrupted.

"You too, Sheriff," Judge Harold said, glancing a warning at Jacob, "shut up."

Jacob rolled his eyes. The prosecutor raised his hand like he was in elementary school. His hesitancy only confirmed to Sidney that there was nothing to worry about from him. Jacob was her real adversary.

"If I may be allowed to speak . . ." the prosecutor asked.

Judge Harold sighed, "No one is allowed to speak except for the God damn defendant. Now just because we haven't had a murder here in six years, it doesn't mean we can't conduct this trial like professionals. I won't have it turned into some kind of barnyard dance with a bunch of backward country farm animals."

He turned toward Dexter, and clasped his hands together on the desk. "Now," he continued, "how do you plead?"

Dexter's mouth worked. He stood up, and shuffled from one foot to the other. Then he sat down again, lacing his fingers together. He looked at Sidney, and she could not help but give him an encouraging nod. He stood up again and looked at Judge Harold.

"Um . . ." he said, "not guilty, Your Honor."

The Judge held his hands toward heaven. "Thank God," he said, "success. Your plea will be entered into the records. Trial is set for one month from today."

"Your Honor," Sidney began, "since my client is a

responsible citizen, I'm requesting he be allowed to stay out on bail in the custody of Samuel . . ."

"A murderer in the custody of a murderer?" Jacob asked incredulously.

"God dammit, Jacob," Judge Harold sighed, "are you the one prosecuting this case? Just shut up for five minutes so we can get this thing over with and all go to dinner." Judge Harold looked at the prosecutor. "Do you have any objections to Dex being released on his *own* recognizance?" he asked him.

"Dex?" Jacob said in disgust.

The Judge ignored him and looked straight at the prosecutor.

"No, Your Honor," he answered. "No I don't."

"Good," the Judge replied, then stood up. He slapped the gavel on his desk and proclaimed dinner time.

Everyone stood up except Dexter. He looked up at the people towering above him. "Is it over?" he asked Sidney.

Before she could answer, Jacob broke in. "Over?" he asked. "It's just beginning."

"Don't you have anything better to do than intimidate my client?" she asked him.

"Hmm, let me think . . ." he said, stroking his chin as if he were deep in thought, "I could go to Rollie's and see if there are any more teenagers hanging out there. Or I could check on Mrs. Dutsin and make sure her dog is staying out of the neighbor's flower bed." He paused then, and looked at Sidney. "No. Come to think of it, there isn't anything better I have to do."

Without taking her eyes from Jacob, Sidney grabbed Dexter's arm. "Come on Dexter," she told him, "stand up."

"Yes! Stand up!" Samuel responded, having overheard only the last of the conversation. "Stop cowering in your chair like the man's going to hit you."

The prosecutor put his hand on Jacob's shoulder. "Come on, Jacob," he said. "We aren't doing any good here."

After the arraignment, Dexter and Sidney sat in the deserted coffee shop two doors down from the police station. This time, Sidney insisted they be alone. He told her that after he and Yolonda left Rollie's bar on the night of the murder, he went one way and she another. And that was the last time he had seen her alive.

Thinking back on the scene on her way to Rudger's housing development, Sidney knew it was going to be a strange, strange trial.

She parked her car across the street from 1686 Easterbrook Drive and laughed when she saw the yellow police tape still encircling the entire house, including the driveway. She wondered briefly why it had been placed so low. *Then again,* she thought, *the town didn't have a lot of practice roping off a crime scene.* As she hopped over the tape, she dropped her book bag. The photos spilled into the dirt and gravel. She picked them up and brushed them off as she walked through the framed door of the unfinished house.

She noticed the chalk outline on the cement floor as soon as she walked in. Several blood stains marked the floor, one huge splatter about ten feet away from the chalk outline. She sat on the floor and leaned against a two by four. The floor felt cold against her bare legs. She studied each picture before placing it on the floor around her.

The first one was of Yolonda with a gaping hole in her neck. The violence of the crime seemed far removed from Dexter's seemingly gentle nature. But she had only met one side of him, and wouldn't be surprised if he turned out to be the murderer.

She placed the next picture on the cold cement floor. This one was of the lower half of Yolonda's body, her denim Wrangler mini skirt pulled over her hips. Sidney remembered questioning Dexter again about his sexual relationship with Yolonda as he sipped his decaffeinated coffee earlier that day. But he told her it wasn't like that. They were just friends. He knew she wasn't a virgin but claimed it wasn't because he'd slept with her. It was because she told him. She was his friend, he insisted again.

The next picture was a close-up of Yolonda's left hand. At first, Sidney thought the girl's red fingernails had been ripped off. But when she looked closer, she saw they were fake. They may have been the acrylic kind, but were probably the cheaper press–on version. Still, even though Dexter wasn't examined by a doctor, she didn't remember seeing any scratches on him.

The next picture was strange: a full body shot of Yolonda. White powder from the cement floor covered her entire body, except for her feet. One high–heeled mule dangled from her toes, but the other was obviously knocked off during the struggle. Still, how could she get white powder on the rest of her body, but not on her feet?

Sidney jumped. She thought she heard footsteps, and the breeze coming through the array of two by fours chilled her. A sound like wood on cement made her jump again, and she tried to laugh away her nervousness. Looking at pictures of dead girls in deserted housing developments was obviously making her nervous. Not wanting to spend another minute in what felt like Yolonda's tomb, she gathered the pictures and threw them into her backpack.

Back on the main road, she noticed the wide fields of the cotton and soybean crops on either side of the car. Row after row zoomed past her windows. She looked at her dash and saw she was almost out of gas. She had been so anxious to get on the road this morning, she had neglected to fill the tank before she left town. The needle was already below the red line, already under the "E."

The car began to sputter, and she pulled to the side of the road.

"Shit," she said and leaned her head against the steering wheel. She would just have to wait until someone passed. She rolled down the windows and lit a cigarette. She took the pictures out again, and begin studying the curious one—the one with Yolonda's clean feet.

"You having a problem?" a voice asked.

She turned to see Jacob leaning in her window. She stuffed the pictures back into her bag before answering him.

"No gas." She waved a hand toward the dashboard.

He laughed. "That's not too smart," he said.

She glared at him. "Are you going to help me or not?" she asked him.

"Give you a ride back to town," he answered, his voice too casual.

She didn't answer him, but rolled up her window and stabbed out the cigarette. She grabbed her bag and opened the car door. They walked to his red Mustang parked behind the Taurus. Sidney was so absorbed in the last picture, she hadn't even heard his car drive up. She wondered how long he had been standing there.

"What year is this car?" she asked him once they were inside.

"Nineteen–sixty–six," he answered.

"Is it a classic?" she continued.

"How long have you been away from Haven?" he countered.

"About five years," she replied turning to him. "I asked if your car was a classic."

"I guess you can see it is," he answered.

"Does it have air conditioning?" she asked. "It's like an oven in here."

"No, it doesn't." Jacob rolled down his window, and

they both got a whiff of sweet manure from the cotton crops.

"How can you live in Mississippi without an air conditioner in your car?" she asked.

Jacob pulled over to the side of the road to let a timber truck traveling in the opposite lane pass.

"The truck's passed by now. You can go," Sidney told him.

Jacob turned off the car. Folding his arms across his chest, he stared at her.

"You've been away from Haven for five years? Don't you have any family here?"

Sidney sighed. "I have a sister and a mother. My sister lives in Vicksburg," she answered.

"But your mother lives here?" he said as if to remind her.

"Yes." She didn't volunteer any more information.

"Are you planning on visiting your sister while you are here?"

Sidney looked at him, but Jacob's face was expressionless.

"I plan to," she answered. "After this is all over."

"And what if it isn't over quickly?" he pressed. "Will you still wait?"

"I don't know," she answered. "I really haven't had time to think about it. Why?"

He shrugged his shoulders. "I don't know," he said. "Just curious, I guess."

"Just curious?" Sidney questioned.

"Yes, I am," he answered. "I mean if I had a sister and was this close, visiting her would be the first thing I'd do."

"So you don't have any brothers or sisters, Sheriff Conrad?" she asked.

"Nope, only child," he explained before turning to her. "And call me Jacob."

She ignored his attempt to be friendly. "Any other family, Sheriff?"

He paused. "No," he finally answered. "My mother is dead—died a long time ago, when I was a teenager," he said, then smiled ruefully. "I guess you can say I'm alone."

"Really?" she replied.

"Really," he answered sarcastically. He turned the ignition, and the engine let out a slight cough, like a TB patient. Sidney's heart skipped a beat at the thought of being alone out here with him. But when he tried again, the ignition only sputtered briefly before turning over. He looked out the window, and waited until a Haven shuttle bus passed before pulling back onto the road.

Sidney shifted in her seat. "I'm sorry," she said. "I didn't mean to bring up any painful memories."

He said nothing, just looked at her briefly in the rearview mirror, his gaze dry and unrevealing. Sidney looked out the window at the fat, white clouds hanging low in the sky, thinking about how alone he must be. Although her family was not the ideal, at least she had one. She couldn't imagine living life without Covina, or her sister Marion.

"Were you going to say something else, Sidney?" he asked her.

"No, nothing in particular," she answered. "I mean it's none of my business."

"Oh, come on," he said. "Just say it."

"Okay," she said. "I was just thinking that you must be truly alone if you don't have a God to turn to."

She felt the car slow down as Jacob subconsciously lifted his foot slightly from the gas pedal. "I have myself to turn to," he said. "Do you believe in God, Sidney?"

"Of course I do," she replied immediately, almost mechanically.

"I did too, when I was growing up," he said. "I was

raised Catholic right up to the point when my mother died. It was stomach cancer; very painful, very fast.''

"You don't have to talk about this if you don't want to," Sidney said. "I don't mean to pry."

"No," he said, shrugging his shoulders. "You asked a question. I want to give you an answer. I found it hard to believe in a God who would allow a woman so devoted to him to go through so much pain. And then there was the police force, where I investigated all those homicides. Dead bodies all over the place, and people getting away with it right and left." As he spoke, his casual voice became insistent, and a little angry.

Sidney answered before thinking. "So, it's not that you don't believe in God, it's just that you are having a spat with him because he's not doing things your way."

Instead of becoming angry, he just laughed and replied, "What floors me most of all, is how people like you, who profess to believe in God, can defend filth like the Havens."

"Have you ever been wrong, Sheriff?" she asked him. "Ever in your whole life?"

"Not often," he said, laughing.

"I don't want to talk about this anymore," she said. "It's beginning to annoy me."

"Fine, we won't," he responded.

Sidney reached for the radio to kill the silence that followed.

"It doesn't work," he said.

"No radio, no air conditioner," Sidney said, shaking her head.

"So what do you think your sister Marion will say when she finds out you are this close but didn't come to see her?"

Sidney looked out the car window to escape his question. She didn't want to admit she was afraid of what Marion might say if she knew she were defending Dexter Haven, that she avoided her sister for that reason and that reason alone.

"Is that a deer?" she asked pointing. *I'll explain it to her after it's over,* she thought.

"You are full of questions," he said, his voice dry. "Did you take Small Talk 101 in law school?"

"Me?" She placed her hand on her chest. "You are the one conducting an interrogation."

"It's because I'm curious," he explained.

"Curious about what?"

"Curious why scum like Dexter Haven would bring you back after all these years."

"What do you know about Dexter Haven? You're just a transplant."

"Oh," he said in that same dry tone, "and how would you know that?"

Sidney hesitated before answering. "Now whose suspicious?" she laughed. "It's hardly a secret."

They passed a bramble of shotgun houses before Jacob spoke again. "I know enough to know your Dexter slit that baby's throat."

"Fourteen is hardly a baby. You need to turn left here, at Johnson's Grocers."

"Too young to have her throat slit by that scum," he said, slowing the car as three laughing children, all black arms and legs, alternately ran and skipped across the street.

"My mother's house is on the right, the small one with the arches," she told him.

He waited until the children passed, then pulled into the driveway.

"And I'm not discussing my client with you," she finished as if there was not a break in their conversation.

After he turned off the engine, he grabbed her hand as she reached for the door handle. Her hand looked small and almost white against his large dark one. Sidney snatched it away. Already sticky and wet from the heat, when he touched her hand, she felt as if she had stuck her hand in a pot full of boiling hot water. Without missing a beat, he grabbed the silky braid that fell down around her shoulders, and twisted it around his fist. She felt a sense of panic as he pulled her toward him.

"Just tell me this. Why in the hell with hair and skin like this did you grow up in the middle of the Bottoms in a house with arches? Do you have any Havens lurking in your closet? Is that why you hot-tailed it back here to defend Dexter Haven?"

Sidney slapped at his hand and twisted her hair away from him until she was free. She had heard about his famous temper, and how it had almost cost him his job more than once in New York. Although she had not had time to find out the details, she knew his accommodations were the only things saving him. And when he decided to stay in Haven after the Heater case was closed, they had given him up willingly.

Sidney also knew he was under no misconception about her heritage. He may have been a transplant, but he was no fool. Her face flushed and red from the exertion, she swiped the hair he had shaken loose out of her face.

She opened the car door and looked him squarely in the face. "I'll see you in court, Sheriff Conrad," she told him before slamming the car door so hard it sounded like a gunshot.

Sidney could not help but notice her mother's house as she walked to the door. She didn't need to examine the neatly cut lawn, the bushes sculpted into the shapes of small unicorns to know the gardener came every Tuesday and Thursday. And she knew the twinkling windows looked almost invisible because her mother had a maid come over every Wednesday and Friday to wash them.

Sidney even teased her about it. *I can't believe you have a maid,* she would tell her. And Covina would answer, *What maid? I just have Miss Mary come over a couple times a week to straighten things up for me. I don't have no maid.*

The marble steps she walked up may have been small in comparison to those at the Haven's mansion, but she knew Jacob was right. A house like this had no business sitting smack dab in the middle of the poorest neighborhood in Haven.

The air conditioner immediately cooled her when she walked into the house. Light spilled into every window. She went to her childhood bedroom, after all these years, still pink and light and safe looking. She started thanking God for the second time since she returned home that her mother wasn't here.

But before she could release the final Amen, a horn blared discordant music through the closed window of the bedroom. It was so loud, Sidney swore people in Vicksburg could probably hear it. She lifted one side of the pink curtain from the window.

In the street driving slowly through a gaggle of children was her mother's long, maroon Buick. The children scattered like chicks to either side of the road, and watched the car turn into the driveway. Sidney stared motionlessly for countless moments, refusing to believe her eyes. *It can't be,* she thought, *it just can't be.* But it was: Covina had come home.

Sidney looked around as if for a place to hide. She knew Covina would have a million and one questions for her, questions she herself did not completely know the answers to. She removed her hand from the curtain, and let it fall in place over the window. She took a deep breath and walked out into the living room, and waited while searching for the right mood in which to greet Covina.

It had been eight months since she had last seen her mother. Covina had flown to Virginia for a three-day visit.

But when Sidney left Julian, her soon to be ex-husband, she swore it felt like three years.

This is stupid, just go answer the door, Sidney. But before she took the first step, the door popped open. Covina tramped in wearing a turban and flared black pants. She had on a saffron–yellow dashiki with a black asymmetrical print.

"Mamma?" Sidney said, her voice a question.

"Yes," Covina replied, kicking the door shut with a foot clad in a chunky black sandal. "Mamma. That's me."

Covina, practically dripping luggage, turned to face Sidney. She had two duffel bags, one slung diagonally over each shoulder. And in both hands she carried two burgundy suitcases trimmed in silver.

"Mamma," Sidney questioned, "what are you doing here?"

"Now is that any way to greet your mother?" she said as she dropped the two suitcases on the floor. "Besides, last I checked, I lived here. This is my house, dammit."

"But I thought you were helping Marion," Sidney said dumbly.

Covina sighed. "Sidney," she said, "could you please come help me with this?"

Sidney walked over to Covina and helped her draw the strap of one duffel bag over her head. When they got the other one off, Covina grabbed Sidney around her neck and pulled her into a tight hug. Sidney smelled the spicy scent of her perfume as Covina smashed her face into the side of her neck.

"I did miss you, girl," she said, then pushed her away so she could study her at arm's length. "But why didn't you tell me you were gon' come down here?"

"How is Marion?" Sidney countered.

"Your sister is fine," Covina said, plumping on the couch. "The doctors in Vicksburg are still making her stay in bed and take medicine so that baby won't come early. But she's fine. It's almost time anyway. I don't see why they just don't go ahead and let it happen.''

Covina unzipped one of the duffel bags and rummaged inside until she pulled out a pack of Newports. She stuck a cigarette between her lips and brought a match up to the tip.

"You started smoking again," she asked, looking at Sidney over the yellow flame.

"No," Sidney said. "No, I'm not."

"Don't lie to me, girl," Covina said as she leaned back against the couch. "I smelled it on you."

Sidney folded her arms. "I only had a couple since I've been here."

"Don't you get started again," Covina said, wagging the burning cigarette at her. "I'm quitting. I'm down to about four cigarettes a day. Even switched from Camels to these things. They not as strong," she finished.

"I won't," Sidney sighed. "Let me help you with the luggage."

She picked up the two duffel bags and carried them into Covina's room. The room was not the stark, well-ordered place it had been when Covina shared it with Carl Haven. But instead, it was a wild garden of colors, crammed with odds and ends of the junk Covina had collected over the years. One of the mahogany night stands was covered with rocks—some of them ugly and jagged, other smooth and translucent.

Covina had followed her into the room. She now stood rummaging among the shot glasses on the antique dresser until she found a crystal ashtray. Though her cigarette was only half gone, she stabbed it out.

"Mamma, what's with all the rocks?" Sidney picked up one, pink and smooth like marble in her palm.

"Oh, them," Covina said, removing her turban. Her

hair was natural and cut low. "I collect them. Every place I go, every time I go, I pick up a rock. And if I can, a shot glass. It reminds me of where I've been."

"And where is that?" Sidney asked conversationally in an attempt to stall.

"Oh, lots of places," Covina said. "Especially since you girls left home. I've been to Shreveport for gambling, and Las Vegas. Even saw me the Hoover Dam, but I had spent so long at the slot machines, all that water just looked like a whole bunch of silver dollars rushing over the edge. Then, a couple of years ago, I even made it to Atlantic City . . ."

Sidney laughed. "So you go places just to gamble, huh?" she asked.

"No," Covina explained. "I looks for things, you know, in people. I love meetin' all kinds of different people. And you sure do get a good mix in a casino. I mean I see ol' people, young people, black people, white people. All sorts of folks. I just never knew there were so many different kinds of people in this one country, coming from Haven and all. You know what I mean Sidney? Where people love to put you in boxes and judge you just for one or two things you done in yo' life."

"Boxes?" Sidney questioned.

"Yeah, boxes," Covina answered. "Some of them love to remind me about me and Carl. I tries not to get mad, tell them it's none of their business. But they think they got me all figured out just 'cause of that one thing."

Covina began taking her rings off one by one, and they fell like raindrops into the shot glasses. "But when I meet people in casinos, I ask all kinds of questions, like where they born, how many brothers and sisters they have, have they ever been in jail . . ."

"Mamma," Sidney laughed, "you don't."

"Sure I do," Covina said, turning her dark eyes to her

daughter. "Most of them answer, especially the real ol' ones. They got no reason to care anymore," she said.

"You're something else," Sidney said, shaking her head.

Covina walked over and stood beside Sidney. "That rock you holding," she said, "I think that's from when I visited you in Virginia, though. It ain't from one of them casino towns. It reminded me of you."

"How do you mean?" Sidney asked her.

"It's all small and fragile looking, like you could crush it if you step on it. But the fact is you probably get nothing more than a sore foot," she said with pride in her voice.

Sidney didn't answer, but looked out the double French doors onto the patio and garden. She noticed that Covina had managed to cut down one of the magnolia trees, but left two others. Their white flowers, encircled by glossy green leaves, drooped heavily from the branches. Covina went to the French doors and opened them.

"Fresh air," she said, sitting on the bed. "Come over here and sit by me, Sidney."

Sidney did as Covina said, and sat close enough to her so their shoulders touched. She couldn't help but think about the time Covina had torn this room apart looking for the paper Carl Haven had given her. It was the paper deeding her the house, and the land. Now, all of that was in jeopardy. But this she could never tell Covina. She was too afraid she would upset what she thought of as her mother's delicate balance.

"Sidney," Covina said suddenly, "is it true what they say? Are you defending Dexter Haven?"

Sidney went to stand up, but Covina pulled her back on the bed.

"How did you find that out?" Sidney asked her.

"I read it," Covina said, her voice strident, "in the Vicksburg Chronicle."

"It was in the paper?" Sidney asked.

"No, no," Covina shook her head. "Not the part about you defending Dexter Haven, but the part about Wilma's girl dying and them arresting Dexter Haven. It was just a little blurb on one of the inside pages. When I called Wilma to tell her I was sorry, she told me you were defending him and you were here at the house."

"Oh," Sidney said, limply.

"You better thank the Lord I didn't tell Marion you were here," Covina said. "She would be too mad that you didn't come down to visit, her being sick and all."

"Mamma," Sidney said and stood up. "I can't talk about this."

"What do you mean you can't talk about it?" Covina said. With a sense of urgency, she grabbed both of Sidney's hands. "You don't know what you are doing—getting mixed up with the Havens is like getting mixed up with the devil."

"But Mamma," Sidney said in a frosty voice, "you did it."

Covina let go of Sidney's hands, and dropped her head. "I know I did, and I'm sorry. It's been so hard on you girls with who your daddy was and all. I've watched you girls growing up, especially you, Sidney, trying so hard to fit in, but just not being able to."

"Mamma, I don't . . ." Sidney began.

"I know you hate talking about it, and Lord knows I hate digging up the past. But I just hope you don't think by defending Dexter Haven they gon' accept you."

"Mamma!" Sidney said. "That's not what I want. I can't go into why I have to do this. But I need you to leave me alone with all these questions. And I don't care—no, I don't want to *know* the whys and the wherefores behind you and Carl Haven!"

"Now, Sidney," Covina said, "I am just tryin' to tell you . . ."

"I'm begging you," Sidney said, swallowing, "to let me do this in peace, for now. When this is over and everything is all right again, I'll tell you more."

Covina stared at her, and Sidney thought how lucky Covina was to be so perfectly beautiful. Her unblemished skin was so pure in its blackness it reminded Sidney of a piece of onyx. The only signs of age were deep creases on either side of her straight nose, and a hardening of the skin between her velvet brows. *How lucky,* Sidney wanted to say to her, *how lucky you are that no one ever asked you what color you are, which can easily translate to where do you belong.* The phone rang, and the tension between them seemed to fall away slightly.

"Okay, okay Sidney," Covina said, and put her hand up in a plea for a truce. "I won't be bothering you with all of this right now, but I'm gon' expect answers to this real soon."

Covina ignored the phone in the bedroom. Instead, she waltzed from the room to get it in the living room. Sidney breathed deeply for a minute, silently thanking her mother for giving her a chance to calm down. She then walked to the living room to hear Covina saying in a loud voice that she was perfectly happy with her long distance bill, and didn't give a damn about ten cents a minute.

Chapter 8

Later that evening, Covina donned a denim blue dress and a white turban for what she termed as an escape to Rollie's bar.

"I can't stay here without asking you what's going on," she said as she used a tissue to blot her burgundy lips, "so I'm gonna leave you in peace tonight and get on down to Rollie's. Tonight is ladies' blues night, all women singing. And I do love women singing the blues."

"You and somebody else I know," Sidney said thinking of Julian and the other secret she had kept from Covina. It would probably be a replay of the Spanish Inquisition if she told Covina she was getting a divorce on top of everything else.

"Don't wait up." Covina flashed Sidney a smile, closing the door on Sidney's don't–worry–I–won't–answer look.

When Grange brought her car by, she was curled up in a Lazy Boy chair wearing a terrycloth robe watching the ten o'clock news. She saw his headlights in the front window. When she opened the door, Grange stepped out of her eggshell–blue Taurus with a big, stupid grin on his face. He met her on the steps, and tipped his hat back.

"Sheriff and I went back after it about a couple of hours ago. Good thing the keys were still in it," he said. "Ran out of gas, did you?"

"Obviously," Sidney answered with her arms folded. "You didn't have to do that. I was going to get it in the morning."

"No bother," he replied. "In this town, we like to take care of folks." He stood looking at her, grinning.

A sound of a blaring horn broke the night. Grange looked back at the red Mustang parked on the curb. Sidney hadn't even noticed it until she heard the horn. Grange took off his hat and pointed toward Jacob's car.

"That's the Sheriff," he said. "He's gonna give me a ride on home."

"Obviously," Sidney repeated as she pulled her robe tighter around her waist.

Grange stood there with his right foot propped on her bottom step looking at her, the grin still splitting his face wide open.

"That Sheriff," he said, "he's something else. Just when you think he ain't got hardly no feelings, he go and do something like this." Grange didn't seem at all in a hurry to leave.

"You want something to drink, some iced tea or something?" Sidney asked, ignoring the comment.

The horn blared again and Grange looked back at the Mustang. "No, I better get," he said. "He might get mad, and leave me."

"Okay," Sidney said. "Tell him thanks."

"No bother, no bother at all, ma'am." Sidney resisted an urge to laugh as Grange tipped his hat toward her.

As Sidney walked to Wilma's house the next morning,

she thought about the incident. She too wondered why
Jacob would be so worried about a car that belonged to
the lawyer representing the man he thought to be as guilty
as original sin.

The sun, barely awakened, had not yet penetrated the
morning coolness. Covina still slept in the mahogany
four-poster bed, a white mask over her eyes like a blind-
fold. Sidney rubbed the sides of her arms and felt goose
bumps there. She wished she had worn her sweater. Her
shorts and white T-shirt were not enough for the unex-
pected morning coolness. Orange-breasted robins skimmed along on the wet dewy grass in the yards she passed.
The smell of bacon cooking and coffee percolating wafted
out of open screen doors. Sidney walked in the street to
avoid the bees buzzing around clumps of honeysuckle.

Wilma's shotgun house stood on the opposite side of
the street about a half mile from Johnson's Grocers. The
house was white with blue trim around the front windows.
Although the front door was open, Sidney could not see
the inside of the house through the screen door because
of the darkened interior. The sound of her knocking was
hollow and metallic.

"Who is it?" a muffled voice asked from inside the
cavern.

"It's me, Wilma," Sidney answered.

"What do you want?" Wilma approached the front door
and put her hand on the latch hook. "You have some
nerve coming up in here."

"Wilma," Sidney sighed. "We have to talk."

"What kind of talking do we have to do?"

"Do you really want to find the person who killed
Yolonda?"

Wilma remained silent for a moment, but the screen
door squeaked when she opened it. When they were both
inside, she turned to Sidney.

"As much as I hate the Havens," she said, "I want to spit in the face of the man who cut my baby's throat, even if it wasn't Dexter Haven."

Sidney looked around the front room of the shack. Braided green and maroon rugs covered parts of the dull hardwood floors. She could see dirt and grease rising through the paint on the walls. *Good Morning America* blared from a big screen TV lodged in a corner.

"Have a seat, I'll be right back." Wilma touched the rake in her fluffy black hair. "I got to finish my hair."

Sidney sat on a forest green leather couch and waited for Wilma. When she saw her walk back in, she carried a jar of Vaseline. She sat in a stout leather chair opposite Sidney, and pulled off the cap.

"You gon' have to excuse me," Wilma said. "I just got out of the tub." She began rubbing Vaseline on her brown legs.

"Wilma," Sidney began, "how long did Yolonda know Dexter?"

Wilma's laugh was short and bitter. "I didn't even know she knew the sonofabitch," she said, then reached in the jar and scooped out some more Vaseline. She held her left arm straight out and begin rubbing it. Sidney could not help but stare at the scar on the soft underside of Wilma's arm.

"You remember how I got that, huh?" Wilma fingered the scar.

"How can I forget?" Sidney replied.

"Me and you," Wilma said, laughing, "jumping the fence behind Johnson's Grocers after stealing that bottle of pop. Tore my arm all open. The only thing that kept Mr. Johnson from killing us."

Wilma's laugh stopped abruptly. "You know," she said, "that's the first time I laughed since my girl died." She clicked the lid back onto the Vaseline jar.

"I'm sorry Wilma," Sidney said again, "but I'm not sure if Dexter did this."

"Too bad we lost touch, huh, Sidney?" Wilma stood up and walked into the last room of the shotgun house. She returned with two cups of black coffee.

"I did write to you, Wilma," Sidney answered, "but you never wrote me back."

"Careful, it's hot," Wilma cautioned as she handed Sidney the cup. "I didn't think you wanted to hear from me, a big-shot lawyer like you."

"Did you know all of Yolonda's friends?" Sidney changed the subject.

"No," Wilma snorted, "of course I didn't. Yeah, I knew she was hanging out down at Rollie's. But what was I supposed to do?" Wilma took a sip of coffee. "At least I knew where she was." She looked at Sidney as if asking her for forgiveness. "Does that sound bad?"

"Then how could you not know Dex and Yolonda knew each other?" Sidney asked, avoiding Wilma's question.

"I don't keep a lot of friends, Sidney." She put the cup on the table. "Not since you left. I didn't have anybody close enough or who cared enough to tell me my daughter was fucking a Haven."

Sidney winced before continuing, "So you think their relationship was sexual?"

Wilma laughed. "What else could he have been doing with that child?" she asked.

"Dex said they were just friends."

"And you believed him?"

Sidney looked Wilma straight in the eyes. "No. I didn't."

"Sidney," Wilma said, "do you know you and me got married on the same day?"

Sidney stood up and wiped the sweat from the back of her legs.

"Wilma, I need to find out about Yolonda." She walked to the opposite side of the room.

"You don't like hearing that, do you?" Wilma asked her. "But we did. The same day." Wilma leaned back in her chair. "I did it on purpose, soon as Covina bragged the date to everybody. I tol' Gil we had to get married on that day. I mean it was about time because we already had Peachy Girl and all. I thought it would make us closer. Where is your husband now?" Wilma asked.

"He's in Virginia," Sidney looked down into her coffee cup. "We're getting a divorce."

"My husband's dead," Wilma said. "Dropped dead one night because of his head. He had a blood clot."

Sidney sighed. "Can we get back to the subject?" she asked.

"Your husband like women?" Wilma continued, looking at Sidney.

"Yes, he did," Sidney said, giving up.

"Mine did, too." Wilma traced the rim of her coffee cup with her forefinger.

Sidney walked back over to the leather couch and sat down. "I'm sorry to hear that, Wilma. When did he die?"

"Seven years ago, right before that boy got murdered. The Heater boy."

"Oh?" Sidney waited for her to finish. It seemed everywhere she turned these days, she heard about the Heater murder.

"Yolonda, my Peachy Girl, took the news about her Daddy's death real hard. She was only seven, but mad as hell."

"Mad at him?"

"Yep, for dying. And mad as hell at the world," Wilma sighed. "That's when I lost control."

A hollow knock on the screen door caused both of them to jump. Without speaking, Wilma answered. She pushed it open slightly, and Sidney could hear an old woman's voice. She stood up and looked around the front room again. Something was wrong here, she thought. Something slightly out of place—like muddy shoes on a kitchen table, or car keys on the back of the toilet.

She looked at the big screen TV, and back over to the leather couch. The braided rugs, though deceptively inexpensive looking, cost at least a couple of hundred dollars. The glass coffee table with its brass legs didn't look like it came from the Levitz in Vicksburg. It was definitely Thomasville.

The pictures on the wall were typical—Yolonda at two sitting on a stool next to a Sears Christmas tree; Wilma on her wedding day in a white dress with a lily in her dark hair. Then, in another frame, there was a picture of Wilma with a group of people carrying signs with UNIONIZE written on them. Samuel Haven was also standing in the background of this picture, frowning. Rupert stood next to Samuel, staring at the crowd, his face frozen. Behind both of them another man peered between their shoulders. It was a white man with curly hair, and although Sidney could only see his eyes and nose, she was sure she had never seen this man before.

"That was Miss Mary," Wilma said, gesturing toward her with a foil–wrapped plate. "She brought me breakfast. You want some?" she asked Sidney.

"No," Sidney turned back to the picture.

"You sure?" Wilma peeked under the foil. "Umm, there's some hominy grits, and bacon ..." She turned the plate around. "And what look like some homemade biscuits."

"Smells good," Sidney said, "but I'm really not hungry."

Wilma crimped the foil around the plate. "Suit yo'self," she said. "You like that picture?"

"It's interesting."

"That was during my protestin' days." Wilma smiled broadly. "We was protestin' for the union." She moved closer to the picture, and her upper arm brushed against Sidney's bare one. "There I am, see?" she said pointing to a woman in braids, wearing a red dress. "Boy, was I skinny then! And, let me see, that's the Heater boy. The one that started it all." She pointed to a young boy with low dark hair and serious eyes, wearing a Malcolm X T-shirt.

"The Havens look fit to be tied," Sidney observed.

"Believe me, chil', they was," Wilma agreed. "I wasn't even working at the mill when I was protesting for them to unionize. I worked at the Havens' mansion, scrubbing they toilets. Believe me, child, they may think their shit don't stink, but they some nasty folks."

Sidney turned to Wilma, perplexed. "Are you still working there?"

"Hell no!" Wilma said as she walked back to the kitchen. "Ain't worked there since all that Heater mess," her voice floated back to Sidney. "Don't want to work for no murderers."

Wilma returned and stood beside Sidney with her arms folded.

"Wilma," Sidney said, still studying the picture, "I recognize Samuel . . ." She placed her finger on the fat man in the picture, "and Englestorm . . ."

"Man's a snake," Wilma hissed, interrupting her.

". . . but who is this man?" Sidney asked, pointing to the face between Rupert and Samuel.

Wilma didn't answer for a few seconds. "Don't know," she said finally. She walked back to the leather chair and picked the remote up from the glass coffee table.

"Oh, come on, Wilma," Sidney chided, "you used to know everything in high school. Remember, telephone, telegraph, tell Wilma?"

"Don't know him," Wilma answered from the leather chair without turning to face Sidney.

"Okay, so you don't know him. What was he doing here, in Haven?" Sidney persisted, still staring at the picture.

"Probably one of those out of town agitators," she answered.

Sidney's laugh did not have any humor attached. "But it looks like he's with the Havens, and they look agitated enough," she said.

"Lot of folks came to Haven during that mess. If I knew him," Wilma said, "I would tell you."

Still bothered, Sidney quietly slipped the picture from the wall. "Wilma," she said and placed a hand on her shoulder, but the woman jerked away, "if you can think of anything unusual, could you please tell me?"

Wilma remained silent. Sidney, not knowing what had changed her mood, said good-bye and walked toward the door. After she unlatched the hook, she heard Wilma's voice.

"You know, we ain't so different, you and me," she said, "we ain't so different at all."

Sidney ignored her and walked out onto the porch. She squinted for a few seconds until her eyes got used to the brightness. For the first time, she noticed a 1994 Grand Prix parked on the curb next to the house.

"Wilma, is this your car parked out here?" she yelled into the darkness.

"And who else's would it be?" came the answer from inside.

Sidney walked down the porch step. She ran her hand over the car, green like the forest at night. *It must be her favorite color,* Sidney thought, thinking of the leather couch and chair. But she also thought that something was wrong here, something was very wrong.

When Sidney reached her mother's house, she stopped,

remembering the first time Julian had seen the house she grew up in. He stood outside their rental car with a look of mock awe on his face. "Baby," he said, "I thought you said you grew up in the Bottoms." And when she answered that she did, he just shook his head and laughed. Pointing to the shotgun house next door which was separated by a patch of dry, brown dirt, he replied, "No, that house over there is in the Bottoms. And the house on the other side, is in the Bottoms. But this . . ."

"This what?" she interrupted him.

"This is a monument to upper middle class security. It has no business being here."

Sidney smiled at him and told him it did have business being there, her mother's business. And if he knew what was good for him, he wouldn't bring it up when he met Covina.

She shook away the memory as she thought again of Wilma. Just as it was odd that her mother's house was in this neighborhood, so it was that Wilma, a widow barely making a living, would have a Panasonic sixty-inch TV in her living room, or a brand-new car parked in the ally of her shotgun shack.

She walked into the house, exhausted. She felt as if she had lived almost a lifetime in the last few days. Before she went to her room, she peeked in on Covina, who still slept peacefully. She laid across her own bed and immediately fell asleep.

Her mother and father argued in the next room. Sidney put her hands over her ears, but could still hear them shout. Her door opened, and her little sister Marion, poked her head inside.

"Can I come in here?" she asked in a small voice.

Sidney took her hands from her ears and waved Marion

inside. The little girl closed the door behind her and climbed on Sidney's pink comforter.

"At least take your shoes off, Marion," Sidney said, disgusted.

"What?" Marion couldn't hear over the shouts.

"I said take your shoes off. You're getting my bed dirty!" Sidney screamed.

"Okay, you don't have to holler." Marion pulled her shoes off one by one. They dropped like rocks to the floor.

"Why don't they fight in their own room?" she asked Sidney.

"I don't know," Sidney answered. "I think it's about money. They were all talking and making nice in the living room."

"Yuck. While you were there?" Marion asked.

"Not that nice, stupid!" Sidney said. "They weren't kissing or anything. I probably would have thrown up. No, Mamma was talking like a white lady and passing around cut–up bologna on Ritz crackers."

Marion giggled. "Was she having one of them weird nice spells . . ." She stopped and scrambled back on the bed when she heard glass breaking.

"I bet you fifty bucks that was the bologna and crackers gone out the window," Sidney said, putting her arm around her sister.

"I hope not," Marion said in a small, light voice. "Because I'm hungry." She rubbed at the sheet wrinkles on the side of her face. Her smooth skin was the color of wheat, almost a shade lighter than Sidney's. Her large eyes were a misty green in her pointed face. Most of her thick red hair was caught up in a blue rubber band, but some short pieces jetted from behind her ear. As Sidney looked at Marion's hair—nappy in some places, curly in others— she realized that Covina had probably not combed it today.

"You're always hungry," she said to Marion.

"What are they yelling about, anyway?" Marion laid down next to Sidney.

"Money."

"Money?" Marion asked, sitting up on her elbows. "Why?"

"Mamma wants more money," Sidney answered, staring at the pink canopy covering her bed.

"For what?"

"For us, stupid," Sidney said and pushed Marion off the bed. "College and stuff."

"Jeez, Sidney," Marion protested and climbed back on the bed. "What's college?" she asked as she brushed her red hair out of her face.

"You don't know nothing, Marion." Sidney looked at her little sister as if the girl were demented.

"I'm only seven. Mamma says I'm not 'posed to know nothing."

The sound of glass shattering reached them again. Marion buried her face in her arms. When it ended, she looked at Sidney. "I bet *that* was the bologna," she said.

Sidney put her arms around her again. "Don't worry about it. I'm sure there's more."

"Why does Mamma want more money?" Marion asked again.

"I don't know, Marion. She just does."

"I built you this house," Carl's voice sounded like a jet plane buzzing through the house, "in this pathetic shit-hole, and you have the nerve to ask me for another penny."

"Carl!" Covina's voice was just as loud. "Them girls growing up. They need some money of their own," she explained to him.

"That's your fault!" he answered her. "You tricked me and had those kids. But I still told you could live anyplace you wanted. But no, you wanted to stay here. To throw everything up in my face. In my family's face. Look how you named those girls!"

"What has being anyplace got to do with how you supportin' me and these girls?" Covina yelled back.

"I got to watch what I do down here. Everything I put in, people notice. Every time you walk around town with another piece of jewelry, people notice. And I'm talking about my people! I'll be damned if I let you walk around all whored–up making a fool of me!"

"I don't want the money for clothes, or jewelry, Carl," Covina replied.

Covina continued, but her voice was so low, Sidney couldn't hear what she said. She jumped over her sister and ran to the door. She cracked it, just a hair.

"Sidney, no!" Marion warned. "They'll get you."

"Shhh," Sidney said and jerked her arm at her sister. "I can't hear." She pressed her ear to the opening until she could hear her mother's voice.

"You think you embarrassed when yo' folks see these girls? Or when I go to Vicksburg and buy me a new dress?" she asked, her voice a low rumble. "Just think how embarrassed you gonna be when I go to the Haven mansion and talk to yo' wife."

Silence followed. Although Carl didn't speak, Sidney could feel his rage.

"I'll bring Marion first, and I'll tell her how she's named after her. Then I'll bring out Sidney. Everybody know who she named for, Carl."

"Shut up," Carl spoke so low, Sidney could barely hear him.

"How she named after Sidney Haven, yo' no good Daddy," Covina finished.

Sidney knew Covina had chosen their names for spite, and always regretted it. Carl knew it too, but chuckled when he heard the names. It was just more proof of her eccentricity. He never thought she would use it as a weapon. If she threw this in the Havens' faces, it would make him a laughing stock.

Sidney heard a whack, skin against skin. Then the sound of furniture falling over. A scream reached her, and she heard Carl grunt. There was more glass breaking and then a deadly silence.

Marion begin to cry as Sidney ran from the room. Carl choked Covina, and his eyes looked as if they were trying to leap from his face. Sidney yelled for him to stop, then jumped on his back. He threw her off as if he were shrugging off a tiresome coat on a warm day.

Sidney's hand closed around a piece of sharp glass. She ran to her father and buried the shard into his shoulder. He screamed and pulled it out. Blood soaked the sleeve of his shirt as Covina crumpled to the ground. Carl walked into the kitchen and grabbed a washcloth. He pushed it against his shoulder. He seemed calmed, as if the pain had brought him to his senses. But Sidney could tell he was still angry.

"I'll kill you next time," he told Covina before leaving. "I'll kill you with my bare hands the next time you threaten me, bitch."

The shrill ringing of the phone woke Sidney. She touched her face and felt tears. She had not thought about that day since it happened. After Carl left, she and Covina cleaned up the living room, carefully putting the sharp glass from the coffee table and broken window into a green Hefty lawn bag.

Marion stayed in Sidney's room, sobbing for the rest of the night. Neither of them—not Sidney, not Covina, not Marion—ever discussed that event. A repair man replaced the window three days later, and Sidney knew that Carl must have phoned him, because Covina said she had not. Carl returned to the house one month later, like the whole thing never happened. Then he died six months later, in Covina's bed.

The phone rang again, insistent. Sidney jumped up and ran into the living room to answer.

"Hello?" she breathed.

"Hi babe, did I wake you up?" Julian asked from the other end of the phone.

Sidney wiped sleep from her eyes. "No. No you didn't," she lied through the fog.

"Sounds like you were sleeping," he sounded worried. "Are you all right?"

"I'm fine. How did you know I was here?"

"I called the University," he explained. "They said you had to leave to go home for an emergency." Even from a thousand miles away, his voice sounded rich and full.

"Oh," Sidney said, still half asleep.

"And since I didn't see you at the penthouse cooking me dinner in that French maid's outfit, I figured they had to mean Haven."

"Julian," Sidney said, disgusted, now fully awake.

"Is your mother all right?" he asked her.

"Everyone's fine," she replied, then sat on the couch and picked up the remote for the TV. She clicked the TV on.

"Then why the hell are you there? You hate that place."

"It's a case, Julian," Sidney hesitated before telling him the truth. "A murder case."

"Who?" Julian asked, confused. "I didn't think they killed folks on a regular basis in Haven. Who are you defending?"

"Dexter Haven."

"Oh, God, Sidney," Julian said, in a voice that now sounded far away.

Sidney could see him sitting up on the bed of their bedroom in Virginia. He'd probably even spilled his scotch.

"You all right?" he asked.

"I'm fine, Julian," she replied.

"Do you need me to come out?"

"No, I don't need you," she answered. "I'm fine."

She was sure she could hear him swallow. She didn't know why she wanted to hurt his feelings, but for some reason, she did.

"There is one thing you can do for me," she said.

"Name it."

"Wilma Brown," she answered. "I need you to find out everything about a woman named Wilma Brown."

"Who's she?" he asked.

"The victim's mother."

"Hold it," he told her, "let me get a pencil." At first, she heard muffled sounds. But after a few seconds, he must have put the phone down, because she heard jazz music in the background. It was Phyllis Hymann, her voice in full control.

"Okay, I'm back. Wilma Brown," he said the name in a long drawl.

"Jesus, Julian," Sidney said, "Isn't it a little too early in the day for you? Shouldn't you be at work?"

"I would be," he said, "but you see, I have a broken heart."

"Yeah, right."

"Sidney, let's not fight, please. Now this Wilma Brown, what kind of stuff are you looking for?"

"You know, the usual. Just run me a credit check, bank accounts," Sidney said as she shrugged her shoulders.

"You got it," Julian said in a way that made her feel like she was the only person who mattered to him. "Anything else?"

"Um, yeah," she said. "Jacob Conrad. But I want to

know other stuff, like where he worked, why he left, any marriages, children . . ." she let out the other half in a rush, feeling vaguely guilty.

"Hey, hey, hey," Julian laughed, "slow down. I don't know shorthand."

Sidney laughed with him, suddenly missing the man she had known for almost ten years. She was about to continue when she heard a woman's voice in the background asking what album to put on next.

"How about Anita Baker?" Sidney said sarcastically.

"Sidney," Julian's voice was so solemn, it was almost funny. "I didn't mean for you to hear that."

"Is that the whore who likes red?" she asked him.

"How many times do I have to tell you she's not a whore."

"So, it's serious?" she asked him.

"Vaguely," he said, "vaguely serious." She could almost see him shrugging his broad shoulders.

"Oh, I see," Sidney said, hurt, "kind of like our marriage."

"Please, Sidney . . ." he began.

"I know. I know," she cut in, "no fights."

"That's right," he answered, "no fights."

"You want to tell me why you're defending Dexter Haven?" he said, trying to change the subject.

"No," Sidney said simply.

"Okay. Okay. We can discuss it later," he told her.

"So will you do that for me then?" Sidney asked, wanting to end the conversation.

"Babe, I'd still do anything for you."

"Yeah, right," Sidney sighed. "Let me know the minute you hear something."

"Sure will, immediately," he said and hung up without saying good-bye.

Sidney tossed the phone on the coffee table and glared

at the television. Susan Lucci wearing a red satin nightgown smiled a Vaseline–toothed smile at a man in a tuxedo. Sidney threw a pillow from the sofa at the TV, hitting the power button. She stared at the empty black screen for a full ten minutes before getting up to take a shower.

After she finished showering, she slid open the shower door and hit her head so hard against the side of it, she saw both sparks and stars.

"Mamma," she breathed, annoyed, "you scared me half to death."

Covina sat on the toilet in a thick white robe and a towel wrapped around her head. She smoked a cigarette, her legs crossed, resting an elbow on her knee.

"Girl," Covina laughed, "are you all right?"

"No, Mamma," Sidney glared at her through the shower–induced fog. "I'm not all right."

"Well," Covina cocked her head at her daughter and blew out a stream of smoke, "at least you ain't bleedin' . . ."

"Mamma," Sidney began, "hand me . . ."

". . . and you ain't knocked out."

". . . a towel, Mamma," Sidney finished. "I need a towel."

Covina looked at the towel hanging on the silver towel rack. "There's one right over there," she said and pointed her cigarette at it.

"Mamma," Sidney said, exasperated, "I'm naked."

"I've seen you naked before," Covina laughed.

Giving up, Sidney walked out of the shower, breathing in the smoke from Covina's cigarette and the soapy, sweet smell from the shower.

"It's not like you got stretch marks like your sister, or a big ass," Covina laughed as she popped Sidney on the butt. "Who was on the phone?" she asked Sidney.

"No one," Sidney lied, walking out of the bathroom.

"Didn't sound like no one," Covina challenged. "Was it Julian?"

"No." Sidney sat on the edge of her canopy bed and began drying off her leg.

"How is he doing?" Covina asked as if she hadn't heard.

She sat on the cotton candy–pink comforter beside Sidney. With her free hand, she smoothed wet strands of Sidney's hair from her face.

"Fine," Sidney said.

"Good," she said. "Where you been this morning?"

"Over at Wilma's," Sidney answered.

Covina sat up, the cigarette's glowing tip dangerously close to the pink comforter.

"I'm surprised she let you in," Covina said.

"Well, she did," she told her mother. "But something is just not setting right."

"No, it ain't right," Covina stood up and strolled over to the white dresser. "Wilma's girl is dead. That don't sound too right now, does it?"

"I'm talking about with Wilma in general, Mamma," Sidney said. "She had a lot of things in the house, you know? Things it would seem like she couldn't afford."

"Really," Covina said absently, running her finger along the frame of a picture of Sidney and Marion.

"Did you know everyone in town during the Heater murder, Mamma?" Sidney asked her suddenly.

Covina turned to stare at Sidney, an old hurt in her eyes. "Oh, now you askin' about the Heater murder," she said. "When I asked for your help when all that mess was happening, you didn't have any time for it."

"Mamma, please," Sidney said as she turned around to put on her bra, "let's not start this again."

"Then why you asking about it?" Covina asked, her hand on her hip.

"It's just when I started asking Wilma about a stranger in one of her strike pictures, she got really strange on me."

"But why do you care about that, Sidney?" Covina asked her.

"I don't know," Sidney said. "Call it instinct, but something just doesn't seem right. It's almost as if she knows something, something about the Heater murder."

Covina shrugged, obviously through with the entire discussion. She brought over the picture she had been holding to Sidney. It was just a snapshot, really. She and Marion sat on the floor in the living room, barefooted and wearing matching summer dresses with red flowers.

"Look at that," Covina now said to Sidney. "I know I made some mistakes, but one thing I never did was sacrifice you girls to anything or anybody."

Sidney looked questioningly at her mother. "I thought we were talking about Wilma, Mamma?" she asked.

"Who said we weren't?" Covina looked back at her.

"What are you trying to say?" Sidney asked.

"What I'm trying to say is," she said as she placed the picture back on the dresser, centering it just so, "if this thing you call instinct telling you to look into this, go do it. Lord knows what Wilma got herself and Peachy Girl into."

Before Sidney could ask Covina what she meant, her mother walked out of the room, announcing it was now her turn to get cleaned up. Sidney did not follow, but instead walked out into the midday light, remembering a stray stretch of river just on the outskirts of Haven proper.

Chapter 9

When she was a girl in Haven, she would use the river as an escape from the fights at home between Covina and Carl. And it worked, for a while. For a long time. But she did not know what she wanted to escape this time. She just knew she had to stop thinking of the Heater murder, and concentrate on Dexter Haven's case. But just on the periphery hovered a shadow of instinct whispering that something more existed, something that may even be connected to Peachy Girl.

At the river, she removed her shoes and stuck her feet in the water. The coolness of the water on this hot Mississippi day surprised Sidney, and it looked like rippling glass running over her bare toes. She watched the water twinkling over her feet, and the light falling like rain from the trees. And like the return of so many memories she had suppressed over the years, she remembered the time C.D. had Haven's complete, rapt attention. Covina sent her newspaper clippings all the way to Virginia when it all started—newspaper clippings that Sidney kept in a box in the back of the closet until they moved from the Anacostia apartment. Newspaper clippings she saved, but never thought of until this very moment.

Sidney believed that when the movement to unionize the mills hit Haven, it was the happiest and purest time of Covina's life. She called Sidney each time something changed, or whenever C.D. was on the news, her voice so breathless with excitement Sidney thought that if the phones did not work, her mother would have shouted the news all the way to Washington. *C.D. had a way of getting folks stirred up,* her mother would tell her.

He was twenty-one in 1988, two years younger than Sidney. Though his father, Randall Heater, managed to return with all of his limbs from the Vietnam war, he lost his arm in an accident at the Haven mill. The Havens generously gave him three hundred dollars severance pay, and sent him on his way. Not enough for the medical bills that had racked up in Vicksburg, and not enough to support his family. So, Randall, thinking he was better off dead than alive, blew his head off in the Heater's bathroom with his one good arm. But his insurance policy would not pay on a suicide.

"I was with Johnie Mae at the hospital," her mother told her one starry night, "and Sidney, little C.D. was there, 'cepting he ain't so little anymore. You remember him, Sidney?"

"No, Mamma," Sidney had answered.

"Girl, you don't remember nothing," her mother sighed into the phone. "Anyway, he was mad. Spittin' and pacin' and screamin' at the doctors, at anybody who would listen."

"Mad?" Sidney had asked absently as she rifled through

the papers on her desk, looking for a case she wanted to use in the gangland murder case that Julian convinced her to take. With luck, she could use it in preparation for a motion to dismiss.

"Yes. Mad. Are you listening, girl?"

"Yes Mamma."

"Okay," Covina continued. "He pissed because he said that the mill is unsafe. Said folks been gettin' parts cut off in there for years and nobody don't care nothing about it."

"Uh huh," Sidney switched on the light at her desk.

"Said that the Havens don't care enough to get insurance for the people working for them. Sidney?"

"Where is it?" Sidney breathed, and pushed her chair out from her desk to peer underneath it for the paperwork she couldn't find.

"Where's what?" Covina asked. "Girl, you even listening?"

"Yes, yes, yes. Please, go on," Sidney said, wishing the conversation were over.

"What's three hundred dollars going to do for anybody Sidney?" she asked her.

"I don't know, Mamma," Sidney responded.

Just then, Julian walked into her office, carrying white take-out bags. The scent of Chinese food filled the air. She smelled fried rice and moo shu pork.

"Who?" he mouthed, pointing to the phone.

When Sidney rolled her eyes, he knew it had to be Covina.

"That's why you have to come home," Covina stated in a flat voice.

"What?" Sidney asked.

"You a lawyer now, ain't you?" Covina answered. "Can't you sue them crazy Havens?"

Sidney watched Julian fold his large frame into a chair.

He pushed aside the mountain of papers and books on her desk, and the case she had been searching for fluttered to the floor. He began plucking at the boxes of Chinese food carefully, as if afraid he would break a nail.

"Did you hear me Sidney?" Covina asked.

"Yes, Mamma. I heard you."

"Well, when you comin'?"

"I can't," she said as Julian set a paper plate with fried rice in front of her.

"Why?" Covina said, as if she had been stung by a wasp. "We in trouble."

"I've got a case, Mamma," Sidney answered. "Maybe Julian . . ." she looked up and saw Julian staring at her with questioning green eyes.

"Never mind, Mamma," she said. "I can give you the names of some good lawyers."

"I don't want no good lawyers," Covina protested. "I want you."

"Mamma, I can't," Sidney answered.

"You never can, Sidney," Covina said, the anger in her voice like a breathing thing. "One day, you gon' know how it feels to think of other people besides yo'self."

"Mamma . . ." Sidney cut in.

"This ain't over," Covina breathed into the phone, "it ain't over."

The second time Covina had called about it, Sidney lay in a scented bubble bath surrounded by candle light. She could almost taste the scent of candle wax and strawberries. Bubbles spilled over the side of the tub and trailed along the floor. She didn't hear the phone ring, but only saw a slightly drunk Julian tripping in with a phone in one hand and a glass of champagne in the other. He almost fell in the water when he bent down to give her the phone. And Sidney jumped as cold champagne fell on her breast.

"For you, my love," he told her.

"Who is it?" she asked.

"Who do you think?" he laughed.

"Mother."

"Yes. Mother," Julian said with a grin before closing the door behind him.

Covina did not wait for Sidney's hello, but instead started talking immediately. C.D. contacted some lawyer from Philadelphia, a place so far away from Covina it might as well have been Africa. Anyway, not only was this lawyer suing the Havens, she was organizing protests.

"A black woman with nappy hair, Sidney," she told her.

"What?" Sidney asked, distracted.

Julian had returned to the bathroom, wearing nothing but a short terry cloth robe. He bent down to kiss her on the lips.

"Nappy hair," Covina explained. "She ain't 'shamed of it neither!"

"Mamma, what do you mean protests?" Sidney asked.

"Well," Covina answered, "she went to Earl at the mill. You remember Earl, don't you?"

"Earl who?"

"Figures," Covina sighed, disgusted. "Anyway, Earl been at the mill longer than anybody. He got a couple of parts missing hisself, 'ceptin it's only his thumb and index finger."

"Get to the point, Mamma," Sidney watched Julian take off the robe and slip it over the shower door.

"Wait a minute. I'm telling this," Covina said.

Sidney could see her sitting on her sofa with an unfiltered Camel dangling from one hand, the smoke curling toward the ceiling. She was sure Covina was all settled in to talk. Sidney remained silent during the pause as Covina took a long drag on her cigarette.

"Lotsa folks respect Earl, you know. The woman lawyer, the one with the nappy hair, Sidney, she asked me who she should be talking to at the mill," Covina said proudly, "who she should be talking to at the mill to get them black folks moving. And I told her, I told her nobody but Earl could help her do that."

"Good Mamma," Sidney murmured as Julian kissed her again.

"Well, she talked to Earl, and guess what chil'?"

"What?"

"Folks be strikin'!" Covina said. Sidney could almost see the smile in her mother's voice.

"Striking what?" Sidney asked, confused.

"Girl! I been talking for ten minutes, and you ain't heard a word. Tell Julian to keep his pants on. I won't be long."

Sidney sat up, embarrassed. Water splashed over the sides of the tub, and Julian almost fell for the second time that night.

"Okay, Okay. I'm listening."

"Good," Covina said. "The mill's shut down."

"What?" Sidney said, this time understanding.

"It's shut down, Sidney. Paper say the Havens losing thousands of dollars a day."

"Mamma," Sidney asked, "how long has this been going on?"

"A week," Covina laughed. "Did you see us on the news?"

"What news?" Sidney was still trying to grasp the fact that the mill, the mill that operated before she was born, had closed down.

"The news, the national news with that cracker Peter Jennings."

Sidney had to admit she hadn't. The case which had

completed yesterday, had consumed her. She had not had time for TV in the last month.

"Sidney," Covina finished. "We joinin' the rest of the country. Them Havens ain't gon' to be allowed to treat us like this anymore without anybody knowing about it. They gon' pay," Covina said, "they gon' pay for all the dirt they done."

Covina called again three weeks later, at dusk. Sidney and Julian picked at their dinner in their Anacostia apartment as the sun set, trailing smoke and fire in the daylight sky. When the phone rang, Julian jumped up from the table, almost knocking over his chair. Sidney just looked at him as he left, and picked at the thyme chicken he had brought home from the trendy restaurant in Crystal City.

Julian, still angry that she had left the ACLU without talking to him first brought home the dinner an hour earlier. He walked past her and slammed it on the chipped Formica table, daring her to challenge him. She knew the dinner had cost at least fifty dollars. It tasted like sandpaper in her mouth.

"It's for you," Julian held the phone in her face, less than an inch from her nose.

She took it from him without speaking.

"Hello," she said.

She heard Covina sobbing into the receiver. She looked at Julian across the table, wondering why he had not warned her.

"Mamma, are you all right?" she asked.

Covina tried to carve her sobs into words, but Sidney still could not understand her.

"Mamma," Sidney broke in, standing up, "is it Marion? Mamma? Did something happen to Marion?"

"No, no," Covina said, taking a deep breath. "It's C.D., Sidney, C.D."

Sidney sat down as irritation overtook her. "Mamma. Come on. You scared me to death."

"He's dead, Sidney," Covina explained. "They killed him."

"Who killed him?" Sidney picked up the phone and walked to the living room, ignoring Julian's quizzical stare.

"Who do you think?" Covina answered. "The Havens. It's over. All over."

"That's terrible," Sidney sat on the couch and put her feet on the coffee table. "But it doesn't have to be over."

"The wind done gone out of folks," Covina explained. "Besides, that lawyer, the one with the nappy hair, is leaving."

"Leaving? Why?"

" 'Cause she got death threats, and a five–year–old little boy. No husband, Sidney. Said she couldn't afford to get killed." Covina answered.

"Mamma," Sidney replied, "I am sorry."

"Don't be sorry," Covina said. "Come help us."

Sidney watched Julian as he walked to the closet door and angrily pulled out his leather jacket. The hanger it was on snapped in two.

"Mamma, you know I can't," Sidney answered.

"I don't know why I asked," Covina said. "You are as selfish as your no–good daddy."

Sidney did not hear the click as Covina hung up over Julian slamming the front door.

Sidney pulled her feet from the water not knowing how long she had been sitting by the river, thinking of the past. She felt coolness touch her feet, and she took a deep breath.

Covina never forgave her for not returning to Haven when C.D. was killed. And she never forgave her for leaving the ACLU to join the Fosters and Fosters law firm. She accused Sidney of choosing sides, trying to be like the Havens. Sidney could almost hear Covina's accusation in her head. *First you marry Julian,* she told her, *a boy almost lighter than you are, and then, you throw away helping people, like maybe C.D., for money and stepping on the side of white folks.* Both things loomed large between them, and they never spoke about it either, until today when Sidney brought up the Heater murder.

She ran her hands over her aching bottom. Older now, she wondered if she could have prevented the boy's death. She wondered about her part in all the things that happened in Haven while she made her career as one of the country's hottest lawyers a thousand miles away from her hometown.

She turned as she heard twigs crack behind her. Dexter stood staring at her, his golden hair competing with the sunlight.

"I'm sorry," he said as he cleared his throat. "I didn't know anyone was here."

Sidney ignored him and turned back to the river. A beaver slid silently into the water and she heard a dog bark, distantly. As she reached to pick up her sandals, she heard Dexter stepping toward her.

"You don't like me much, do you?" Dexter's voice was as soft as the water trickling over the rocks in the river.

"Why do you ask me that?"

Sidney straightened up and looked at him. Gone was the boy so unsure of himself at his uncle's house and in the judge's chamber. He looked as if he didn't have a care in the world.

"I love this river," he said. "It makes me forget everything. The trial," he said as he bowed his head, "even Yolonda."

Sidney sat down on the ground to fasten the straps on her sandals.

"Seems to have that effect on a lot of people," she mumbled, wishing he would go away. She knew she should be talking to him, but now wasn't the time. And she was not in the mood.

"I am not my father," Dexter kneeled beside her. He hesitated a moment, and then picked a leaf, moist with life, from a bush next to him. Sidney watched as he used his thumbnail to separate the leaf from its veins.

"You could have fooled me," Sidney said, and turned away to fasten her other sandal.

"You know," Dexter continued, "I saw you that day. The day of our father's funeral. Your legs were all scratched up. And your sister, the one with the funny red hair, had on dirty white tights. I saw you hiding in the bushes."

Sidney ignored him.

"Do you remember the funeral?" he asked.

"It's one of the few things," Sidney breathed.

She stood up. When he grabbed her wrists, she wondered briefly if she should be afraid. The man was quite possibly a murderer. His hands, though soft and cool, were strong.

"Please," he said, "talk to me for a minute. I've wanted to talk to you since that day. I wanted to know the father you knew," he barked out a bitter laugh, "but Uncle Samuel, he pulled me back. I thought he was going to break my shoulder."

"Look . . ." Sidney said, embarrassed, "we can talk about the case later."

He let her go then and sat down by the river's edge. She watched as he removed his shoes and socks to stick his feet in the water.

"You and your sister, Marion," he said laughing. "Both

standing there barely visible. It was your pink halter I saw first." He turned to look at her. "You looked so out of place."

"We felt out of place," Sidney said. She couldn't decide if she wanted to be angry.

"Imagine feeling that way your whole life," he said.

Sidney laughed then, and sat down beside him.

"I don't have to." She grabbed a handful of twigs and stones and started throwing them, one by one, into the river.

"You are more like him than you think," he said.

"Who?" Sidney turned to find him staring at her.

"My father," he finished. "Our father."

"What?" Sidney looked at him as if she wanted to hit him. She had made up her mind—she was angry.

"I don't mean to be insulting," he laughed. "Most people would consider that a compliment."

"Well, I don't," she answered.

"I know you don't, but I remember when I saw you and your sister. I saw your gray eyes. He had gray eyes. Gray and angry like yours. And I remember thinking how much you looked like him."

"What were you doing hanging around a fourteen-year-old girl?" Sidney asked him suddenly.

Dexter waved his feet back and forth over the rocks in the water. He then bent over and splashed water over his face, over his hair.

"It's hot," he said in a way of explanation. Droplets of water glittered like small diamonds on his face.

"I asked you a question."

"As my lawyer or my sister," he mocked.

"I'm not your sister," Sidney spat.

As Dexter shrugged his shoulders, Sidney realized she had underestimated him. He was more than the man who fumbled his plea in Judge Harold's chamber. He had more spirit than the man who had cowered in front of his uncle when she first met him.

"Okay," he said, looking at her with an odd twinkle in his eyes. "I guess it's as my lawyer. I told you earlier. I thought she was twenty."

"So you lied. She was more than a friend."

"Yes. I lied. When I found out how old she really was, I panicked. She was my girlfriend."

"So you slept with her," she said. It was more of a statement than a question. Disgusted, she reached over to plunge her hands in the river. She watched the dirt from her hands disappear into the water.

Dexter laughed. "You sleep with your boyfriend?" he asked. He leaned back on his elbows and looked at the blue sky. "But I didn't kill her," he defended.

"How long did you date her?"

"Six months."

"So you mean to tell me in six months no one told you how old she really was? As much time as you two spent hanging down in Rollie's bar?"

"No one talked to us when we went to Rollie's," he explained.

Sidney stood up and dried her hands on her shorts. "Anything else you want to tell me?"

Dexter said nothing for a moment, just sat back on his elbows. They watched as the beaver who had slipped into the water earlier fought with a silver fish.

"No," he said, squinting against the sun. "I don't have anything else to tell you."

Sidney watched him for a little while longer. She watched until gray rain clouds covered and claimed the noon sun. She left him sitting there, watching the river and smiling peacefully.

As she negotiated up the hill to her Taurus parked along the side of the dirt road near the river, she realized her mother was right six years ago. Someone had to make the Havens pay for that boy's murder; and if they were responsible for Yolonda's Brown murder, they had to pay for that too.

To be able to sit by the river at peace and be accused of murdering a fourteen-year-old girl at the same time, was the epitome of arrogance. Only a Haven could be able to do that—squint at the sun without a care in the world while on trial for their life.

She pulled open the car door so hard she broke a nail. Her book bag had fallen onto the driver's seat, and when she picked it up to move, she felt the heavy weight of the gavel at the bottom. She reached in and fished it out. Why had she carried it all these years? This personal connection to her father? At first, she did it as a reminder of the Havens and how she had to make them pay. Make them pay by becoming the best damn lawyer she knew how to be. Success was the best revenge.

And now, standing on a dirt road near a river where Dexter Haven stood looking out on the glinting water, she realized why she carried it. A plea, a hope for acceptance. Disgusted, she threw the book bag on the passenger seat. Probably the same reason she defended one of them now. The gavel rolled off the seat, abandoned, and fell to the floor.

Chapter 10

The old woman stood on the sidewalk in front of Haven's secondhand store with a bag of oranges. A red head scarf covered her gray hair. Sidney slowed her car to a stop at the light on the corner of First and Main. She was on her way to visit Grayson of the *Haven Crier* to research the Heater murder. It was only an hour after she talked with Dexter Haven, but that seemed like a lifetime ago.

Sidney looked again at the old woman standing so tentatively on the side of the road, and recognized her as the one who had sat beside her at Yolonda Brown's funeral. She stared at the woman until the light flicked from red to green. A car horn blared behind her. She didn't hear it. Finally, the driver swerved around her unmoving car, barely missing her fender.

The old woman stared back at Sidney, silent and expectant as death. Her mouth remained closed, unsmiling. She clutched at the bag of oranges as if she were afraid Sidney would jump from the car and snatch them from her. As

Sidney heard another horn pierce the early afternoon, she realized the light had already turned from green to yellow to red.

The old woman took a step, and the bag of oranges slipped open. Plump oranges rolled into the gutter and under Sidney's car. The woman looked right and left, then put one foot into the street, but retracted it immediately when another car swerved around Sidney's.

Sidney opened the door and left the car. She stooped down and began picking up oranges. They were still cool to the touch. When the old woman saw Sidney in the street, she stepped from the curb. Her knees cracked as she bent down to help.

"Thank you. Thank you," she said. "You've always been a helpful girl."

Sidney looked up, surprised. There was a light in the old woman's eyes.

"You don't remember me, do you?" she asked, her voice a rustle of fall leaves.

"Not really," Sidney said truthfully.

The old woman's laugh reminded her of tart lemons. "Wilma was right about you," she said. "You don't even know how to lie when it suits you."

Sidney dropped two oranges into the plastic shopping bag. She and the old woman were shoulder to shoulder, and Sidney could smell mint leaves on the old woman's breath.

"I'm Miss Johnie Mae," she said. "C.D.'s grandmother."

"C.D. Heater?" Sidney asked.

"Same. The same." Miss Johnie Mae crawled toward the front of the car. Sidney followed.

"Be careful," Sidney warned.

"I'm too old to be too careful," she laughed. "Ain't got too much left to be careful for."

Sidney pushed her car door closed to retrieve a rolling orange.

"Seems like I made a mess," Miss Johnie Mae called from the front of the car.

Sidney could only see the corner of the woman's blue and white flower dress.

"Just a little," she mumbled under her breath.

The woman crawled back to where Sidney stooped on the curb. "Come sit with me for a while, child." She patted the asphalt next to her as if it were the sofa in her living room.

Sidney glanced back at the car blocking the intersection, then at Miss Johnie Mae sitting on the curb. The old woman's legs were slightly open, and she could see the roll of stockings on her thighs. A piece of the woman's gleaming white underwear peeked out from under her dress.

"Just for a little while," she told Sidney, "ain't nobody gon' bother that car."

Sidney stood up and opened the car door. She reached in and turned on the flashers, then joined Miss Johnie Mae on the curb. The asphalt burned against her bare thighs.

"Young folks," she laughed. "Always worried about something." Johnie Mae wiped the sweat from her forehead with a damp handkerchief. "Whew, I'm tired," she finished.

"Do you need a ride somewhere?" Sidney plucked imaginary threads from her shorts and rubbed her hands together. First Wilma, then Miss Johnie Mae. She couldn't believe she sat curbside with another woman the Havens were accused of wronging.

"No. I hate ridin'," Miss Johnie Mae answered. "I like to walk. I just need to sit here for a while." She reached into her black bag and pulled out a bottle of water. "And

I just need to have a drink of water." She jabbed the bottle at Sidney. "Have some?"

"No," Sidney said, shaking her head.

The old woman tipped the bottle to her wrinkled lips and took a long swallow. When she finished, she wiped around the rim of the bottle, and stared at it. "My grandson bought this here water bottle for me in Vicksburg," she said. "Not C.D., but my other grandson, Albert. C.D. been dead going on six years now."

"I know." Sidney grabbed the bag of oranges and hoisted them into her lap.

"The boy always was hot-tempered," Miss Johnie Mae said. She then pulled a wallet from her purse to show Sidney a picture of a black boy. "That's him. C.D., I mean."

"I know."

"Havens killed him," she said. She put the picture back into her purse.

"Do you have any proof?" Sidney wiped her legs with the palm of her hands. The heat had made them slick with sweat.

"Don't need proof. I just need to know," Miss Johnie Mae answered. "And believe me, I know."

"Then why don't you go to the police."

The old woman snorted and took another swig of water. "Ain't no police care up in this town when C.D. got killed," she said. "When the new Sheriff first came, he knew who murdered my grandson too, but he couldn't do nothing about it."

Sidney picked up a pebble and began rolling it between her fingers, wishing the old woman were finished. The pebble reminded her of C.D., of the time they both cut school to hang out at the creek. She remembered him now, sucking on pebbles until they would shine. He claimed he could taste sea salt on them. And Miss Johnie Mae, who lived near the river, caught both of them.

"Don't be puttin' them nasty things in your mouth, boy!" She ran to C.D. and slapped the rocks from his hands. "I don't believe this. Most children play hooky would be going to the movies or something." She grabbed both children by the hands and pulled them to their feet. "But not you two, you sit by the creek eating dirt." She dragged both of them to her house.

"You know, boy," she said, "if I didn't know yo' Mamma would beat the snot out of you, I'd take yo' butt home." She then looked over at Sidney's flushed face. "But I ain't even bothering with yo' Mamma," she said.

She took them to her house that day, and Sidney remembered red and purple and green patchwork quilts thrown everywhere. On the wooden table, across a plaid brown couch, even at the feet of a big rocking chair. The house was dank and dark, but it felt safe to Sidney. Miss Johnie Mae let them help her make hot water corn bread. And Sidney remembered sitting on the back porch with the old woman and C.D. eating corn bread and drinking cold buttermilk as they watched chickens pluck at the hard ground.

"You remember my boy, don't you?" she asked Sidney again.

Sidney smiled slightly. She and C.D. weren't great friends after that summer. The boy was two years behind her, and Sidney, except for her friendship with Wilma, remained a loner in school. She hadn't thought of that day by the river since it happened. For the first time since arriving home, she realized how much she had buried memories of Haven within her.

"Yes," she finally answered. "I remember him."

Johnie Mae shook her head. "Them Havens. Something in them make them want to kill children."

"Then you think Dexter Haven is guilty, too?" Sidney asked.

"Humph," She snorted in reply, "don't know if he is, don't know if he ain't. But his family responsible. Just the same. They responsible. Just as responsible as if they held the knives what cut both of their throats."

"C.D. had his throat cut?" Sidney sat up in surprise.

"Where you been, girl?" Johnie Mae answered, disgusted. "Yeah, he had his throat cut, about the same place Peachy Girl did." The woman scratched her chin, " 'Ceptin' wasn't no houses out there then."

"You think there is some sort of connection?"

"Yep. They be connectin'. Everybody in this town, same as me, know who murdered C.D. But Wilma the only person made somethin' out of it." She looked at Sidney. "And it be funny her girl be the one don' got kilt," she finished.

"What do you mean?" Sidney stared intently at the old woman, at the folds and wrinkles on her face.

A car door slammed and they both jumped as if they had been caught gossiping. Jacob strolled to them, his red Mustang gleaming in the sun behind him. His white shirt looked damp in the heat. Sidney couldn't see the expression on his face behind the sunglasses covering his eyes.

"Trouble?" he asked, his voice was smooth as silk. He placed a foot next to Sidney, where she sat on the curb. It almost touched her bare thigh.

"Ain't no trouble here, son," Miss Johnie Mae said. "Just an old woman runnin' off at the mouth."

Jacob did not look at the old woman, but kept his gaze on Sidney. Sidney avoided him by pretending to look around the curb for her keys.

"If you are looking for your keys, you left them in the car." He pointed to the rental.

"Now you gonna help an old lady up, or are you gonna just stand there and stare at the girl's legs all day long?" Miss Johnie Mae's voice cracked.

Jacob's face remained expressionless, unsmiling. He

reached down and pulled Miss Johnie Mae to her feet.
When she was standing, he pointed toward the bag in
Sidney's lap.

"Yours?" he asked Miss Johnie Mae.

"Yep, they mine," she answered.

He reached down and grabbed the bag, his face almost
touching Sidney's. He tied the top of the bag into a knot,
creating makeshift handles. He gave it to Miss Johnie Mae.

"Thank you, son. Thank you," she said. "Well, I guess
I'll be on my way. Thanks for helping, girl." She patted
Sidney's shoulder as she made her way down the street.

Jacob watched the woman for a few seconds as she walked
away. He took off his sunglasses and stuck them in his shirt
pocket before turning to gaze fully at Sidney.

"Trouble?" he asked again.

"No. No trouble," she answered.

When he didn't step aside, Sidney stood up. She was so
close to him, she could smell his spicy cologne mixed with
perspiration.

"Like the lady said, no trouble at all." She stepped
backward in an attempt to get away from him. When she
stumbled a little as her feet made contact with the curb,
he grabbed her bare waist. His hands were rough and hot
and moist, not soft like Julian's. Sidney cursed the skimpy
halter she wore as the man's belt buckle dug into her bare
midriff.

"You normally block traffic to sit on the curb and talk
to old women?"

Sidney made her body still, and waited for him to let go
of her waist. She looked into his face, but it was still as
stone.

"It's a long story." When it became clear that he was
not going to be the first to let go, she peeled his hands
from around her waist.

"I got time," he said, smiling a little.

"Well. I don't." Sidney stepped around him to get to the car. He reached it first, and stood blocking the driver side door.

"What were you talking about?" He folded his arms.

"Why?" Sidney asked, genuinely surprised.

"Do you know her?"

"Of course I know her," Sidney's voice was huffy. "I'm from here, remember?"

"Talking about the murder?" he persisted.

"None of your business," she said.

He was like a mountain blocking the door. A big stone mountain. Sidney wished she had the strength to shove him backwards.

"I could arrest you for this, you know?" His straight white teeth gleamed as he grinned at her.

"Arrest me for what?" Sidney challenged.

He shrugged his broad shoulders. "Blocking traffic, public nuisance," he said.

"You're the only nuisance around here right now, Sheriff," she sighed. "So arrest me or get out of the way."

Jacob stared at her for almost a minute. A green pickup truck swerved around their parked cars. The driver leaned out the window and gave both of them the finger. Sidney rubbed hair away from her face and stared at the pickup careening down Main Street. She looked back at Jacob.

"Well?" she asked.

His full mouth curved into a smile, as if he knew a secret she did not.

"Your carriage, Madam," he said, then opened the car door wide enough for her to enter.

"Yeah right." Sidney rolled her eyes and climbed in the car.

Jacob slammed the door and leaned into the window.

"Next time," he warned, "I will arrest you."

"You know," Sidney said with her eyes narrowed, "I believe you are twisted enough to do it."

He smiled, tapped the car door, and winked. He stepped on the sidewalk and folded his arms. Sidney cursed the light until it turned green again. It seemed like an eternity. As she pressed the gas pedal, she knew Jacob still stared after her car. She ignored the thrill of relief as she turned down Second and knew he could no longer see her.

She also ignored the brief thought flashing in her mind that Jacob had purposely pulled her toward him as she stumbled. But she told herself that it was only the heat causing her imagination to go into overdrive.

When she returned home, she found nothing except a terse note from Covina that she was spending the evening playing bingo. Again, she was told not to wait up.

Chapter 11

It started with a phone call the next day. Sidney answered it in the early morning, expecting to hear Julian's warm voice. But instead, she heard Rupert, his voice like a low train whistle.

"Get over to my house. Immediately," he said. "We must talk."

Sidney grabbed the covers to her chest, ran her fingers though her hair. For a minute, she forgot where she was, didn't recognize the room. Then she remembered she was at her mother's house in Haven, Mississippi. And yesterday, on her way to talk to the small town reporter named Grayson, she had met an old woman in the streets who told her more than he ever could. She had driven home immediately after meeting Miss Johnie Mae, and canceled her appointment with Grayson by virtue of not showing up.

"Sidney," he said again.

"What's this about, Englestorm." She couldn't help but

recognize his low, intense voice. She fumbled for the alarm clock.

"It's five–thirty in the morning. Don't you sleep?" She fell back into bed.

"Dexter Haven. Jacob Conrad," he replied, as if that were enough information.

"Get a life, Englestorm." Sidney hung up the phone and rolled over. It rang again, but she ignored it. She knew it would not disturb Covina, because she had stayed out late last night. Besides, the woman slept like the dead. Fifteen minutes later, it started ringing again.

"What?!" Sidney barked into the phone when she realized the man was not going to just give up.

"This is no joke," Rupert's voice was still low.

"Oh, did you mean it to be?"

"Okay," he relented. "I'll give you until seven o'clock. But be here."

"You know what, Englestorm?" Sidney sat up in bed.

"What?"

"You're all heart."

"I'll see you at seven then," he responded.

Sidney hung up the phone and stared at it, half expecting it to ring again, not believing that Rupert would summon her with so little information. But the phone remained silent.

Rupert lived in a house two blocks south of the Haven Mansion. More modest, it was a narrow house with bright red brick and green trim. Three cement steps led up to a lacquered green door. Sidney lifted the brass knocker, then let it drop from her hands. It clattered in the early morning silence.

She was a little more than surprised when a woman answered. She had never thought of Rupert Englestorm as married. The woman wore a chiffon dress with smeared red roses which reminded Sidney of blood stains.

"Why, hello," she said, "you must be Sidney." She smiled brightly, and looked at a spot just over Sidney's shoulder. She had small, hooded eyes and the skin hung from her face like the chiffon hung from her body. Two bright stains of rouge competed with the small, hooded eyes.

Sidney cleared her throat before replying, "Yes, Engl . . ." she stopped. "I mean, Mr. Englestorm asked to see me."

"You are late," Rupert's voice reached Sidney. "Myra," he said before taking his wife by the arm and gently moving her aside, "thank you, I'll take care of the rest."

He motioned her inside the house, and Sidney found herself standing on a patch of polished hardwood floor. She was surprised at how open the house appeared. The entrance gave way to a gray carpeted room that was obviously the living area. A folded paper and a pair of slippers lay on the floor next to a Lazy Boy chair. She noticed a pair of reading glasses on the coffee table. They must have belonged to Myra, because Sidney couldn't remember seeing Rupert in glasses.

"How about some tea?" The woman looked in Sidney's direction. "Or some coffee . . ." she offered.

"Yes, yes, that will be quite fine," Rupert smiled at his wife.

After Myra left, he turned to Sidney. "I'm taking my breakfast out on the terrace. Won't you join me?" he asked politely.

Sidney returned his fake smile. "Do I have a choice?" she asked.

"Frankly, no."

He turned and walked in the same direction as Myra had earlier. They reached a large, sunny kitchen with natural-looking, brown stone floors and gleaming copper

pots hanging from the ceiling. Neither of them acknowledged Myra standing by a coffee pot pouring coffee into
china doll cups. Her hands shook so badly that coffee
spilled in pools on the kitchen counter. Rupert opened
the French doors and walked outside.

The terrace was made of red brick shaped into a semi–
circle. It seemed to spill from the back of the house. Grass
as green as summer surrounded the semi–circle and ended
in a natural tangle of trees and underbrush. She could see
wild red and white roses among the wood.

"I always tell Myra we should chop that down," he
explained when he saw her looking at the uncivilized land-
scape capping his back yard.

"But she likes it," he continued, "calls it nature."

He walked to a white lattice table in the middle of the
terrace and pulled out a padded chair. Sidney walked down
the steps to the table and sat down. Rupert moved aside
his newspaper so she could lay her book bag on the table.

"Why do you carry that tattered thing around?" he asked
her.

"Don't know," Sidney said squinting in the sunlight. "I
guess it reminds me of where I've been."

Rupert laughed then. "Was that supposed to sound
noble?" He reached for a pitcher of orange juice in front
of him and poured some into his glass. "I understand your
father treated you quite well."

"The man was an asshole," Sidney said, annoyed.
"Besides, what would you know about it?"

Rupert shrugged. "I've known Carl Haven all of my
life," he said matter-of-factly.

"You didn't know him like I did." Sidney reached for
an empty glass, and filled it with orange juice.

"Well," he said, and smiled. "I guess I didn't."

He took another drink. "But I paid the bills. And you
didn't suffer."

"Money isn't everything," Sidney said as she crossed her legs, and leaned back in her chair.

Rupert laughed this time. "How inanely stupid, Sidney," he answered her. "Money's the only thing. And you know it."

"Englestorm," Sidney said, tired of his games, "what do you want?"

Before he could answer, Myra floated out of the kitchen. She carried a silver tray in her arms, staring at it as she walked over to them. It was as if she were daring the tray to fall. Instead of standing up to help, Rupert began clearing away china plates so she would have a place to set it.

"I'm sorry it took so long," she said, her voice sounding like a nest of humming bees, "but I knocked the other cups off the counter and into the sink. I broke two of our best cups."

"That's quite all right." Rupert patted her hands. "Did you get burned?"

"No," she breathed, "the cups were empty, thank goodness. But I'm afraid I have a mess of broken glass in the sink. How do you like your coffee?" She turned to Sidney.

"Black," Sidney said flatly.

Myra put a cup in front of Sidney. Both she and Rupert sat in silence as Myra prepared her husband's coffee with cream and sugar. She was just turning away when Samuel Haven blustered through the patio doors.

"I see you haven't the good manners to wait on me, Rupert." He walked over to Myra and kissed her on the cheek.

"Oh, Samuel," she said stepping away from him, "it's good to see you. You should come over to the house more often. Would you like some coffee? How's the family?"

"Yes, dear, coffee would be delightful. And I shipped the entire clan except Marion off to Vicksburg to wait out this mess." He sat down in the chair between Rupert and

Sidney. After Myra left, he reached inside his jacket and pulled out a flat, silver flask. It glittered brilliant in the sun.

"Rupert?" He lifted the flask toward Rupert's cup, ignoring Sidney.

Rupert shook his head. "Too early for my blood, Samuel. But please go ahead," he said.

"Intend to," Samuel grunted.

"Anyone want to tell me what's going on?" Sidney asked.

"I hope you don't mind, but I asked Samuel to stop by for this meeting."

She looked over at Samuel Haven. He reminded her of a sausage stuffed into a blue linen suit. His shirt was open at the throat, and black hair stuck to his chest from the heat. The coffee cup looked like a doll's cup in his meaty hands. He took a long swallow from it while studiously avoiding her gaze.

"Would someone clue me in?" she asked.

"You didn't tell her?" Samuel questioned, looking at Rupert.

"Tell me what?" Sidney looked at Rupert's frowning face.

"That half the town saw you and the Sheriff playing house in the middle of the street yesterday morning."

Sidney swallowed, and stared at the woods at the edge of the yard. She could see the wild, red roses glinting red fire through the trees.

"Then half the town needs to get a life," she said, her voice calm as wind.

"You can't defend my nephew and fuck the Sheriff at the same time." Samuel jabbed a meaty finger toward her.

"Now Samuel," Rupert protested, "there is no cause for that kind of language." He looked around until he was sure his wife was out of earshot. "Myra might hear."

He turned toward Sidney and laced his fingers together

in his lap. "We just want to make sure you are coming along with the case," he told her. "And to also tell you that scenes like yesterday could be, uh, misconstrued."

Sidney gaped at Rupert, trying to keep her mouth from flying open in surprise. The man was actually chastising her.

"The case is coming along fine," she said. "And what I do in the streets is my business."

"Nothing's your business when you are defending my Dexter," Samuel said through a muffin stuffed in his mouth.

"Sidney, we need an update," Rupert said, ignoring Samuel.

"Actually," Sidney answered Rupert, her eyes never leaving Samuel, "I'm coming along fine. But I'm running into some rather curious situations, though."

"Oh?" Rupert raised an eyebrow. "Such as?"

"Wilma Brown," she answered.

Samuel's cup paused in mid-air. "What's that whore got to do with it?" he asked.

Sidney laughed, "She's the victim's mother. I say she's got plenty to do with it."

Rupert motioned for Samuel to be quiet. "What have you found, Sidney?"

"Well, for one thing," she said, "she used to work for the Havens."

"So what?" Samuel grunted. "I hardly remember her."

Sidney looked at Rupert. "Don't you think that's something you should have told me?" she asked him.

"It's not important," Rupert answered.

"And another thing," she continued, "she's living in a shotgun shack with a big screen TV and a thirty–thousand dollar car." She looked pointedly at Samuel Haven.

"So what?" he said again.

"The woman's on welfare."

"That's all very interesting, Sidney. But what has that got to do with the case?"

Sidney didn't answer. She fished out the picture she had taken from Wilma's house.

"Do you remember this picture?" She shoved it in Samuel's face.

He frowned. "Yes, I do," he said. "That was from the mess the Heater boy stirred up."

"Who's that man standing behind you, Rupert?" Sidney asked.

Rupert took the picture from her and stared it for a moment.

"I don't remember that man," he said. "Samuel, do you?"

"This!" Samuel stood up. "This is what you've been working on?" he bellowed. "What in Sam hell does this have to do with Dexter going to jail?"

Sidney leaned forward in her chair. "Do you know that C.D. Heater had his throat cut?" She stared up at them, innocently. "In almost the same place Yolonda Brown had her throat cut?"

Samuel's face melted into a Halloween mask of fury. "What are you trying to do?" he said, his voice was hoarse with anger.

"Samuel is quite right, Sidney," Rupert broke in. "We need to be working on a strategy for Dexter's defense, not some murder that occurred over six years ago."

"Strategy for his defense?" Sidney let out a sharp laugh. "Have you read the police report, Englestorm?" She stood up and walked around the table. "They have witnesses who saw him with the girl on the same night she was murdered." She threw her arms into the air. "Hell, they even have his semen in her vagina."

"The DNA's not back yet," Rupert tried.

"What are you saying?" Samuel asked. Fear had so over-whelmed him, he had not heard Rupert's last comment.

"What I'm saying, Haven," Sidney spoke as if she were talking to a four–year–old, "is that we don't have much of a case right now. And if he is innocent, that's the only thing he's got going for him at this moment. And that's not much."

"So," Rupert said slowly, "you are going to try and introduce another murderer? Some mysterious stranger who runs around town every five years or so murdering black children?"

Sidney looked at him. She did not know if he was being sarcastic or not. And for the first time in years, she questioned herself. Ever since she had arrived in Haven, she could not focus. Her childhood became a cloak, rising up and wrapping itself around her, clouding her view. She admitted to herself that she did not know why the Heater murder fascinated her, but it did. It sparked every particle of her lawyer's instinct. These murders were connected, somehow. All she had to do was prove it.

"And what if your man in the picture turns out to be some fry cook at the McDonald's in Vicksburg?" Rupert asked her. "A devoted family man with dozens of witnesses to swear he hadn't been in Haven in years."

"This is crazy!" Samuel finally found his voice again. "This whole thing is ridiculous. You are going to botch this."

"Samuel's right," Rupert said, thrusting the picture toward her. "It's ridiculous."

Sidney shrugged and dropped the picture in her book bag. She was more convinced than ever that there was something here.

"I've got at least a month before jury selection. I'm just exploring my options," she said.

"Exploring your options?" Spittle rained from Sam's

mouth. "You are wasting time, that's what you're doing. You should be out talking to witnesses! Finding dirt on that whore, Yolonda Brown," he said, his eyes boring into Sidney's. "Not trying to bed the very man who wants my nephew in prison."

Sidney folded her arms across her chest and looked at Samuel. "Just what are you afraid of?" she asked him.

Samuel ran his hand over his gray hair. "Losing Dexter," he breathed, "he's like a son to me." He turned his back to her and grabbed the back of the chair to keep his balance.

Rupert walked around Samuel and took Sidney by the arm as she stood up to leave. "Leave it alone," he whispered to her. "You should not be focusing on the Heater case. You should be focused on this one."

When Sidney tried to jerk her arm from his grasp, he only held it tighter as he guided her to the front door. When they reached the entrance, he paused, still holding her arm.

"You don't like me very much, do you?" he said. His smile reminded her of a hissing rattler.

"No," she answered. "I don't."

"I was very young when I started working for the Havens," he said. "But I've grown up since then. I don't approve of everything they do."

"Then why do you protect them?" she asked.

"Because," he said looking at her squarely in the eyes, "I've known them all of my life. Myra is actually a distant cousin of Sam's. I protect them because I love them." He opened the door for Sidney. "They are my family."

During the drive back to Covina's house, she thought about the meeting, and wondered if the Havens really deserved Rupert's loyalty. When she arrived, there was a message from Jacob on the answering machine. In a stiff voice, he told her that he had Covina down at the Haven jail. He didn't elaborate on why; only said that she was fine, and that Covina was insisting Sidney come down to the station and take her home.

Sidney pushed down the panic she felt stirring in her chest. After all, she didn't have all the facts yet. There could be a perfectly reasonable explanation. By the time she reached the station, the faint panic she felt in the beginning had given way to a weary curiosity.

When she got inside, she saw Covina and Jacob facing each other outside his office. Sidney could see her mother was angry. She had a hand knurled into a fist on her hip. And the plastic bracelet she wore jostled against her wrist as she shook one finger in Jacob's face. Except for that, others may have considered Covina orderly. She wore a white cotton shirt colored with inky blue flowers, and matching white shorts. She looked to Sidney like what she would soon be when Marion gave birth—somebody's grandmother.

Jacob just stood, nodding periodically with a bemused smile on his face. Sidney could not hear what they were saying, and wasn't sure she wanted to. She liked seeing her mother at least looking respectable. Who cares if it was in the middle of a police station? At least it was not behind bars.

"Sidney?" Grange, sitting at his desk, called her name. Both Covina and Jacob turned toward her. "You all," he said to Jacob and Covina, "Sidney's here."

"We can see that," Jacob said, striding toward her. Even after being berated by Covina, the man still had a presence. He wore neatly pressed jeans and a cream-colored polo shirt which blended nicely with his dark skin. Sidney felt her heart speed up slightly. But before he could reach her, Covina flew between them.

"Jacob Conrad," she said, "don't walk away from me while I'm talking to you."

Sidney brought her fingers up to her temple. "Mamma, please," she said. "I've already had a rough morning. Don't make it worse."

"Can I get you some coffee?" Grange asked from behind his desk. "How about I get everyone some coffee and we'll sit down and discuss this."

"Thanks, Grange," Jacob answered. He pointed to his open office door. "Shall we use my office?"

"I don't need to go into nobody's office," Covina said, her voice high and shrill. "I can tell it right here."

Sidney looked around the Haven jail. Late morning light fell through the slated bars covering the windows. Anyone could walk in at any moment and see her mother like this. She could tell Covina was on edge. She needed to get her home.

"Look, is she free to go home?" she asked Jacob.

"Of course she is," he answered, a little insulted.

"Then why didn't you take her home?" Sidney asked. She felt suddenly angry that he had brought her mother here to be the weekday matinee for anyone who might pay Jacob or Grange a visit.

Jacob sighed. "I didn't take her home," he said, "because she wouldn't let me. Besides, I didn't think she should be alone in her state. I called, but you were not there."

"State?" Covina said indignantly. "I ain't in no state!"

"It's okay, Mamma," Sidney said softly, taking her by the arm, "let's just go home."

But Covina jerked away. "No," she said. "I want you both to know what happened. This ain't all my fault. And Sidney," she said, turning toward her daughter, "stop using that crazy lady talk on me."

"Okay, what happened then?" Sidney asked, more annoyed now than ever.

"There was a disturbance at Rollie's bar," Jacob explained. "Rollie wanted your mother to leave, and she wouldn't."

"Mamma," Sidney said, passing a confused look to Covina, "what were you doing at a bar this time of the morning?"

"Don't be a damn fool, Sidney," Covina said. "Rollie serves food, too. I went there to have breakfast with Reverend Robinson. Just like I do every Saturday. The man been trying to save my soul ever since Carl died."

"Anyway," Jacob said, still looking at Sidney, "someone insulted your mother and she became upset. It escalated."

"Boy," Covina cut in, "that ain't the way it happened at all and you know it. That's way too clean sounding. I know you from New York, but you've been living in Haven long enough to talk like you got some sense."

Sidney knew her mother well enough to know when to give up. Defeated, she sat down in one of the hard chairs opposite Grange's desk. Jacob, as if taking a cue from Sidney, sat in the empty chair next to her. He presented a large hand to Covina. "You have the floor," he said.

But before Covina could get started, Grange came in holding three steaming mugs of coffee. As he handed them out, Covina consciously tried to control her breathing. Grange sat back behind his desk and swiveled to face Covina.

"What's going on?" he asked.

"Why don't you get a cup of coffee for yourself, Grange," Sidney said. "We are about to have a show."

Covina cocked her head at Sidney. "Now that ain't right." She looked at Jacob. "Was that right?" she asked him.

Jacob gave Sidney a blistering look of disapproval. "No," he said. "That was not right at all. No one should talk about their mother like that."

"Why are you being such a kiss—up?" Sidney asked him, as she placed her coffee cup on Grange's desk.

"You get to leave," Jacob smiled at her. "I have to stay here."

"I've already had my coffee," Grange grinned, always the last to catch up. They all three turned to look at him. Undaunted, he returned their stares and clasped his hands on his desk, waiting for Covina to speak.

"Anyway," Covina said in a calmer voice, "at Rollie's, I ordered the biscuits and sausage gravy like I always do, and coffee. I always order coffee." As if that reminded her of the coffee she held, she took a sip, and placed the cup on Grange's desk. Sidney dropped her head into her hands. "And Reverend Robinson, he had the big boy breakfast—ham, eggs, plus sausage and grits. And a big ol' glass of orange juice. Do you know how many calories in orange juice, Sidney? I can't believe how much that man ate, big as he is. It's like he's asking for a heart attack."

"Mamma," Sidney groaned.

"Okay, okay, I'm getting to it. Well, that waitress, some-body's daughter in Haven who only comes visiting in the summer. What's her name Grange, Tina, Trina?"

"You talking about that girl with the funny hair and the earring in her nose? Her name is Tina," Grange answered.

"Okay, Tina," Covina said. She paced up and down as she spoke. "Well, anyway, she started acting funny the minute she saw me up in there. I never seen her at night, so I'm guessin' she only works the day shift."

"Funny?" Sidney asked. "Funny how?"

"Well, you know, funny. Like she didn't come and tell me where to sit right away. I had to wait 'til Reverend Robinson came. Then she kept bringing the wrong food out. I told her biscuit and sausage gravy, but she brought out just one ol' hard, plain biscuit and nothing else. Not even coffee. At first, I thought it was just a mistake."

"Well maybe it was," Sidney ventured. Jacob remained silent.

"Well it wasn't no mistake," Covina insisted. "Because after I tol' her she got my food wrong and the biscuit wasn't even fresh, she just kind of sniffed and took it back. And she got the Reverend's order right the first time. The next time she come out with the right food, but the coffee was ice cold." Covina sat on the edge of Grange's desk before continuing. "So I asked her for the exact nature of her problem . . ."

"But not in those words, am I right?" Jacob asked.

Covina pretended not to hear. ". . . and she said she didn't want to serve nobody hooked up with the Havens, with the killings and all."

"Mamma, what did you do?" Sidney asked

"Well," Covina answered, "since I didn't want no foolishness in front of clergy, I dragged her little behind outside to teach her some manners."

"And that's where I came in," Jacob told Sidney. "Rollie called and requested I remove Covina from the premises."

"Mamma," Sidney asked, deflated, "you didn't hit her did you?"

"No," she answered, "but I did insist she come outside with me. And when she did, I proceeded to tell young fresh Miss Ann that she didn't know nothin' about my business. And had no right—bein' here only in the summers and all—to think she knew anything about the Havens or killings or this town. I take enough shit from people who've been here for years to take it from the likes of her."

"Is that it?" Sidney asked. She looked at Jacob, who returned her gaze. "Why isn't this Trina person down here?"

"Tina," Grange corrected. "I never liked her no-how.

Kind of stuck up," Grange explained, nodding and smiling.

"Don't I know it," Covina agreed.

Jacob crossed his long, muscled leg, and looked at Sidney with a small smile. "Why do you think I should have brought her down here?" he questioned.

"Because she obviously instigated, I mean she insult-ed . . ." Sidney stopped, suddenly realizing how ridiculous it sounded.

"Look," Jacob said, not unsympathetically, "I'm sorry I had to bring Covina down here, but like I said, she was a little unruly. And when she calmed down, she didn't want me take her home. She asked me to call you."

Sidney looked for any hint of sarcasm, but there was none. "Okay, thanks," she said. "Mamma, let's go."

She barely heard Jacob's response as she and her mother left the police station. Only one thought occupied her mind, and that was to finish up her business with Dexter Haven and get the hell out of this God–forsaken town.

It had just turned noon when Covina and Sidney stepped out the door of the Haven jail. The sun seemed to be at its hottest and brightest. Though Sidney could tell her mother had finally calmed down, she could still see the aura of disappointment in the slump of her shoulders as she walked out the door.

That was one thing Sidney did not have to see her mother suffer: rejection, accusation. Before Carl Haven died, Covina would barely go out in public. Carl hired someone to bring in groceries and run the errands. After he died, Covina forced herself to spend more time out of the house—grocery shopping, or spending time at Rollie's. There was never any brash coldness, but a few people pretended not to see her in order to avoid speaking. Others just happened to stare too long.

Instead of going to the car, Covina walked to the corner and stood with her arms folded. On the street, a couple of noon shoppers glanced at the two of them curiously.

"Sidney," Covina asked, "do you mind if we don't go home right away? I need some air for a minute."

"No problem," Sidney said. "Do you want to go for a walk?"

"A walk sure do sound fine," Covina answered.

About two blocks from the Haven Jail, and just before the courthouse, they came to a patch of green grass with two big weeping willows at either end. In the center was a statue of the first Samuel Haven, the Haven who had founded the town in the mid-19th century. Two stone benches, yellowed by the sun, flocked the statue on either side. Their once ornate carvings were now only faint ridges.

"You know, I really didn't mean to get this mixed up with them Havens," she said, sitting down on one of the benches.

Sidney sat down beside her, feeling the heat of the cement on her thighs. She rubbed the top of her legs and then the back of her neck. She was already damp and sticky from the Mississippi heat, and the day was barely half over.

"How do you mean, Mamma?" Sidney asked.

"I thought you said you didn't want to hear about all of that?" Covina accused. "Let me see if I can remember how you put it?" Covina said, screwing her face into a look of mock concentration. "Oh, now I remember, you said you didn't want to know the whys and wherefores behind me and Carl Haven. Ain't that what you tol' me the other day?"

"Whatever, Mamma," Sidney answered, suddenly exhausted. "I don't want to get into a fight about it."

Covina sighed. "You are right," she said, "ain't no use
fighting about what's passed. But I do ask myself from time
to time how did I let it go so far and on for so long. I
should have left him a long time ago. Way before giving
him a chance to die in my bed."

"And why didn't you?"

"Because I had gotten used to him. Besides, it was too
late by the time I had you girls. If I had left him, you
wouldn't have had anything growing up."

They sat quiet for a moment, watching pink–billed
pigeons as they lifted and landed on the statue.

"You know we ain't originally from Haven, Sidney?"
Covina asked suddenly.

"Yes," Sidney answered.

"Me, my sister and my daddy used to ride the train cars
after my mother ran off." Covina slapped a ladybug from
the side of her leg with her purse. "And we stayed in Haven
because he was able to make enough money working the
crops. He drank a lot, died when I was going on fourteen.
Funny how my sister ended up drinkin' herself to death,
too."

The park was beginning to fill up. Not too far from
them, a couple with a small child shook out a red throw.
It billowed out like a flag before floating onto the rich
green grass. Covina didn't seem to notice them.

"Before my daddy died, Carl Haven used to come
around and collect the rent. We stayed in one of them
shacks, you know, the ones way out by Rudger's housing
development just before you hit town. We had to stuff
magazines and newspapers in the holes in the walls to keep
the wind out. But Carl, I could tell he liked me. I was
pretty, prettier than I am now."

"How did you feel about Carl?" Sidney asked, curious.

"How do you think I felt?" she said. "I just knew he
was rich, and sometimes, because he liked me, he would

forget to come to our shack on rent collectin' days. Some months, we didn't have to pay nothing."

"And that's how you ended up with him?"

"Well, that's how it started anyway. I guess in the beginning, I could have said no. But we all had been hungry too many times. I remember once we had to eat an onion raw, like an apple, because we didn't have any food. And then when Carl came around, we seemed to have food all the time. I got other things too, a bottle of perfume, some underwear sometimes, candy."

Sidney didn't say anything, just thought about Yolonda Brown.

"Same thing Peachy Girl probably got from Dexter," Covina said as if reading her mind. "And then when my daddy died, Carl came around with these plans for this house. So I said yes, and that's how we both ended up here."

"So, Mamma, do you regret it?" Sidney asked.

Covina waited before answering. "Sometimes I wish people didn't make such a big thing out of it. I went with Carl because he gave me things no black boy in Haven could at the time."

Covina leaned back and breathed in to gather strength before continuing, "I was only sixteen at the time and pregnant with you, but he didn't know it."

"Where was Aunt Margo?" Sidney asked.

"Oh, she'd run off way before that," Covina explained. "Like I said, we weren't originally from Haven, and I didn't know nobody willing to put up with me for too long, except Carl. But I think I more than made up for it. I'm free of him now. I don't put up with nothing from those Havens now. I mean, you should have seen me when Black folks got together to unionize the mills. I was right up there in it." Covina stood up, ready to leave. "And for awhile, didn't nobody care about who I slept with."

"But that just sounds like a bunch of excuses," Sidney said. "I asked you if you regretted it."

"No," Covina explained as she sat back down. "Because if I did, that would be like regretting you girls."

They sat a little longer, watching the couple with the red blanket. The woman pulled sandwiches wrapped in paper towels from a wicker basket, and little doll–size bags of Ruffle potato chips. The child chased a yellow balloon around the blanket, laughing and tripping over both mother and father. They looked happy, safe, and normal. Sidney was surprised such a thing could exist in Haven.

"Come on," Covina said, and stood up again. "I'm hungry. Let's go." And this time, she turned to leave, not waiting to see if Sidney followed.

Chapter 12

From a plastic chair at the glass picnic table, Sidney watched Covina part and braid her low Afro into many tiny plaits. Covina sat on one of the green and white lawn chairs on the patio, with her legs crossed and jar of Blue Magic in her lap. As she worked a braid into one part of her head, she would leave the comb hooked in another, letting it dangle in her face.

Crime scene photos of Yolonda Brown and the police report, the pages separated like blades of a broken fan, covered the round picnic table. She and Covina had barely spoken a word since coming home, but the silence between them was comfortable. Sidney could not remember the last time she felt this close to her mother.

"Those glasses make you look ol'," Covina said as she plaited her hair. "Why don't you wear contacts?"

Sidney adjusted the frame of the black–rimmed reading glasses on her face. "They are reading glasses, Mamma. I only need them sometimes when I read. I don't need contacts."

Wind lifted the papers, and Sidney had to cover them with the palm of her hand to keep them from blowing off the table. She looked up. Several of the branches on the magnolia trees began to sway. She could smell rain in the air.

"Looks like it's gonna rain," Covina said, looking up at the nighttime sky. "Maybe we should go inside."

"Maybe," Sidney said, but neither one of them moved, as if afraid it would break the newfound bond between them.

"What time is it?" Covina asked.

"Just past six," Sidney replied.

"Well," Covina said, "I need to get on the road. I don't want to be driving down to Vicksburg too late, especially if it's going to rain."

"Mamma," Sidney said, "are you sure you need to go?"

"Yes, I think so. I don't want Marion having that baby without me. Besides, she didn't sound too hot when I talked to her earlier," she replied.

Soon after they arrived home, Covina told Sidney she was going back to Vicksburg to be near Marion. Sidney did not ask her how much that decision had to do with what had happened at Rollie's today, and Covina did not volunteer a reason.

Sidney returned to the papers spread across the table. She thought about how little she had found out about the Heater murder, though it occupied her thoughts almost as much as Dexter's defense did. She realized that she and Miss Johnie Mae had not finished their conversation earlier.

She and Covina said good-bye at the door. Covina kissed Sidney's cheek as she draped one of the black duffel bags over her shoulder.

"Drive careful, Mamma," Sidney said.

"I always do," Covina lied. "You'll call me if there is any trouble or anything new happens, right?"

"Of course I will," Sidney answered. "Tell Marion to take care."

Covina shook her head, the gold hoop earrings she wore bouncing against her cheeks. "Look," she said, "if I told Marion you were here, she'd be expecting you in Vicksburg the day after. So, just between you and me, I ain't seen you."

Sidney laughed, "Okay, Mamma." She helped carry Covina's other bags to the maroon Buick and waited until Covina started the car and backed out of the driveway.

Before going back to the house, she looked up at the sky. Instead of being smooth and black and clear, it was tinged with gray rain clouds no star could break through. She knew she would have to hurry in order to avoid the rain.

She steered the car toward the old shack where she, a boy and an old woman had once sat on the porch eating fried cornbread and watching chickens in the backyard.

When she nosed the car into Miss Johnie Mae's yard, she didn't hear any chickens—only the blare of the TV from the screen door of the living room. Miss Johnie Mae sat on the front porch, rocking back and forth. As she walked up the rickety steps, Sidney was afraid the rocker would collapse under the strain.

"Don't be worrying about this rocker none," Miss Johnie Mae said noticing the worry in Sidney's eyes. "It done lasted me through two husbands, two wars, a son, and two grandsons." She looked Sidney in the eye. "Sit yo'self down," she said. "I'll get you some lemonade."

"I don't need anything, Miss Johnie Mae." Sidney sat

down on the steps, not wanting to begin questioning her right away. Though she had driven to her house, she felt a stitch in her side; her chest felt tight as if she had run a long way.

"Nonsense," Miss Johnie Mae answered back. "Look like you been running from ghosts." She opened the screen door, then turned and looked back at Sidney. "Or running to them, whichever way you want to see it," she finished.

Sidney turned away as she heard the screen door bang against the wooden frame of the door. She looked out on Miss Johnie Mae's front yard. How beautiful, she thought. One untouched place of Haven filled with trees that must have been one hundred years old, and all kinds of flowers—honeysuckle, black–eyed susans, and poppies. A beautiful, wild old garden.

"I love this place," Miss Johnie Mae said as she handed Sidney a narrow, red Tupperware glass filled with lemonade. "I hope you like your lemonade sweet."

"I do." Sidney took a long swallow and leaned back against the porch rails. She listened to the sounds the yard made. Neither she nor Miss Johnie Mae spoke for awhile.

"Looks like you got something big on your mind," the old woman asked her.

"Sort of." Sidney took a long swallow of lemonade. "Miss Johnie Mae," she asked, "you own this house?"

"Yep," she said. "Sure do. And some of the land. I own it out back down to the creek." She pulled a square of Day's Work tobacco from inside her blouse. Sidney watched as she broke off a piece. "And out front." She tucked the piece of tobacco in her cheek. "I own that down to the road." She gestured down to the dirt road. "And about a mile off to both sides." She held her arms out as if she was about to fly.

"Lot of black folks own land around here?" Sidney asked, avoiding the real reason she had come.

"Yep," Miss Johnie Mae spat tobacco into a Pepsi can. "Sure do. Mr. Sam, I mean Big Sam—not that sorry one down there in town, ran up on a bad spell once where he run out of money. Had to pay some of the black folks off in land to keep 'em working."

Miss Johnie Mae rocked back and forth for awhile before continuing on. "Some folks, they sold it back for money when thangs got better for the Havens. Like Wilma's Mamma and Granddaddy. That's why she ended up in that shack in the Bottoms. Others, like my granddaddy and daddy, kept it in the family and passed it on to us."

"Why don't you do anything with it?" Sidney asked.

"Am doing something with it," she laughed. "Living on it. Why you so interested?"

"Why don't you sell it?" Sidney asked.

When Miss Johnie Mae stopped rocking long enough to stare at Sidney, Sidney realized she had obviously hit a nerve with the old woman. A black kitten in white socks slinked over to the Pepsi can. Without taking her eyes from Sidney, Miss Johnie Mae waved it away.

"Why?" her voice was strident. "If I'd sold it, still wouldn't have kept my fool son Randall from killing himself. 'Cause then, he would not only have been crippled, but homeless." She began rocking again. "My folks came by this land honest, and they kept it. Not like some folks I know. Not like Wilma."

"I didn't mean anything by that, Miss Johnie Mae." Sidney put the cup back on the step and stood up. "I shouldn't have come here," she finished.

"Yes." Johnie Mae looked her straight in the eyes. "Yes. You should have come. 'Cause you finally trying to do what's right. Now take that cup back in the kitchen 'fore that stupid cat drown hisself."

Sidney looked down and saw that the kitten had stuck his entire face up to his whiskers inside the red cup. She hesitated only a moment before taking the cup inside the house.

When she returned, she sat in a metal garden chair next to Miss Johnie Mae.

"Now you didn't come here to talk about C.D. and his fool Daddy," Miss Johnie Mae continued. "You come here to finish our conversation of yesterday morning."

Sidney looked at the old woman. "Yes, I have," Sidney answered. "You said Wilma profited from your grandson's murder."

"Yep," Miss Johnie Mae answered. "But I ain't got no proof." She squinted her eyes out into the front yard. The kitten chased a firefly down the steps, and tumbled out into the yard after it.

"What makes you think that?" Sidney asked. "What makes you think Wilma knows something?"

" 'Cause right after, she started buying lots of things," the old woman answered. "Even after she quit her job with the Havens and went on welfare."

"That doesn't mean a whole lot," she answered her. "It could have been anything."

"It doesn't mean a lot," the woman conceded. "But it means something."

"What did the police think?" Sidney asked.

"You mean the Sheriff?" the old woman huffed. "He ain't from around here. I don't think it meant nothing to him. He didn't notice." Miss Johnie Mae spat another long stream of tobacco with the precision of a stealth bomber into the Pepsi can. "And I don't think he cared."

"Somebody should have told him." Sidney said.

"Wasn't nobody here had the notion."

"Not even you?" Sidney asked.

"Not even me," Johnie Mae answered. "It don't matter

to me no—how. Samuel Haven wasn't going to jail, anyway, and that little bit of money Wilma get ain't gon' bring my boy back."

The old woman rocked on. "Besides," she said. "Wilma be paying for it now. Paying for it in spades."

The rain finally broke through as Sidney drove from Miss Johnie Mae's house. It was still raining as she stepped from the car into the driveway of her mother's house, the only house with arches that close to the Bottoms in Haven, Mississippi. It sizzled from the sky in a hot slow drizzle piercing her skin through her thin halter and shorts. Warm mud—soaked rain oozed between the leather straps of her sandals.

She left everything in the car—her book bag, her purse, her notes, and even the police reports from Yolonda Brown's murder she had hastily thrown in the car before visiting Miss Johnie Mae. She could feel her nerves jangling just behind her eyes.

Once in the house, she stripped off her clothes on her way to the shower in her mother's room. The shower was bigger than hers, and available now that Covina was away. She let the water run until it was hotter than the rain outside. She let it pound the back of her neck, her shoulders. She stayed in the shower until the glass door and bathroom mirror were thick with steam.

She stepped from the shower and grabbed a white towel from the towel rack. When she opened the bathroom door, she saw a man standing by the French doors, staring at the garden of magnolia trees. His hands were in his pockets as he watched the rain.

"Oh Jesus," Sidney breathed and fell against the bathroom door.

"I didn't meant to scare you." Jacob turned at the sound of her voice.

"Don't you knock?" she asked him as she brushed the wet hair from her forehead.

Jacob walked around her mother's four-poster bed, one hand still in his pocket, the other twirling around the bed post.

"I did, several times," he answered. "You didn't answer."

"So that gives you the right to just barge in here?" Sidney put her hand over her chest; her heart pounded so hard it hurt.

"I wanted to make sure you were all right," he said.

"Bullshit," Sidney said as she walked to the closet and pulled down her mother's red and black checked robe. "You did it to spy on me. Turn around."

Jacob stared at her for a long time, noticing how the towel she clutched so tightly barely covered her breasts. Then he shrugged his shoulders and turned to the French doors. Sidney let the towel fall to the ground as she put on the robe. She didn't say anything to him as she left her mother's room for the kitchen.

She flicked on the lights and went to the cupboard. She knew Jacob had followed and now stood behind her, but she ignored him.

"Suspicious." There was amusement in his voice as he watched her measure the Hershey's cocoa into a big blue mug. "I'll have you know I'm here on official business."

She stabbed a glare in his direction, then reached for the sugar bowl. He walked into the kitchen and stood so close behind her, she could feel his breath on her neck. He leaned one hand on the counter, blocking her way to the refrigerator.

"Do you mind?" Sidney pushed his arm away and opened the refrigerator door.

"Aren't you even curious to know why I'm here?"

She opened a carton of lowfat milk, and poured a long

stream of white into her mug. As the milk heated in the microwave, she turned to stare him. She folded her arms, not knowing what to feel.

She now had to admit, the man was handsome. Not in Julian's pretty–boy way. Jacob was over six feet tall, with raven black skin. And his eyes were an even darker liquid black, like crude oil.

"Take a picture," Jacob chuckled. "It'll last longer."

Sidney kept staring in a frank unabashed appraisal as if she were inspecting a bug on a pin.

"Do I pass inspection?" he held out his arms to his sides and whirled around.

Sidney kept staring at him until the microwave beeped.

"Barely," she said as she opened the door to the microwave, "you barely pass."

"I'm flattered," he smiled wryly and bowed from his waist.

Sidney stirred the chocolate and took a sip. The hot liquid scalded her tongue.

"As I was saying," he asked as he followed Sidney into the living room. "Aren't you even curious as to why I'm here?"

"No." Sidney plumped on her mother's couch, and picked up the remote to the TV. She flicked the channels until she found a rerun of 'M*A*S*H' on one of the cable stations. She leaned her head back on the couch and propped her feet on the coffee table.

"Your car," he said, as if that explained everything.

"What about my car?" She looked at him sideways.

"The door was open in the rain." Jacob clicked off the TV. "The lights were on. And your neighbors were worried."

"You could have called." Sidney pointed the remote back at the TV as if she were aiming a weapon. She clicked it back on without waiting for his answer.

"I did call." He hit the power switch on the TV itself. He bent and took the remote from her hands. "No answer."

Sidney looked up at Jacob and ignored the anger in his eyes.

"Okay," she said, "as you can see, I'm fine."

She stood up and snatched the remote from him. "Now," she said and looked up at him and smiled, "get out."

When she turned the TV back on, the light played on both of their faces. Jacob stomped over to the TV and turned it off again. He reached down and pulled Sidney up by the shoulders. He clamped her so close to him, she could feel every line and bend of his muscled body.

"You are just like them aren't you?" he said, shaking her a little. "The Havens."

"Sheriff," she said, and jerked away. "Do you mind?"

He sighed and let her go. "I apologize," he said. "I let my temper get away from me sometimes."

"*You* are telling me," Sidney said, looking at him warily. She felt suddenly conscious about how naked she was under her robe. Jacob sat on the couch, and looked up at her with his large, dark eyes.

"Can we start over, please?" he asked. "Pretend I just came to visit?"

Sidney searched his face, trying to determine if he were serious or not. She couldn't tell if it was anger she saw flashing in his dark eyes.

"Maybe we can start at the point where you ask me if I want something to drink?" he smiled widely.

She regarded him silently, knowing she should tell him there could be no truce for them as long as she defended Dexter Haven. Instead, as she stared at his broad, handsome face, she decided to trust him just a little, just for tonight.

"Okay," she said finally. "Would you like something to drink?"

"Yes," he said and sat back on the couch. "A Coke would be nice."

"That would be nice, wouldn't it?" Sidney agreed. "But we don't have any."

"No Coke," he said, his face falling dramatically. "What do you have?"

"Kool-Aid," Sidney stated flatly. "Grape."

"Why, that would be fine," he said, getting up and following her to the kitchen.

"You don't have to follow me," she said over her shoulder. "I know where the kitchen is."

But he followed anyway, and once in the kitchen, leaned against the counter as she took a clear glass from the cupboard.

"Where is Covina?" he asked.

"Hmm," she opened the refrigerator and took out a clear pitcher. Ice and purple Kool-Aid clamored into the clear glass as she poured. "Oh. She had to go back to Vicksburg to be with Marion, my sister. She's pregnant, and has to stay in bed. Mamma has been helping her on and off for the last couple of months."

"I know that," Jacob responded.

"And how is that?" Sidney eyed him, the suspicion back.

Jacob took a sip of the Kool-Aid and grimaced. He pulled it back from his lips and stared into the glass. "It's kind of bitter, isn't it?" he asked.

"How do you know Covina went to Vicksburg?" she persisted.

"I didn't say I knew she went tonight," he defended quietly. "But I knew she has been going back and forth for quite awhile. She usually calls to have Grange or myself drive by the house while she is away," he said as he set the glass on the counter.

"That all sounds very logical," she answered. "Except this is Haven, and people hardly lock their doors at night."

"Can I ask you a question?" he asked, staring at her.

She didn't answer, but instead closed the throat of her robe, knowing how she must look to him. Before she took a shower, she couldn't help but notice the large dark circles under her eyes, and tiny worry lines around her mouth.

"Why are you so suspicious of me?" he asked her.

"Why?" she asked. "Why not? Everytime I turn around you are there, like a damn bad penny. You just keep turning up."

"You want to elaborate?"

She started counting off points on her hand. "You followed me outside the church at Yolonda Brown's funeral, then you . . ."

"*You* are being ridiculous," Jacob said, cutting her off and folding his arms over his broad chest.

". . . just happened to be there both when my car ran out of gas, and when I was talking to Miss Johnie Mae in town. Then today—to top everything off—you arrest my mother. Now tonight, here you stand here with some inane excuse about a call."

He cocked a black eyebrow at her. "It wasn't inane," he said. "You know as well as I do there is a perfectly good explanation for all of that."

"Do you have anything better to do than spy on me?" she asked him.

He laughed suddenly. "What do you think I'm doing? Stalking you?"

"Maybe," she said, staring at him unflinchingly.

"Don't flatter yourself," he replied, shaking his head. "Really, don't. I mean why would I?" he asked, laughing.

"Because you are obsessed with the Havens," she said, ignoring his surprised laughter. "You want revenge because you think Samuel Haven killed C.D. Heater and got away with it."

Jacob's reply was sudden. "Me?" he said, pointing to his chest. "I'm obsessed? Who traveled all the way from Washington to defend a murderer just because he happens to be a Haven."

"See," Sidney said pointing at him, "the Havens again. You can't get them out of your head. You are scared, scared I'm going to win this case, and make you look like an ass."

He stopped for a long moment, as if he were really thinking about her last statement. Sidney turned away from him and stared at the rain slithering sideways across the glass in the kitchen window. It was coming down in torrents.

"There is one thing I can say about you," he said. "You got guts, lady."

"Get out," she told him again. "Get out before I have you arrested, yourself, for harassment."

"Don't get excited. I am leaving, because this is useless," he said. "Do me a favor, though, and lock the door behind me."

Sidney didn't know why she didn't feel more relieved. When he reached the front door, he turned back around and paused for a moment.

"Oh," he paused with his hand on the door knob, "there is one more thing."

"What?" Sidney didn't bother to hide the irritation in her voice. He walked over to where she stood. "What?" she asked him again.

He gently placed his hand at the point where her neck curved into her shoulder and looked into her eyes. "Everything isn't always about the Havens, you know. Their family may have found this spot, but it took a whole lot of people to make it. This town is full of people that have absolutely nothing to do with them. You need to see that."

She stood for a moment, stilled by his callused hand on her neck. He leaned forward, and for a minute she thought he might kiss her. The phone rang, breaking the spell. She jerked away, and he turned and left. She quickly clicked the dead bolt into place, surprised at herself for not feeling more relieved at his departure. She then ran to get the phone before it stopped ringing.

"Babe?" It was Julian.

"Julian," she sighed. "Julian. Hi." she said, trying to steady her breathing.

"Are you all right?" he asked her.

"Yes. Yes. I'm fine," she insisted.

Julian started talking, but Sidney couldn't make any logical sense out of what he was saying. Her mind was still on the conversation she had had with Jacob, and the almost tangible thing that had passed between them at the door. Julian kept talking though, and after a minute or two, Sidney let the phone slide from her ear. She turned tentatively around. She could hear the rain blowing sideways into the door by the wind. If Julian hadn't been on the other end of the phone connecting her with the reality she knew, she would have thought it was all a dream.

After she hung up the phone with Julian, she tested the silver bolt to make sure it was locked. It felt cold in her hands. She poured the chocolate down the sink and ran water in the cup until it looked like new.

Chapter 13

The pounding in her head turned to an insistent pounding at the door. Sidney leaned up on her elbows in her mother's bed, remembering she had taken two sleeping pills after Jacob left. Rain still fell sideways onto the panes of the French glass doors. Tree branches swayed past the window, blowing in the wind.

She didn't know whether fear made her heart jump as she stuck her feet into the red slippers by her bed. She shrugged into her robe as she ran to the door. The pounding came again. In her mind's eye, she could see the side of a black fist hitting the door.

"I'm coming, I'm coming," she said sleepily. "Pipe down, you are going to wake the whole neighborhood."

She slapped the bolt on the door open. When she swung open the door, her face fell. Julian stood there in an Eddie Bauer waterproof jacket, the rain glistening on his light skin and shining like diamonds in his hair. His smile lit up the darkness.

"You look a little disappointed," he said. His green eyes twinkled.

Sidney put one hand on her hip, the other to her fore-head.

"Julian," she said, "what are you doing here?"

"Were you expecting someone else?" he asked her.

"Well, I wasn't expecting you," she quipped, dodging the question.

"Sorry to disappoint you." He reached down and planted a brotherly kiss on her cheek. "Are you going to let me in, or make me stand out in the rain all night?" he asked.

Sidney waved him in and closed the door behind him.

"What are you doing here?" she asked him again.

"What can I do with my wet things?" he replied.

She folded his jacket over the sink in the guest bathroom next to the hallway. He asked if he could take a shower, and she pointed him toward her mother's room. She made a pot of coffee while he showered.

Julian emerged from the bedroom the same time she stepped out of the kitchen with two steaming hot cups. He was shirtless, with a towel over his head. She noticed he had on dry Levi's.

"Thanks," he told her as he balled up the towel and dropped it on the coffee table. "That's just what I need. I just hope it's decaf." He sat on the couch and took a long drink of the black coffee.

"Julian, why did you drive all the way down here in this storm?"

"Why else?" he said, winking at her. "Because of you. I was worried about you tonight. I know how much you hate this place," he told her.

"So after you talked to me . . ." she began.

"That's right, I took the first flight out, rented a car in Vicksburg. And here I am."

"I don't know why you bothered," she said to him.

"I bothered because I also have some information for you," he said. He dug into the suitcase he brought with him and pulled out some papers. He handed Wilma Brown's credit checks to her.

"Oh," he said as an afterthought, "I almost forgot this." He gave her a vanilla file folder. Inside there was an 8 x 10 glossy of Jacob in a police academy uniform. He didn't smile, and his eyes stared straight into the camera. She quickly closed the folder and started looking at Wilma Brown's records.

"That's funny," she said. "The woman didn't even have a checking account until 1989."

Julian laughed. "I know. I thought the same thing. A $500.00 deposit that same year, then no more for six months," he said, leaning in close. Sidney hardly noticed the smell of the Ivory soap her mother used.

She flipped through the pages and then noticed another large deposit.

"Two thousand dollars?" she exclaimed to Julian.

"I know," he said again. "It's a trip, huh? And then five thousand dollars every month since."

"Julian," Sidney turned to him, "do you know where she got this kind of money?"

"Probably the same way Covina got hers," he chuckled.

"That wasn't necessary, Julian." Sidney jumped up and took his empty mug into the kitchen.

"Why?" he asked, following behind her. "It's the truth."

"Besides," she said as she placed his mug in the sink beside the one she had earlier in the night, "I don't think that's happening here."

"Why?" he asked.

Sidney folded her arms and stared at him. "Too much of a coincidence," she said. "I mean, right after the Heater murder, she takes a Sugar Daddy. I just don't think she would do it, Julian.''

"Why?" he laughed again. "It wouldn't be the first time."

Sidney ignored the overwhelming urge to slap him. "Why are you here, Julian?" she asked.

He dragged his fingers through his hair, laughed, then stopped abruptly. "I told you. I was worried about you," he finally said.

She looked at him for several moments. "You can take my mother's room. I'll sleep in my old room."

"Don't you want the other information I got for you?"

"What other information?"

"On your Sheriff Conrad," he answered.

"He's not my Sheriff Conrad," she snapped at him.

"You're touchy." He cocked his head and looked at her.

She walked out of the living room and he hurried after her. He retrieved the file from the coffee table.

"Okay, let's see," he said. He plumped on the couch and put his bare feet on the coffee table. "Police Academy, 1982." He yawned.

Sidney pursed her lips, and grabbed two sheets from the linen closet.

"You won't need a blanket," she told him. "Even though it's raining, it's hot."

"Yeah, I bet," he chuckled.

"What's that supposed to mean?" she said, and stopped with the sheets in her hand.

"Nothing, nothing at all." He looked back down at the file. "Never married," he said.

"You know what I can't understand?" she asked him, "I can't understand why a man like that would want to stay in Haven."

Julian held up a piece of paper from Jacob's file. "I can," he said cheerfully, waving it in the air. "Right here."

She walked behind the couch and took the paper from his hand.

"What's this?" she asked him.

"Notes from your Sheriff . . . excuse me, Sheriff Conrad's session with his psychologist."

"Psychologist?" Sidney dropped the paper as if it caught fire. "Julian, you didn't . . ." she started.

"You said everything; I got you everything," he said, staring at her. "You are not getting squeamish on me, are you, Sid?" he asked.

"But these are confidential. How did you ever get these?"

"I have friends in low places," he said as he flashed another smile at her. "You want me to continue?"

"No," she answered flatly.

"The man was fed up," he said. "Sick of crime, sick of law. Would you believe he told the psychologist he was afraid he was going to hurt somebody?"

"Then why would they send him here to help with the Heater murder?"

"It was perfect. A perfect chance to get rid of him. Besides, he wasn't really a bad cop. I mean, he got an accommodation in 1983 for bravery, another one three years later. Eventually got promoted to homicide detective."

"Julian," Sidney interrupted him, "I don't want to know this."

"Yes you do," he said quietly. "They made him leave, Sidney."

He walked behind the sofa and picked up the paper that had floated to the floor.

"This," he said, "this is just a summary of those sessions."

"Why would a man like that go to a psychologist?" she asked him.

"They made him," Julian's voice was serious. Sidney was shocked. She could count on her hands the number of times in their marriage Julian was serious.

"He killed somebody," he said in that same serious tone.

"Don't be naïve, Julian," she spat at him. "The man was a homicide detective. That's not unusual."

The rain paddled the windows during the silence. *It's going to be muddy tomorrow,* Sidney thought, trying to take her mind off of the conversation.

"Why are you defending him?" he asked as he walked around her. "It wasn't his first kill, Sidney. And you know as well as I do there are cops that go their whole career without ever pulling the trigger."

"That's why you are here," she said. "Isn't it, Julian? You are afraid of him."

"Okay, that's part of the reason," he admitted. "Besides I thought you could use this in the trial. There is more in here. The man is clearly unstable."

"You know damn well I can't use that," she told him.

"Maybe not directly," he shrugged. "But you could sub-poena it, or even allude to it, choose something else like it. There's more in here, Sidney," he said again.

"What's the other reason?" she asked him, wanting to change the subject.

"The other reason what?" he asked her. He turned his back, pretending to be engrossed in reassembling Jacob's file.

"The other reason you are here," she said. "Just spit it out, Julian."

He placed the file on top of Wilma's and turned to her. He put his thumbs in his front belt loops, rocked on his heels. He watched her for a minute before reaching down into his briefcase and handing her a large 10 x 13 brown envelope. The minute he gave it to her, she knew what it was. She didn't have to open it to know the envelope was filled with divorce papers.

"You came all this way," she started, "you came all this way, in this storm, to serve me?"

"Something like that. Partly," he admitted.

Sidney laughed then until her gut ached. She fell on the couch laughing and threw the papers on the coffee table. They skidded off onto the green carpet.

"It's not funny," Julian told her, still serious.

"You are getting married, aren't you?" she asked him.

"Yes," he said grimly. "As soon as the divorce is final, I'm getting married in Mexico."

Sidney stood up and faced him then. "You know Julian," she told him, "you have always been something else. Always willing to leap tall buildings when you have your own self–interest at heart."

"You know what, sweetheart?" he said, and smiled at her without his eyes, "I learn from the best."

"What's that supposed to mean?" she asked him.

"Nothing," he said, holding up his hands. "It means nothing."

Sidney and Julian stared at each other from across the room. *Adversaries at last,* she thought. She got up from the couch and went to the bay window next to the door. Pulling aside the curtain, she looked outside. Because only a small dim lamp lit the living room, she could see just beyond her own reflection into the rain–slicked street. Oval patches of light from the street lamps lay on the street, producing a pitiful shine. Wind pulled the pattering rain sideways, and caused tree branches to scrape wetly across the window. As she watched, the sky illuminated flatly and completely, throwing the entire scene into a spotlight for less than a millisecond.

She pretended to be engrossed in the scene, not wanting to talk to Julian just yet. She touched her throat and swallowed. Her fingers felt like ice, and her mouth was so dry she tasted cotton. Julian wisely kept silent. He had always avoided direct confrontations, which was probably one of the reasons his career never took off, as hers did.

"Look," Julian said finally, but hesitantly, "I'm sorry I said it . . . I mean, I shouldn't have said it."

Sidney ran her fingertips over her throat, softly. "I just want to know what you meant by that, Julian. That's all," she said.

But that was not all, and they both knew it. She leaned her forehead against the window, and closed her eyes. She remembered the first time she had caught Julian cheating on her. Of course, she had always suspected. During the first year after leaving the ACLU, she had the usual clues. Phone calls with no one at the other end. Julian out late and long, but always with an excuse. She never had any real proof and she had so immersed herself in her new job, she talked herself out of suspicion.

Then, two years later, she arrived home from a business trip to find a woman—petite and blonde—in their condo. She had on little gym shorts with a sports bra, and running shoes so new and white, they could have never touched dirt. Sidney thought she looked sweatless—one of those women who wouldn't break a sweat in hell. Sidney took one look at her and knew why she was there. Before even putting her luggage down, she told her, calmly, to leave. After the woman left, Julian came down the metal spiral staircase. *Not in my house,* she remembered telling him, *Just not in my house.* And that was all. They had never really discussed it.

She said aloud, "What was her name, anyway?"

"Whose name?" Julian asked.

"That woman," Sidney explained, "the bouncy blonde I caught in the condo when I got back from California a few years back. Tell me, was she the first?" She let the curtain fall and walked back into the room. Julian didn't answer right away. He stood with his hands on his hips, a look of mild surprise on his face.

"You are not going to play the wronged wife on me, are you, Sid?" he asked.

"For just once in your life, can you answer a question directly, Julian?" she said tiredly.

He took a deep breath, then plunged. "Very well," he said, "since we are talking about this. No, she wasn't. I slept around before that. And the wisecrack about learning from the best, I was obviously referring to you. You always put yourself and your career first, no matter what. You didn't give a damn what it did to me, or our marriage."

Sidney felt the rage she had pushed down all the years she stayed married to him boil over. She walked over to him, then reached out and slapped him squarely on the face. He put his hand to his face the minute she drew back her own. She watched a range of emotions—from surprise to anger to hurt—pass over his face like a series of rain clouds.

"That's a damn lame excuse and you know it, Julian," she said. "I didn't deserve to be treated like that. I just didn't deserve it."

"How dare you?" he asked, quietly angry. "Now, after there is no chance left for us, you decide to take exception to my behavior."

"I took exception long before," she shot back.

"Bullshit," he said. "You were so caught up in your career, you barely knew I was alive. It has been over for us for a long, long time . . ."

"Yes," she interrupted, "the minute I left the ACLU, the minute I didn't do what you wanted me to."

"Don't try that on me!" he said. "We never should have gotten married, and you know it."

"Yes, how did that happen in the first place? Oh, I

remember, you wanted to use me because you knew your own career had gone flat," Sidney said, sarcastically.

That stunned him into silence. He bent down, swiped up the envelope containing the divorce papers from the floor.

"That wasn't fair," he said. "That wasn't fair and you know it. We got married because we were friends, and we mistakenly thought that was all we needed to make a successful marriage."

"If it was over for a long time," Sidney challenged, "why weren't you the one asking for a divorce?"

Julian made a time-out signal with his hands. "Wait," he said, "didn't you hear what I said, friends? Like I thought we still could be."

"Why, Julian?" she persisted.

He didn't say anything at first. They both just listened to the rain dwindle, and finally lift.

"Simple," he said finally, "you were just too damn busy."

They stood facing each other across the room, their arms folded. Sidney didn't know what to feel, only knew in some ways, he was right. She had always been too damn busy.

"The rain stopped," Julian said, gently.

"I can see that," Sidney answered.

"Look," Julian said, walking over to her and taking her hands in his, "can we at least try and get through this like two civilized people?"

She wanted to scream at him. Tell him no, hell no. How dare he find someone first? But she just didn't have the energy. Instead, she looked at him with her hands lying limp in his. "For now. I guess for now we can," she said finally.

The next day was clear and bright, almost sunny. Julian stayed, attempting to be jovial, pretending like the night before didn't happen. *As usual,* Sidney thought to herself.

For the most part, she ignored him. The trial would be starting in a couple of weeks, and she didn't want to get past jury selection. With the overwhelming evidence against Dexter, her best strategy would be to avoid this trial, period. And if she couldn't avoid it, she had to introduce another theory, another murderer. She needed to get the attention focused away from Dexter Haven.

She started with Jacob's file not caring a fig for the prosecutor, because she knew this man was just a shadow. He hardly spoke up during the arraignment and she knew the whole thing put a sour taste in his mouth. The man lived in Haven his entire life. He owned a hardware store on Main Street, and became a lawyer simply because the town needed someone to process wills and the occasional divorces.

She read the entire file on Jacob while Julian cooked breakfast in his pajama pants, barefoot. It turned out that Julian was only able to get a summary of Jacob's mandatory sessions with the psychologist. And she didn't learn anything he hadn't already told her. The summary was peppered with phrases like *battle fatigue* and *needs a rest* and *callous view of right and wrong which may sometimes lead to questionable behavior*.

Dexter came to the house at eight in the morning to discuss the case. He talked for four hours, recounting his every move while eyeing Julian distrustfully. Sidney didn't even bother to introduce him. *Yes, he had sex with Yolonda Brown on the night of the murder. No, he didn't rape her. They had sex in his uncle's car. And no and no and no he didn't know how old she was.*

"I keep telling you, I thought she was twenty," he said. He jumped up at last and stuffed his hands in the pockets of his navy blue Ralph Lauren sweat pants. "Who is that anyway?" he asked, and jabbed a hand toward the kitchen as a whistling Julian cleaned up the breakfast dishes.

"Don't worry about who that is," she answered. "He's the least of your problems right now."

Dexter sighed and turned to her. "My uncle will be happy, at least," he said.

She looked up from her notebook. "Oh? Why is that?" she asked him.

"He thought you and the Sheriff had something going on," he said. "I would really be happy if he were here. My uncle I mean."

"Why?" Sidney asked. "Do you think if he were here you wouldn't have to answer so many questions?"

"I just wish he were here, that's all," Dexter explained. "I'd be more comfortable."

Sidney walked over to him. "Look, there is a reason I asked you not to tell Samuel about this," she said, arms folded. She measured her phrases in doses as if she were giving medicine to a child. "If you have to testify, you are not going to be able to take your uncle on the stand with you. And you are certainly not going to be able to take him to jail with you, that is, if you are convicted," she finished.

"Jail!" Dexter exclaimed. "I'm not going jail."

Sidney had wondered what happened to the confident boy by the river. But here he was, in his full Haven glory, standing by the window, light glinting in his golden hair. Julian dropped a plate in the kitchen, shattering the silence.

"What about him?" he asked. "I don't like him being here."

"Is that why you are so jumpy? Julian?" she asked. "Who cares about him; he's not even paying attention. Let's get on with it."

She moved on with more questions before he could protest. *How many times had he seen Yolonda? How many times had they had sex? Did they fight in public? Did they fight, period?*

And fatigue punctuated his features as he answered: *a couple of dozen, about ten, no they didn't fight, especially not in public.*

"Did you pay her?"

"No," he said.

She waited.

"Okay, yes," he finally admitted. "But not in money. I bought her clothes, took her shopping in Vicksburg. And when we hung out at Rollie's, I paid for everything."

And it went on like that until noon. Julian came out of the kitchen balancing three glasses of orange juice in one hand and a plate of bear claws in another.

"Okay, folks, nourishment," he said, carefully setting the food and juice on the coffee table. He stared down proudly.

Sidney still ignored him and continued, the questions falling like a steady, sure rain. What was Yolonda like? Did she have other boyfriends? How well did he know Wilma? When Dexter reached for a bear claw, she slapped his hands. The orange juice had long separated in the glass, the pulp settling to the bottom.

"Sidney, come on," Julian protested, "give him a break."

"Go away, Julian," she told him without looking at him. And he did.

"Did you want anything else from me?" Dexter asked, five minutes after Julian had slammed out of the house. Sidney scribbled furiously, not looking up.

"I'll take that as a no." Dexter answered his own question and left without bothering to close the door.

The next person she talked to was Rupert Englestorm. At first he protested, telling her she was not going to interrogate him like some convict. But she wore him down. *No, the Havens were not making payments to Wilma Brown. Why would they? Yes, he would know. Didn't he pay all the bills? No, he didn't know that Dexter was seeing Yolonda.*

After speaking with Rupert, she went to see Wilma. The car was gone, and when she walked into the open house, she realized why they called it a shotgun house. Standing at the front door, she could see daylight shining through the back door. The harsh light illuminated balls of dust scurrying across the bare, buckled wooden floors of the empty house. If she had a shotgun, she would have sworn she could have fired a bullet through the front door, and it would fly into the sunlight streaming through the back.

She ended the day at Miss Johnie Mae's house, sitting on the front porch drinking peach moonshine from a Mason jar and listening to cicadas make their music in the darkness. The sound reminded Sidney of a cross between fingers on a blackboard and violin music from heaven.

Miss Johnie Mae spat the juice from the Day's Work tobacco into an empty can of Stagg's chili. Sidney concentrated on the sound hitting the bottom of the can, and the music of the cicadas. She sat close to Miss Johnie Mae, and when the old woman leaned forward to spit in the empty can, she could smell sweet tobacco.

Sidney watched the fire Miss Johnie Mae lit in a rusty tin tub, to keep the bugs away, dance orange against the night sky. Sidney sat watching, listening, and Miss Johnie Mae sat rocking and spitting for a long time in silence. Eventually, she got up to put another twig on the fire. It sparked blue, then green.

"I 'spectin' that one was too green," she told Sidney as she climbed back on the porch.

"Yes," Sidney answered, distracted, "too green."

The old woman picked up a pickle jar filled with clear liquid. The glass tinkled as Miss Johnie Mae refilled Sidney's cup. The old woman pushed her full skirt between her legs, and guided herself back into the rocker.

"So," she said, turning to Sidney, "who be that man you got living at your mother's house?"

Sidney twirled her braid between her fingers and looked at the fire. "It doesn't matter," she said absently.

"What do you mean it doesn't matter?" she responded. "Plenty folks say it matter a lot when you got a man living at your house."

Sidney laughed and looked toward the old woman. "News sure travels fast around here. He's only been there one night. He's my husband," she answered.

Miss Johnie Mae's chair creaked in the darkness. The cicadas paused for a moment, and began again. The fire sparked up.

"Oh, yeah," the old woman said. She pulled at two long gray whiskers growing from a mole on her chin. "That's right, folks said you got married."

"Well, don't worry about it," Sidney said, then took another drink of the moonshine. Peach fire burned her throat. She laughed. "He'll only be my husband for about another minute and a half. We're getting a divorce."

"Oh," Miss Johnie Mae said, laughing, "you young folks that go away always marrying and divorcing. When I was young, the men just come. They sat a while, and when they got tired they left. And when we women want some company, we just invite another man over to sit." She laughed and stumped her bare feet on the porch at her own joke. The rocking chair squeaked faster. "None of this fancy stuff. This marrying up and then divorcing."

Sidney smiled and looked at the old woman. There was something she desperately needed to know. She could not help thinking about what Julian had said about her the night he came, about learning from the best. Was she being selfish when she left the ACLU; and was she being selfish when she refused to come to help Haven unionize six years ago?

"Miss Johnie Mae, what do people around here say about me?" she asked.

The creaking stopped for a minute, then started again. "What you be worried about that for?" she asked Sidney. "People always gon' talk."

"I'm just curious." Sidney took another sip, but the jar was empty. She was surprised she had drunk so much. Her nose felt cold and numb, and she felt as if she was floating a little.

"They always say stuff."

"Like what?"

"Well," Miss Johnie Mae said, the rocker slowing a little as she thought, "they say you selfish . . ."

Sidney laughed. "Tell me something I don't know. If I had a nickel for every time I heard that . . ."

"They say that, too . . ." Miss Johnie Mae cut her off. "They say you care so much about money you didn't come out to help out the union when Covina asked."

"And what did you think about that?" she asked her.

"Well," she said, "I figure Covina had nerve. She sold herself to the Havens for a lotta years, and then when somebody else getting theirs, she jump mad because they ain't move fast enough when she snap her fingers. Beside, what you care about that for?"

Sidney lightly tapped the rim of the jelly jar on her chin. "Well, first, the trial," she replied, "and because I've been . . ."

"I know what you been," Miss Johnie Mae said as she kicked the pickle jar over to her with a bare brown foot. Moonshine sloshed slightly over the rim as Sidney picked it up and refilled her glass. Overflow fell onto her lap and it felt cool, like rubbing alcohol.

"You been questioning yo'self. And I say it ain't no cause to go doing that," she continued.

"Why?"

"Because it ain't about what people say, it's about what's inside of you that count," she said while bending sideways over the arm of the rocker to pick up the empty can. "And if you do things 'cause of what people say, and how it look, you ain't never gon' to get to the part that count inside."

Sidney took a long swig of the moonshine.

"And if you don't take it easy on that stuff," Miss Johnie Mae warned, "it gone turn them same insides into mush."

Sidney laughed, stumbled up and put more sticks on the fire. When she finished, she sat down on the steps. This was a peaceful escape from the day for Sidney, and she was glad for not having to talk about the Brown murder. Or Wilma being gone, which she found out the whole town knew, except herself.

Both she and the old woman laughed and rocked, rocked and laughed until Haven's only police cruiser bumped along the uneven rocky yard to park itself at the mouth of the steps, next to the burning trash can.

Chapter 14

From a distance, the fire seemed a living, breathing thing spitting sparks every now and then into the night air. Jacob saw it from the road as he made his rounds. He made it a point to drive past Miss Johnie Mae's house on a regular basis because he knew the old woman was alone, and probably afraid. He had to admit feeling guilt about never making the Havens pay for the murder of her grandson, but she never spoke of it, and he felt glad about that.

He stopped the police car alongside Timber Road and watched the fire for a few seconds. He knew that many times the old woman lit a fire in a trash can to keep the bugs away. But he feared the one time he did not check, there would be a fire the old woman could not control.

He put the car into reverse and backed up until he faced the part in the trees he knew to be the road to her house. The trees, their green leaves faded by the darkness, closed around his car as the road thinned. Just when he thought the cruiser would be swallowed by pure wood, the path opened and the shack stood in a clearing. No matter how many times he traveled that road, he felt relieved when he saw the structure that the forest belied, existed.

The old woman rocked in the old rocker he thought would one day fall apart with her in it. Someone sat on the top step holding a clear jar. He did not have to see the gray eyes and raven hair to know it was Sidney.

He ignored the knot of fear at the pit of his stomach. He didn't know why Sidney scared him so much, but she did. She represented everything he hated in the Havens, and it didn't help that he was attracted to her. He walked up the dirt walk, placed his foot on the bottom of the wooden step.

"Miss Johnie Mae," he said around the stick of Juicy Fruit he had in his mouth, "now, I've told you about that fire, haven't I?"

The old woman rocked and looked past him to the police cruiser. "Yep, I reckon you did," was all she said.

It was the same conversation they had every time he caught her burning a fire at night.

"Well," he said, studiously ignoring Sidney staring at him from the steps, "I think you need to put it out."

"Why?" Miss Johnie Mae asked. "You tellin' me I can't burn a fire on my own place?"

"Only if you want to burn it down," he told her.

Miss Johnie Mae responded with laughter. "Boy, I been burning fires around here for years. 'Fore you were born, and ain't nothing burned down yet."

Jacob looked at the ground for a moment. He could see the dirt and weeds through the gap between the first and second step. He could also see empty wrappers of Day's Work crumbled among the weeds. He looked up again at the two women on the porch—first at Sidney on the steps, then at the old woman steadily rocking. He took a deep breath, and the smoke made his eyes water a little bit.

"Now Miss Johnie Mae," he said, "I don't want to have to give you a citation."

"Citation for what?" Sidney piped in, her words slurred just a bit.

Jacob turned toward her and ran his eyes up her bare legs to the denim shirt she wore with a bikini top underneath.

"Burning a fire without a permit," he said flatly.

Sidney laughed again, in a gurgle that sounded like water boiling. "Bullshit," she replied.

"Ain't no cause for that kind of language," Miss Johnie Mae said absentmindedly.

"But Miss Johnie Mae," Sidney said as she waved her hand over at Jacob, "he can't give you a ticket for burning trash."

"That's not trash," Jacob contradicted.

Sidney leaned forward to get a better look at him. "It's a trash can, isn't it?" she said. "How do you know there's not trash in it?"

"Because I know," Jacob responded.

"Well, I don't think you do." Sidney sat back up, folded her arms. "Why don't you go and dig around in it and then come back and tell us what it is."

"Now children," Miss Johnie Mae chimed in, "ain't no cause for all that. Put out the fire if you want. I'm gon' to bed anyway."

The old woman stood up cautiously. She placed one foot in front of the other, as if she walked on a tight rope, and went into the house. Sidney grabbed her arm in order to steady her. Jacob watched both of them disappear behind the screen door. Then he went to the side of the house to get the hose. He turned the water on until it flowed in a steady clear stream. He sprayed clear water on the fire until it turned blue. Turned blue and died without so much as a protesting spark.

* * *

While Jacob put out the fire, Sidney helped Miss Johnie Mae take her dress off and get into a soft flannel nightgown. She let the old woman lean on her arm as they walked from the bathroom to the big four-poster bed in the front room.

"When my grandchildren left," the old woman told her as she helped her under the covers, "I didn't think there was no reason to keep the bed in the middle room all the time. Too much junk in there, anyway, and I didn't have a lot of people coming over to keep up a living room."

Sidney said nothing, but pulled back the old green and purple quilt and helped her into the tall bed. She didn't realize how much she had drunk until she stood up earlier; now she concentrated on not throwing up on Miss Johnie Mae's stainless sheets. She noticed the washboard in the claw-footed tub earlier, and knew Miss Johnie May did her laundry by hand. Her forehead felt warm and moist.

"Need some help?" Jacob asked from the doorway.

"I don't need your kind of help, Sheriff," Sidney said without looking at him, remembering the feel of his hand on her bare shoulder the previous night.

Jacob sighed. "Well, it looks like you could use a ride home," he said.

"Nope," she replied.

"You're staying here tonight?" he said, clearly confused.

"Nope," she said, still not looking at him.

"You are not thinking of driving, are you?" he asked incredulously. "Are you?"

This time Sidney did look at him. "My, you are a detective!" she said. "Now I know why you were elected Sheriff."

He walked into the room, and looked over at Miss Johnie Mae snoring peacefully. *She obviously had had her share to drink tonight also,* he thought. He took Sidney by her upper arm. She pulled away as if she had been burned.

"You take one step toward that car, and I will arrest you," he told her.

"I don't feel like this right now," Sidney told him. "I'm tired and my head hurts."

"And yet you want to drive?"

Sidney thought a long moment. "Okay, you are right." Anything to make him go away. "I'll sleep here tonight. Now do me a favor and leave me alone."

"And just where are you going to sleep?" he asked her, annoyed.

Sidney took her time in answering him. She looked around the front room—the big four–poster bed with the purple and green handmade quilt; the couch with stuffing coming up on the opposite wall. The middle room—the parlor as Miss Johnie Mae liked to call it—only had a big Lazy Boy chair, an ottoman, and an old black and white TV with foil on the arrows.

And all that was left beside the cracker box bathroom was the kitchen with its white counters and wooden floor gone colorless over the years.

"Are you going to sleep with Miss Johnie Mae?" Jacob chided.

"Sheriff," she said, and looked him square in the eyes, "it's none of your business where I sleep."

He pressed his lips together in a frown, studied her for a moment, and then held out his palm. Sidney noticed how dark the palms of his hands were, so foreign from Julian's.

"What?" she asked him.

"Keys," he answered.

"What?" she asked him again, still not understanding.

"If you are going to stay here tonight, give me your keys, and I'll drop them by in the morning."

"Don't bother," Sidney said, annoyed, and brushed her way past him to the front porch. The queasiness in her stomach subsided with the cool night air, but she could still taste the burning peach moonshine lingering in her throat.

She made her way to the book bag she had thrown in the corner of the porch earlier today. She cursed as one of her bare feet slid off the head of a nail sticking out of the splintered porch. She looked down at the side of her foot. There was only a stain of blood where a patch of skin no bigger than a stamp was missing. It should have hurt like hell, but she barely felt it.

She pretended not to notice Jacob turning the inside lock on Miss Johnie Mae's door. He shut it slowly behind him. *The bastard didn't even bother to ask if she needed anything from inside the house,* she thought to herself.

"Eureka," she said as she located her keys. She had momentarily forgotten what they had been arguing about in the house earlier. "I thought I was going to have to send out a search party," she said as she held them up. They gleamed in the moonlight.

Jacob said nothing, but reached behind his jacket and brought out a pair of silver handcuffs. Sidney stumbled off the porch, and Jacob caught her arm. She jerked away.

"You are under arrest." He reached out and grabbed her arm again.

"For what?" Sidney asked, confused.

"Attempting to drive under the influence," he answered.

"Bullshit," Sidney laughed.

"Didn't they teach you any other word besides that in law school?"

"Under the influence of what?" Sidney ignored the barb.

"I'm serious," he answered.

Sidney laughed until her chest hurt. Jacob grabbed both of her wrists and half—walked, half-carried her to the car. When they got to the car, he leaned her against the passenger door on the driver's side. He pulled open the door. Sidney fell sideways, and he used his right hand to steady her.

"Aren't you going to frisk me?" she asked, still laughing.

Jacob grimaced as he guided her into the seat.

"Don't I get to be handcuffed to?"

Jacob paused for a moment, his black eyes flashing steel. "Since you mentioned it," he said, before slapping the cuffs on her wrists and closing the door on her laughter.

Sidney leaned her head against the car window. Bright—colored lights—reds and blues—flashed behind her eyes as the cruiser bounced along the dirt road leading away from Miss Johnie Mae's shack. She felt her wrists press against the bracelets of the handcuffs. Tomorrow, she would be bruised. But for now, there was no pain. She opened her eyes, then closed them, then opened them again. In her off—balance state, pieces of the car's interior weaved in and out of sight. The passenger side headrest floated past the rearview mirror. And the mirror itself looked to Sidney like a square, silver eye edged in blackness.

The leather creaked as she struggled upward into a sitting position, and leaned as close to Jacob as the seat belt would allow. When her face touched the net separating the driver and passenger's compartment, she felt as if she had walked into a spider web.

"Hey," she said, her voice rough from liquor, "you want to do me favor and take these things off? They are starting to bug me."

She saw a muscle twitch in his square jaw. "Why should I?" he asked.

"Look," she said, and plopped back against the seat,

"don't be such a hard ass, okay? Besides, I think I may be getting sick."

His hand twisted against the wheel as he considered. Then he sighed, pulled the car over, and let her out. Stepping out of the car was like stepping back into reality. The fresh air closed around her. *I'm probably only one drink away from being totally wasted,* she thought to herself. One drink away in her eyes, maybe, but with Jacob it was probably a different story. She began to feel slightly embarrassed about even attempting to drive.

"Hold still," she heard Jacob's voice in her ear as he unlocked the cuffs. "There, I got it."

"Hey," Sidney said suddenly, forgetting about her embarrassment, "do you know where we are?" He didn't answer, and she took advantage of his hesitation. "We are at the river," she said, pointing down the embankment along the side of the road. "Do you know how much time I spent at this place when I was a kid?"

"No," he said. "How would I?"

She ran to the edge where the road slanted down into a small valley below. She could almost hear the river running, finding its way through the rocks.

"Do you mind if we go down there for awhile?" she asked.

"Yes," he said, but not moving toward the car. "It's late, and I need to take you home."

Home, she thought, *Shit, Julian.* She had forgotten about him. She wondered why Julian had not left after their fight last night. *Maybe he truly is worried,* she thought. He was right, though: they had been friends in the beginning. But during their marriage, they had drifted apart. It probably began even before the cheating, though she was not ready to admit that to him.

"I don't want to go home," she said. "I just want to go down by the river, and listen to the water for a little while."

He let out an exasperated sigh. She heard the crunch of gravel beneath his shoes as he turned to the police cruiser.

"Let's go," he said, plainly this time, and more sure of his intent.

But she had already started to maneuver her way down the sloping hill. The first two steps had been sure, but then she slid. Dirt and rock scraped her thighs.

"Sidney," he called sharply, reaching to pull her up by her elbows. He spun her round to face him, breathing heavily. They stared at each other a full moment before he spoke.

"Look," he said finally, "tomorrow you can come by this river and sit and listen—or whatever the hell it is you do—until the second millennium. But tonight, you are going home."

"Why?" she asked him, pushing down the bubble of peach bile in her throat.

"Isn't it obvious?" he said shaking his head. "You are drunk, it's late and it's the right thing to do."

"I'm not drunk," she said, laughing a little.

"I beg to differ," he contradicted.

Sidney laughed fully now, and waved her arms to the heavens. "Would you look at this night?" she yelled upward, stumbling a little. "It's beautiful, it's clear, and it smells good. Do you always, always do what's right?" she teased.

Jacob regarded her for moment. Remnants of laughter still lingered on her face. A breeze wound its way through the trees and lifted a strand of hair across her face. Using both hands, she smoothed it back into the braid laying on her shoulder. He frowned, looking at his watch.

"It's almost one o'clock in the morning," he wavered.

"Just for half an hour," Sidney said in a soft, reasoning voice. She had to concentrate hard to make her words clear. "We can sit for a while and forget this entire crazy mess—Dexter Haven, and . . ." she stopped suddenly. She almost said "Julian."

". . . and what?" Jacob said, his voice oddly quietly in the stillness that followed her laughter.

"Nothing." She grabbed one of his hands with both of her own. "Let's go."

"Let me get this straight," he said. "Earlier, you wanted nothing to do with me. Why now?"

"Oh, come on! Now who's suspicious?" Sidney dropped his hand. It fell like dead weight to his side. "What do you think I'm going to do? Get you down there and bean you in the head with a rock? You have the car, for heaven's sake. I want you to go with me so I won't have to hitchhike back home."

"Just for a little while," he said finally.

"Thank you, kind sir," Sidney said, smiling.

She walked up to him and placed both hands around his neck. By reflex, he placed both his hands around her waist. They were strong, and smooth at the same time.

"You will have to carry me you know," she said, almost laughing again, but out of nervousness this time. "I don't have any shoes on, and I haven't been doing my feet any favors tonight."

He shook his head. "Why not?" he breathed, exasperated. He picked her up, and carefully carried her until they reached the river's edge.

"What are you going to do?" she asked him after he didn't put her down immediately. "Throw me in?"

He said nothing, just lowered her to the ground, then took a few steps away. She leaned back on her hands, listened to the ebb and flow of the glittering water between the rocks. Jacob leaned against what looked to be a tree stump in the darkness. Sidney could feel his eyes on her.

At night, the river did not look as peaceful. The wild

iris and black-eyed susans, whose brilliant colors would shine so brightly in the daytime, now lay hidden under the darkness. Boulders became only murky shapes, their jagged surfaces deceptively smooth. The moon, full and luminous, burned a hole into the black, velvet sky. Sidney heard a nighthawk call, its lucid cry like a warning in the still night.

She drew her knees up to her chest. Turning her head toward Jacob, she rested her cheek against her knees. He remained unsmiling. His white polo shirt fit him so perfectly, she could tell even in the darkness it was without wrinkle. He would be able to just swipe away the dust that clung to his highly polished black leather oxfords. Even his jeans were pressed. She thought about the file Julian had on him, wondered if it was true.

"Tell me, Sheriff, is it perfectly stressful to be so damn right all the time?" she asked.

He laughed a little, and crossed his legs at the ankles. "Are you trying to piss me off, now?" he asked.

She shrugged her shoulders. "No," she denied. "You always just seem so sure of yourself, like you have privy to some secret code or something."

He nodded and walked over to her. "Now you are talking about the Havens," he said.

"How can you be so sure Dexter Haven is guilty?" she asked him.

She was surprised when he sat down beside her. Their shoulders touched. He turned to look at her, their faces inches apart.

"You've seen the evidence, Counselor," he responded.

"Evidence," she challenged. "That matters to you, does it?"

She could feel his shoulders stiffen against hers. He picked up a stick and tossed it toward the river. It disappeared into the darkness with only a faint splash when it hit the water.

"I'm sure you are going to explain yourself," he said in a deliberately mild voice.

"You hate them," she said. "It's almost pathological."

"Not all of them," he said, a bemused smile on his face. "Unfortunately."

Confused, Sidney stared at him. "What do you mean by that?" she asked him.

He reached over and put his hand on her face, buried his fingers in her hair. He leaned over, and kissed her softly. At first she drew back, afraid. But his mouth was strong and sure. She found herself kissing him back in search of that same surety. She closed her eyes and felt as if she was walking out into cloudless yellow sunshine for the first time in years—everything beautiful and right. Then, clear as a stone dropping into the water, Jacob's words hit her: *not all of them, unfortunately*. She pulled her face away from Jacob, and slapped his hand away.

"I'm not like them," she spat. "You don't even know me."

Jacob sat up and brought his hands up to his lips, almost in prayer. "Carl Haven was your father," he said with infuriating logic. "You are defending your half brother, Dexter, for murder. That makes you a part of them, whether you like it or not."

By pure reflex, she reached out to slap his face. But he caught her wrist in mid-air and she felt the blood flow stop in her hand.

"Don't," he said distinctly, "just don't."

She stood up, and almost fell over. Jacob kept his distance.

"Take me home." She flung over her shoulder as she navigated up the hill. In her anger, she forgot about her bare feet.

"My pleasure," he said, sounding unconvinced by his own words.

The next morning, light poured through the thin ruffled curtains of Sidney's childhood room like the curtains didn't exist. It fell in warm splashes across her bare legs and back. Sidney didn't remember much about the ride home, except that she and Jacob sat in a charged silence for the entire drive to her mother's house. He had graciously allowed her the front seat. Then there was Julian, standing in the doorway with a pool of light from the entryway spilling around him. She hopped out of the car before it rolled to a stop in the driveway and rushed past Julian's surprised silence into her room.

Now this morning, her entire body felt stiff, glued to the bed. Her head simply pounded. Heaving herself up on her elbows, she rolled over onto her back. Julian stood at the doorway, shirtless again, his arms folded. His hair, glossy and black, was wet, as if he had just gotten out of the shower. But Sidney noticed he had dark circles under his eyes. He had obviously been up for hours. She could tell by the fixed position of his mouth that he was deathly angry.

"It's ten o'clock in the morning," he said, sounding petulant, like a child. "You need to get up."

Instead of speaking, she turned toward the ceiling and placed her hand on her forehead.

"Just what do you think you are doing, Sidney?" he asked, walking into the room. "Have you lost your mind?"

"Julian," she said, "do me a favor, and get the hell out of here."

"The room, or the house?" he asked.

She sat up. As she moved, hair fell away from her face

and shoulders in sticky clumps. *God,* she thought, *I feel like shit.* But she knew she probably looked even worse.

"You decide," she said as he placed her feet on the side of the bed. She noticed that they were scratched mercilessly, and there was a long bruise just under her big toe. "I'll be in the shower."

As she showered, she tried not to think of Jacob, or Julian, but wondered what her life would have been like if things had been different. *If only,* she thought, *if only I had stayed with the ACLU; if only Julian hadn't cheated; if only I hadn't concentrated on my career.* And finally, *if only my mother had not slept with Carl Haven.* What would have happened? Would she be the person she is right now? She wanted to stay there in the shower forever.

Dressed in a white cotton shirt dress, she walked out into the living room to a silent Julian. She couldn't remember the last time she saw him so angry. He still did not talk to her while she collected the files and police reports from the coffee table in the living room. He watched her spread everything on the kitchen table while the silence between them grew like a rain forest.

He poured coffee into a ceramic blue cup and set it in front of her without a word. He only began speaking when he had his own coffee, and had folded his long body into the chair opposite her.

"Did you sleep with him?" he asked.

Sidney let the pencil she was using fall from her hand. It landed on the stack of papers by her coffee cup. "Julian," she said, "I really don't think that is any of your business."

"You are still my wife," he said, his voice quiet.

The table jostled when Sidney stood up. Coffee spilled over the rim of her coffee cup, making a brown stain on one of the documents.

"Damn it, Julian," she said, using a paper towel to soak

up the stain. "You have some nerve, after all the sleeping around you did."

He pointed his finger at her, "But I never threw it in your face, now did I? I never had the entire town talking about it. Don't you think this makes me look like a damn fool, Sidney?"

"Oh, I see," Sidney said and sat down. "That's all you care about? Looking like a damn fool?"

"That's not true and you know it," he said.

"Then tell me Julian, what is true?" she asked.

"I still care about you, Sidney." He stared down into his black coffee. "You are still my wife."

Sidney barked out a laugh. "For about another minute and a half. The divorce is final at the end of this week." She leaned across the table, and looked directly into his eyes. "My God, Julian," she said, "you are getting married in Mexico. Remember?"

"You are making a mistake with this Sheriff Conrad," he said.

"Mistake?" Sidney questioned, waving her hands as if she were trying to wash something away. "There is no mistake. There is nothing between us, Julian," she finished. She walked over to the counter top and clicked off the coffee pot. She pushed it to the wall without looking at him.

Julian waited until she sat back down. "Nothing between us," he said, "or nothing between you and that lunatic?"

Sidney gripped the coffee cup between her hands. "Both," she said. "I'm sick to death of both of you. Besides, nothing happened."

"Give me a break," Julian laughed harshly. "You come in here at two-thirty in the morning, reeking of alcohol, and you have the nerve to tell me nothing happened. If you didn't sleep with him, then explain to me what's going on."

"I'm not going to discuss this with you," she said, and resolutely picked up her pencil again. "It's none of your business," she repeated, wanting to hurt him. "You've made it none of your business."

"Okay. Okay," he replied. "We'll leave it at that. But don't come running to me when . . ."

"Julian, please," she cut him off.

"Okay fine, it's none of my business. As far as I'm concerned, the subject is closed," he said.

"Good," she sighed, relieved that it was over.

"What are you doing anyway?" He touched the papers she had been rifling through.

"Motion," Sidney said, looking up at him with a splashy smile, "to dismiss."

Julian sat back in his chair, laughing. "Your balls are bigger than mine, lady," he said.

"Will you help me?" she asked, still smiling.

"You know I will," he said as he stood up and rinsed his coffee cup in the sink. "I just can't help myself."

Chapter 15

Sidney met with Rupert, Samuel, and Dexter for dinner at the Haven mansion two nights later. Marion, Carl's widow, was there, too. But wan and hushed as a ghost. Samuel insisted that Marion and Sidney sit right next to each other. *Probably for the entertainment value,* Sidney thought.

Marion wore a wispy, pale blue dress ruffled at the neck and wrists. She didn't speak through the entire dinner. As Sidney watched her, she understood what it meant when people described an older person as faded. Because that's exactly the word that came to mind when she looked at Marion. Instead of being deeply wrinkled, the lines on her face looked soft and powdery. Her hair had been dyed so many times, it looked like a series of cotton puffs painted watercolor brown.

If it weren't for Marion's eyes—darting between Sidney and Dexter—she would have been mistaken for a ghost. Sidney caught her staring several times. She wondered if

Marion was comparing her to her Dexter. She noted the way Sidney held her fork, or raised the crystal goblet to her lips. During the first few minutes of dinner, Sidney was uncomfortable. But the woman was so quiet and pale, Sidney soon forgot she was even there.

Dinner was served in the smaller dining room next to Samuel's study. The table was glass on a gold stand, the chairs overstuffed and covered with a red rose tapestry. A low floral arrangement of roses, daisies and magnolias radiated a honeyed fragrance into the air around the table. Jason, the butler, stood by the side of the table waiting for the slightest movement from Samuel Haven before refilling an empty water goblet or coffee cup. There was also a maid in a shiny wig and white cap, standing next to Jason like a wooden soldier.

Sidney sat back a little from the round table in her own overstuffed arm chair. She watched the candlelight flicker in and out of the Waterford crystal goblets. She listened to the click–clack of Samuel's fork and knife as he attacked his rosemary garlic lamb like it was a living thing. Rupert also ate heartily, but carefully. His fork followed the same path again and again to his mouth as he devoured his dinner, seemingly out of necessity more than pleasure. Dexter picked at his food, pushing the lamb to the edge of his gold–rimmed plate while alternately staring at Sidney, Rupert and Samuel. He rarely looked at Marion, his mother. And she didn't eat at all.

Samuel pushed his plate away, and Jason quickly scooped it onto a bright silver tray. Jason cocked an eyebrow at Sidney and touched her full plate. When she shook her head, he placed her plate over Samuel's empty one. He took both Marion and Dexter's full plates without even asking them if they were done.

"What, you don't like lamb?" Samuel asked Sidney.

"I'm not hungry," she said, and sent him a closed–mouth smile.

"Well, I was starving," Samuel said, vigorously wiping his hands on a white linen napkin. "Jason!" he yelled toward the kitchen. "Bring out the dessert!"

"Samuel, really," Rupert protested mildly.

Samuel ignored him and began sucking his teeth. While he picked at them with his pinkie finger, the light from his diamond ring twisted in the candlelight.

He leered at Sidney. "I didn't know you cleaned up so good," he said, still picking at his teeth.

"Samuel," Rupert warned again, this time disgusted.

"What?" Samuel turned his big head in Rupert's direction. "The girl looks good."

Sidney held back a bubble of annoyance. She did dress for the part tonight, for dinner at the Havens. She didn't want her usual shorts and flip–flops to distract them from the business at hand. She wanted them to take her seriously. So for tonight, she wore a white backless dress with a flared skirt and black pumps. She had twisted her long hair into a roll, and it lay heavily on the back of her neck.

But still, when she told them she had filed a motion to dismiss, Samuel rolled with laughter, holding his fleshy gut. Rupert sat up in surprise, and Dexter choked on the water he had been drinking. Not wanting to ruin dinner, Samuel declared they would discuss it after they ate.

Now, as Jason cleared away the dinner dishes, she felt glad they were about to get down to business. Samuel scooped up a big piece of his German chocolate cake. Before he stuffed it in his mouth, he looked at Sidney.

All of a sudden, Sidney caught a whiff of perfume, light and flowery. She looked up to find that Marion had leaned so far over to stare at her, the woman's nose almost touched her shoulder. Sidney drew back.

"Marion," Samuel said around the chocolate cake in

his mouth, "get the hell out of here. We are about to discuss business."

Marion floated up from her chair and left the room without making a sound.

"Now what's all this about a motion to dismiss," Samuel asked her.

Instead of answering him, Sidney removed a file folder from her book bag and handed it to Rupert. Rupert looked into her eyes for a long time before taking it from her. He opened it and began skimming the pages.

"Well?" Samuel asked, looking from one of them to the other.

Rupert ignored him. Watching Rupert from across the table as he read, Sidney took a sip from the heavy crystal.

"I thought they had a lot of evidence," Dexter piped up.

"They do," Sidney said, "but it's all circumstantial."

"Is this a waste of time?" Samuel grunted. "Huh? Rupert?"

He looked over at Rupert, who flipped through two or more pages of the document he read.

"We don't have anything to lose," Sidney answered for him.

"But I slept with her. They found . . ." Dexter blushed. "People saw me with her."

Sidney looked at him surprised at how his personality wilted when he was in Samuel's presence.

"The DNA isn't back yet," she said. "And so what if it's a match? So what?" She took another sip from her water glass. "All it means is that you slept with her."

Rupert held his hand up for silence. "I'm trying to concentrate," he said.

Samuel gulped dessert wine from his goblet, and wiped his mouth with the back of his hand. Rupert closed the file folder and looked up at Sidney as if he had never seen her before. She saw something in his eyes that made her drop her own.

"Sheriff Conrad," was all Rupert said.

"What about Sheriff Conrad?" Samuel asked, still not understanding.

"She intends to argue the Sheriff tampered with evidence, that the arrest was malicious. Malicious and personal," Rupert said, still not taking his eyes from Sidney.

"He has a history we could use." Her voice was cool, impersonal as the air–conditioned room. "And he did clean up the vomit."

"Vomit?" Samuel asked. "What vomit?" His fork clattered against his plate. "Would someone please tell me what's going on here?" he bellowed. "I feel like the class dunce!"

Rupert turned to Samuel with a sigh. "Apparently, there was trace evidence of vomit on Yolonda's feet. But none in the crime scene photos. Sidney found out from Reverend Robinson that Grayson threw up all over her. Someone cleaned it up."

"Why would someone do that?" Dexter asked, perplexed.

"I don't know," Rupert shook his head. "But I can't believe the Sheriff would be so dumb as to do a fool thing like that."

"It doesn't matter who did it," Sidney said finally, and then raised her eyebrows at Rupert. In her heart, she didn't believe Jacob did it either, but rushed on anyway. "The fact is that it was done. It means the other evidence at the crime scene could have been tainted."

"Is that it?" Samuel asked. "You mean to tell me you are going to build an entire motion to dismiss on just that?"

"No," Sidney answered flatly, "not just that."

"You know," Rupert said pensively, "I always wondered

why Sheriff Conrad would choose this town over New York. I wondered why he didn't go back there after the Heater case."

"So, you found something, right?" Samuel asked.

"He's been accused of planting evidence before, some police brutality," Rupert said and tossed the file folder on the table. "But nothing really stuck."

"Hot damn," Samuel said as he rubbed his hands together. "How did you find out about that? Pillow talk?" he asked, turning toward Sidney

"Don't be a damn fool," Sidney said. Her eyes pierced his across the table.

"Will it work?" he asked, looking again from her to Rupert.

Rupert looked at Jason and the maid waiting patiently by their table. Samuel caught his glance and waved both of them away. They left without a word.

"So?" he said when the door closed behind them.

Rupert didn't answer for a long moment, and Sidney stared out the window of the dining room. She could hardly discern the wide green lawn in the darkness, but she saw the faint shapes of willows sway in the light wind.

"It'll give Judge Harold an excuse," Rupert answered. "Probably wouldn't stand a chance if this weren't Haven."

Samuel laughed so loud, Sidney resisted an urge to cover her ears. Rupert stood up and threw the napkin he had been using on the table. He walked over to the window with his back to them.

"I don't like this," he began.

Samuel looked at Rupert's slender back. He picked up his napkin and wiped the tears of laughter from his eyes.

"Why?" he questioned.

"It's not right," Rupert finished.

It was Sidney's turn to laugh. "Right?" she asked him in a high voice. "You have the nerve to blackmail me to get me out here to defend Dexter? And now you stand here and tell me what's right?'' She couldn't believe her ears.

"That's how you got her here?" Dexter said as he stood up. "By blackmailing her?"

"Rupert," Samuel said, "don't be stupid. If it's going to work, who cares?"

"I care," Rupert said. He turned to face them again. "And you should care, Samuel. You too, Dex." He looked at Sidney's angry eyes. "And this is totally different from how you got out here. We intend to compensate you fully for your work."

"We do?" Samuel grunted, confused.

Rupert ignored him. "If we do this, and this thing goes through, the town will always believe Dex is a murderer, just like they do you, Samuel. It's like cheating. We just shouldn't."

"Now just wait a damn minute," Sidney said. She walked around the table to where Rupert stood. "If we go to trial, there's a chance we won't win at all. And it's a certainty we will lose if we don't mention Sheriff Conrad's past," she told him.

"So you want to ruin a reputation of a good man rather than find an ethical way to win this case?" Rupert asked her.

"First of all," she said, "this is the *only* way to win this case. Second of all, how do you know he's a good man?"

"All I know is the town thinks highly of the Sheriff— black and white. And the Havens won't win any points by dragging him through the mud. Again." He stared pointedly at Samuel.

"Rupert!" Samuel pushed himself back from the table, causing a water glass to fall over. Water and ice formed puddles on the glass table.

"I'll get Jason," Dexter said.

"Sit your ass down, Dex," Samuel bellowed. "We aren't finished here. Rupert," he said, turning his large frame toward the little man, "I don't give a damn about that nigger and his reputation. All I want is for my nephew, my *heir,* to stay out of jail. If this gal has to ruin the reputation of Jesus to keep him from prison, I'll be standing right behind her cheering her on." Samuel's voice had changed to a low growl.

"Lower your bloody voice, Samuel," Rupert said. "You sound like a damned animal act. The whole house can hear you."

Sidney walked back to the table and picked up the file. It felt hot in her hands.

"Well, my dear," Rupert said, "I see how you maintain your reputation, and keep your winning record." He smiled at her without his eyes.

"Judge Harold will hear arguments in his chamber on the first of September. Dex, you need to be there."

She turned toward Rupert. They stared at each other.

"Rupert, you and your scruples," she said as she stuffed the file back into her book bag, "can stay the fuck out."

Rupert ignored the comment, including Samuel's laughter following it. Instead, he tipped a fluted wine glass to her. "Congratulations, you have just become an honorary member of the Haven family," he said.

He took a small sip from the glass and placed it back on the table. "I can find my own way out, Samuel," he said before brushing past Sidney and walking out the door.

Sidney sat down at the table for a few minutes on the pretense of finishing her wine. But the real reason was because she felt shaken. This was nothing new to her; all routine. But Rupert's attitude not only surprised her, it made her feel a guilt she had never felt before.

"Well, my dear," Samuel said, almost beaming at her, "why don't you have a piece of cake?"

"No, I can't stay," she said as she stood up to leave.

Dexter looked at her questioningly. "Is this the right thing?"

"Did you kill Yolonda Brown?" she countered.

He lowered his head. "No," he said.

She looked at him without smiling. "Then it's the right thing," she said and walked out of the door. Jason caught up with her in the hallway.

"I'll see you out," he said. He charged in front of her and pushed open the front door, smiling.

She walked out into the balmy night. She had parked her car across the street, in the same place she had the first time she visited the mansion. In the dark, the street seemed wider, and Sidney suddenly didn't have the energy to cross it.

"Is there something wrong?" Jason asked with that same smile on his face. It looked fake, and the skin around his mouth glowed gray in the moonlight.

"No, nothing is wrong," she shivered, "nothing at all."

She walked across the street concentrating on the clicking sound her high heels made on the pavement. The rented car smelled of stale cigarettes and mildew. The light from the dashboard cast green shadows on her face when she flicked the lights on.

She had just turned onto Grove Street when she noticed flashing lights in her rearview mirror. At first she ignored them, and contemplated not stopping. But then she knew he wouldn't give up. She pulled over to the side of the road, cut the ignition and folded her arms, and waited.

Jacob left the lights flashing as he walked over to Sidney's Taurus. She watched him in the rearview mirror, remembering his broad shoulders and muscled arms as they kissed at the river the other night. She flushed crimson, and locked the memories in another part of her mind. She couldn't afford to think about that right now. She rolled down the window.

"Get out of the car," Jacob said before she could speak, his lips tight.

"What do you want?" Sidney said stubbornly.

"I won't tell you again." His words fell like drops of steel from his mouth.

Sidney studied him for a moment, feeling his anger. Had he heard about the motion? And then she knew he couldn't have. She had filed it just yesterday afternoon, and she knew the prosecutor had left for Vicksburg on a personal emergency, telling her he wouldn't be able to meet with Jacob right away. He even asked Judge Harold to delay the hearing until the first of September.

She twisted the door open. Jacob inhaled deeply, almost as if relieved, and took a step backward. Sidney leaned against the car with her arms still folded.

"What do you want?" she asked him again.

His eyes searched every inch of her as she leaned against the car, her white skirt like a flat cloud against the sky blue Taurus.

"I see you got your car back," he commented.

"Julian gave me a ride." She looked him directly in the eyes.

"And this was the man at your house when I took you home the other night? Do I get to find out who he is?"

"Is that why you are so angry?" she asked him.

"You could have at least told me, Sidney," he said quietly.

"You mean, you don't know?" she asked him. "He's my husband."

He took another deep breath, then leaned beside her on the car and folded his arms over his chest. "Would you believe I didn't know until I asked Grange?" he said. "It seems I haven't been in town long enough to become an official part of the rumor mill."

"Well," Sidney said, looking down at the pavement, "now you do."

"Tell me, just what did you tell him?" he asked.

"That's none of your business," she said. "What do you want? Why did you stop me?"

"We need to talk."

"Look," Sidney sighed, "there's nothing to talk about. And I shouldn't be talking to you. Period. Not while this trial is going on."

Jacob laughed, bitterly. "You weren't saying that the other night," he told her.

Sidney made a conscious effort to keep her face the same. "That," she almost laughed, "that was nothing, and besides, I was drunk, and it was a mistake."

"You weren't that drunk," he said, touching the side of her face, "and it didn't feel like a mistake."

She jerked away from him.

"I don't get you," he said, genuinely confused.

"This isn't smart, Sheriff," she told him, her voice soft.

He stepped backwards, stuck his hands in his pockets. He looked at her and laughed. "Sheriff? After all we've been through together, don't you think you should use my first name? Please, call me Jacob," he said and held his hands out to her as if he were giving her a gift.

Without taking her eyes from him, she turned to open the door of the car.

"Look," she said and gazed over her shoulder at him, "I have a job to do. There is nothing between you and me, and you will be Sheriff Conrad to me as long as this trial is going on." The handle of the door felt cool in the night air. She opened the door, dismissing him.

But before she could get into the car, he was behind her quick as lightening. He had moved so fast, she didn't even hear his footsteps. He reached over her shoulder and shut the door again, hard. It sounded like a shotgun blast on the quiet street.

He put the palm of his hand on the back of her neck, brought it around until his fingers caressed her throat. His touch was soft and dry, and his hand was like felt touching her throat. He pressed his body into hers and bent his lips to her ear.

"Do you know what you are?" he asked her.

Sidney kept her body still, tried to steady her breathing. But everywhere he touched, her body flamed. "Let go," she whispered.

"You are a snake, cold," he said distinctly. "Just like every one of those Havens."

Sidney tried to move away, but he jerked her backward again. "You can't separate yourself from the crap you are doing for them, Sidney," he told her.

"You're hurting me," she said quietly, and she felt his grip immediately relax. "And you have no idea what you are talking about. I don't owe you or them a damn thing," she finished, her voice tight.

He kept her close to him for awhile, and she thought she heard him swallow in the noiseless night. Suddenly, his mood changed, and he gave her neck a tight squeeze before turning away.

Even though the night was warm, she felt an empty cold pierce through her dress as he left. She didn't move until she heard his door slam and the police car drive away. She looked up and saw her reflection in the driver's side window. Her face was wet with tears.

Chapter 16

The minute Sidney opened her eyes the morning of September 1st, she remembered the hearing. She reached a hand from underneath the blanket and twisted the red face of the clock toward her. Her eyes focused on 6:30 am. She didn't have to be in court until nine, but already she could smell coffee brewing and bacon sizzling in the kitchen. She could hear Julian singing aloud as he cooked.

She sat up in bed and put her face in her hands. It felt as if she had been drinking, and her head hurt. She and Julian stayed awake late the night before, reviewing the motion while she gripped cup after cup of coffee and he gulped glass after glass of Jack Daniel's. It was almost like old times. *He should be the one with the headache, not me,* she thought as she threw the covers aside and padded barefoot into the kitchen.

"Hi Babe." Julian smiled at her, his eyes twinkling.

"Julian," Sidney said and sat at the kitchen counter,

"Why so early? And it's freezing in here." She folded her arms and looked around.

Julian poured eggs into a skillet on the stove. "Cold is good for you," he said, "wakes you up and gets you going." He placed a plate and a mug in front of her. "I thought we would review one more time before we left for court," he told her.

She looked at the empty blue ceramic plate in front of her, still not awake.

"There's nothing to review," she said and sat back as he poured coffee into her cup. "It's a cinch."

"Cocky, aren't you?" he replied.

"No," she smiled wryly, "just confident."

He leaned on his elbows against the counter top. His green eyes turned serious.

"I've decided not to leave until next week," he said.

Sidney had already brought the cup halfway to her lips. "Why?" she asked.

"Because," he said, "there is no telling what may happen after the hearing today."

Silence washed over both of them. Julian left the counter and stirred the eggs on the stove, turning over the bacon.

"What are you getting at, Julian?" she asked him.

"You know damn well what I'm getting at," he said. "The man's not stable."

"You mean Jacob Conrad?"

Julian sighed and opened the cabinet to get a plate. He concentrated on scooping eggs onto the plate as he answered her. "Yes," he said, "I mean Jacob Conrad."

Sidney stood up and went to stand beside him. "Julian," she told him seriously, "don't put your life on hold because of me; besides, this is just business. He shouldn't take it personally."

Julian barked out a laugh. "He's not going to see it that way," he told her.

"We aren't married anymore, Julian," she snapped at him. "Get on with your life, and stop trying to run mine. The man is not stupid."

Julian studied her a long moment. She avoided his gaze. "Have it your way," he said, before grabbing her plate.

As they ate breakfast, the conversation they had about Jacob lingered. Suddenly, she felt the urge to ask Julian to stay. But she didn't. Because if she did, that meant she would have to believe what she was about to tell Judge Harold in court. And for some reason, she didn't want to do that.

Before she could get dressed, the phone rang. Julian reached it before she did, and picked it up. "Oh," he said, "hold on."

At first, Sidney thought it was Jacob because of Julian's tone, but when she put the phone to her ear, she heard Covina's voice all bubbly and happy with excitement.

"Sidney," she said, laughingly, "guess what? Marion had the baby—six pounds two ounces."

"That's great, Mamma," Sidney said, gripping the mouthpiece with her hand. She looked over at Julian who had retreated back to the kitchen. He and Covina never got along. It seemed they had distrusted each other from the first moment they met. Covina said he smiled too much, talked too much and just plain winked too much. She accused him of not only looking down at her, but also trying to hide it. Sidney didn't know what to think. She just knew she found herself forever between the two of them.

She turned her attention back to Covina, who still babbled on excitedly, ". . . and Sidney, I got to see! They let me right in the delivery room. That ole husband of hers was 'bout as useless as a three–dollar bill at a slot machine. Fool almost fainted when her water broke."

"Boy or a girl, Mamma?" Sidney asked, her voice artificially bright. Maybe Covina would forget to ask what Julian was doing there.

"It was a boy," Covina announced. "Can you believe it Sidney? Our first boy in the family! Now, I know I had me two babies, but there ain't nothing like being on the other end of it, Sidney. I just never knew there was so much blood, and then there is all this stuff that come out after the baby . . . ."

"Mamma," Sidney stopped her, "what did they name him?"

"Name who?" Covina asked, thrown off track. "Oh, you mean the baby! They ain't naming him. I am," Covina said.

Sidney laughed, "Mamma, now how do you figure? That's their baby, not yours."

"But Sidney," she began loudly, "do you know what they want to name that baby? They want to name him Early. Now what kind of a damn fool name is 'Early'? Why not just plain 'late' or how about 'right on time'?"

"Come on, Mamma," Sidney said, laughing. "Early is a perfectly good name."

"But a name ought to mean something, Sidney . . ." Covina said, and continued to talk.

"Yeah, like mine, like Marion's," Sidney mumbled under her breath.

". . . did you say something, Sidney?" Covina asked.

"No, I didn't, Mamma," she lied, not wanting to get into an argument.

"Oh," Covina said, not quite believing her. "Well, anyway, I told them I was naming the baby Adam, 'cause he is the first male of the family."

"And they are going to let you do that?" Sidney challenged, amused.

"Ain't no lettin' got anything to do with it," Covina said.

"Well, Mamma," Sidney said as she bent to hang up the

phone, "give them my love. Tell Marion I'll be down to see them soon."

"Wait, wait," Covina stopped her. "What's Julian doing there?"

Sidney didn't answer right away. "I am married to the man, Mamma," she said finally.

"Not for long," Covina said. "Y'all getting a divorce, right?"

"How do you know that?" Sidney asked.

"Girl, the entire town knows it. Folks calling Marion trying to find out what's going on. But I don't let her near the phone."

Julian came from the kitchen and stood beside her. She turned her back to him.

"Okay, yes," she agreed, "we are."

"That's about the smartest thing you did in a month of Sundays, but why is he at my house?"

"He wanted me to sign the divorce papers."

"Well, sign 'em girl, and kick his lying-cheating-talking-winking-ass out," Covina clamored.

"I can't, Mamma. He's helping me with the trial,"

She heard Covina sigh into the phone. "You kids and your foolishness. So you telling me you are going to walk up into that courthouse and speak for a Haven?"

"Mamma," Sidney said quietly, "I don't know what you want me to say."

"You can't say nothing to make me like your doing this. Go on, then, but remember who you gon' have to look in the mirror, in the morning."

"Bye, Mamma," Sidney said, and hung up before Covina could say anything else.

She turned around and saw Julian staring at her in surprise. "You hung up on Covina?" he asked, laughing. "Boy, you are going to have to pay for that one."

"I'm already paying for it," she replied, not laughing at all. Not even one chuckle.

When she walked into the Haven courthouse at nine that morning, Sidney noticed the building—really noticed it—for the first time since she had been back in Haven. The courthouse was a narrow but elegant building designed by Samuel's father. It had two narrow windows on either side of a wide staircase with intricately carved stone handrails. The stained glass windows reminded Sidney of two elegant ladies.

Sidney felt a surety that her motion would prevail when she saw Grayson sitting in the judge's chamber, a notebook in his hand. Judge Harold did not acknowledge him, but instead waved Sidney and Julian to leather armchairs on the left side of his desk. The prosecutor already sat in the other chair, clutching the handle of his briefcase with both hands, even though it sat securely on his lap.

Both she and Julian ignored Jacob, as if he didn't exist. He sat easily in a big chair opposite Grayson with his hands crossed in his lap. Only his eyes betrayed his anger. They were like obsidian.

Ten minutes after nine, Judge Harold checked his watch. Dexter and Samuel had not arrived. The Judge threw a look of annoyance at Sidney. Grayson alternately looked at Sidney and scribbled furiously on his notepad. If she didn't have a sure victory, Sidney thought, no way would Judge Harold open the hearing to a reporter, even if it was Grayson. Even he wouldn't splash a guilty Haven all over the front page of the *Haven Crier*.

Sidney felt Julian's breath in her ear, and leaned toward him. "You sure you don't want me to stay?" he whispered. She faked a laugh as if he had said something funny.

She didn't want them to know how nervous she really was. "Positive," she answered.

"Counselor," Judge Harold spoke up, "your client . . ."

". . . is on the way," Sidney finished smoothly for him though she had no idea where the Havens were.

"And who is this?" Judge Harold pointed at Julian.

"Co-counsel, Your Honor," she said. "Julian McCa-laster."

Judge Harold sighed again and looked at his watch. He opened his mouth to speak, but Samuel blustered in the door. He shook everyone's hand except Jacob's before easing himself into an armchair next to Grayson. Dexter slipped in behind Samuel, sat next to his uncle, and looked at the floor.

"You are late." The Judge directed his comments to Samuel.

"I know. I know," he said. "Just couldn't seem to drag myself out of bed this morning, George," he laughed. "You should have had this hearing a little later in the day, not this ungodly hour."

Instead of answering him, Judge Harold picked up the papers and motioned toward Sidney. "Now I know where you get your reputation, young lady," he said before putting on his glasses. "Willie," he said, looking over the top of his reading glasses toward the prosecutor, "have you read this?"

"Of course, I have, Your Honor." His voice seemed to come from a long way off. The grandfather clock against the wall chimed to mark half past the hour.

"Okay." He turned toward Sidney. "Counselor, let's hear it."

Sidney started her arguments in a clean voice, only drawing one weakened objection from the prosecutor when she mentioned the vomit found on Yolonda Brown's feet.

"I, uh, object to that, Your Honor," he said. "That's

irrelevant. That vomit could have occurred anywhere. Not necessarily at the scene . . .''

Sidney watched Judge Harold as Willie, the prosecutor, spoke in a halting voice. The judge barely listened, but instead twisted a paper clip apart in his hands. He leaned back in his chair as if he were watching a rerun of a sitcom he already knew the ending to.

"Overruled," he said casually over Willie's weak voice.

"But Judge Harold," Willie continued the protest.

"I said—or can't you hear, man—overruled. I want to hear what the girl has to say."

She went on, in the same monotone. She told them of the statement she was able to obtain from Reverend Robinson, which indicated that Mr. Grayson had become ill at the scene. As she talked, she looked around Judge Harold's chamber.

The room was not well lit. It had one window to the left, but it was skinny, and covered by a heavy, velvet maroon curtain. The walls were painted a dull green, and there was a stuffed catfish hanging on the wall behind Judge Harold's head.

Then suddenly, she stopped. On Judge Harold's desk was a framed picture of him and Samuel Haven in fishing gear at the river. They leaned over the carcass of that same dead fish hanging above Judge Harold's head. They were shaking hands and laughing as the river flowed behind them. *Why hadn't I noticed this before?* she thought.

"You were saying?" Judge Harold asked her.

"What?" Sidney asked. She felt the entire room staring at her. She looked at Julian, who glanced at her quizzically, then gave her an encouraging smile.

"You were saying that if someone cleaned up the vomit, it could logically . . ."

"Oh yes," Sidney said, remembering where she was. She

felt oddly dirty. "It could logically be assumed that other evidence could have been tampered with," she explained.

"Your Honor?" Willie spoke up tentatively. "I'd like to say something here."

Judge Harold sighed, "What is it, Willie?"

"This is preposterous," he said. "There is no reason to assume anything. Sheriff Conrad had no reason to plant evidence against Dexter Haven."

Sidney continued, as if on autopilot. "Your Honor," she said, "Sheriff Conrad had engaged in a six-year feud with the Havens, ever since he failed to pin a murder conviction on Samuel Haven for the death of C.D. Heater. He is hardly objective."

"That's right, that's right," Judge Harold agreed too enthusiastically, letting the chair he had been leaning back in fall to the floor. He pointed his gavel at Jacob. "I remember you being pretty damn riled up over that one, Jacob," he said.

"Is that an overrule of the District Attorney's objection, Your Honor?" Julian asked, sarcastically. He didn't move as Sidney kicked him, and only looked at her in disgust.

"Who is he again?" Judge Harold asked Sidney.

"His part of our defense team, Your Honor," Sidney said, then elbowed Julian in the ribs for emphasis.

"Then tell him to shut up and remember whose side he's on," he said, then turned to Willie. "Overruled. Keep going, Sidney."

Sidney felt a lump at the back of her throat, so large she doubted if she could even speak. She looked again at the picture of Judge Harold and Samuel Haven on the desk. It brashly faced outward so everyone could see it. *This case was over before it started*, she thought to herself, *I didn't have to drag Jacob's past in this to win.*

"Is that it?" the judge asked in mild surprise. He already had her motion. He knew what else was in it.

"No," Julian broke in, smoothly.

"Wait," Dexter said in a thin voice, "I don't think we need to go on with this."

He stood up, his gray suit jacket hanging on his lanky frame. He had at least gotten a haircut for the occasion, and his curly blond hair covered his head in tiny yellow ringlets. He looked like Shirley Temple gone horribly wrong. Samuel jumped up and tried to forcibly re-seat him.

"Dexter, I swear boy," he started.

"Samuel," Judge Harold sighed, "leave him alone." He turned to Sidney. "Counselor, your client."

"Dex," Sidney said calmly, placing her hand on his arm, "please sit down."

"But I didn't kill Yolonda, Sidney," he said. "What if Rupert is right, and everybody thinks . . ."

"Shut up, Dexter." This time it was Julian who spoke. "As I was saying . . ." he told them of the investigations he was able to do in New York. "And through confidential but reliable sources, we've learned he may have a seeming propensity to alter evidence to fit his view of the facts."

What the hell does that mean? Sidney thought to herself. But Judge Harold smiled and nodded as Julian spoke. Sidney could tell he approved greatly of him. Dexter looked at Jacob as Julian droned on, and Sidney thought she saw something that looked a little like pity on Dexter's face. She risked a look at Jacob, and saw that he sat like a stone statue.

All of a sudden she thought about Covina's boxes. *The reason I go to the casinos,* she heard Covina's voice in her head, *is because people there ain't in boxes. They don't know me well enough to judge the strength of my whole life on the one or two bad things I might've done.*

Here, in Judge Harold's chamber, Covina would probably say they were all in boxes. Dexter would always be known for sleeping with and maybe killing a fourteen–

year—old girl; Jacob for his transgressions in New York; Julian for his sleeping around. Then there was Samuel Haven, the third. He would always be known for getting away with murder. His name would never be mentioned again without being in conjunction with C.D. Heater. Now, as she sat there, she wondered if she had just stepped into her own box: Sydney Adamson McCalaster, famous for helping murderers go free.

Judge Harold called for a mid-morning recess as he considered his decision. Sidney and Julian stood facing each other on the steps of the courthouse. Dexter and Samuel were nowhere to be seen, but Sidney guessed they probably went to the diner for lunch.

"What do you think?" she whispered to Julian, standing so close to him she could smell his aftershave.

"Are you kidding?" he asked, and smiled at her. "Do you really think he's in there making up his mind?"

"What do you think he's doing?"

"Playing solitaire," he said, looking briefly around the courthouse steps. "He's already made up his mind."

Sidney looked to the right of the courthouse and saw the park she and Covina sat in the other day. Suddenly, she missed her mother.

"Julian," she said hesitantly, "thanks for picking up in there. You didn't have to do that."

"Hey," Julian joked, "no problem, just looking out for my partner."

"Why did you do it?" she questioned.

His face turned serious for a moment. "Look," he said, "you have to live here, or at least keep coming back here as long as Covina stays. I don't. After we are divorced, I am no longer obligated to darken the doorstep of Haven, Mississippi."

"Have you seen Jacob?" she asked, changing the subject.

"Nope," he answered. "But Grayson said he slipped out the back shortly after the hearing."

"Good," she relaxed, stepping away from him.

At one o'clock, they all filed back into the Judge's chamber. All except Jacob—the chair he had occupied earlier sat accusing and empty.

Chapter 17

This kind of victory was nothing new to Sidney McCalaster. Julian had called it before a questionable victory—when you win at something but are not sure if it was the right thing to do. Sidney called it falling into a pile of shit, and then magically rising and smelling like roses—at least in the eyes of the law.

She remembered the first case she won, the first case where she knew the defendants were guilty beyond a shadow of a doubt—in her mind, at least. The thought of them being innocent crossed her mind only once, and briefly at that. Leon and Anton Donavon, both brothers and both arrested for gunning down a child about the same age as Yolonda was when she died.

When she first met them in Julian's office at the ACLU, they still had on their gang colors. Crudely drawn tattoos in green ink covered Leon's entire left arm. She remembered her mouth filling with distaste at the sight of them. But after that initial meeting, when it started to look like she had a chance at pulling it off, the trial became like a football game. It boiled down to who had the best strategy, the best players, and the best defense.

In the end, she had won, and it was the first time she had felt this feeling—proud of her victory, but ashamed at the same time. But in the end, even that turned out all right. Two months after they were freed, Leon and Anton were found shot to death only two blocks from their home. Leon would have lived, except one bullet hit him in the mouth, knocking his gold front teeth into his throat. He choked to death on his own teeth before the ambulance arrived. She didn't feel anything about their deaths other than a grim satisfaction. In the end, they got what they deserved, and their case helped launch her career.

She learned from that first big case that justice somehow took care of itself, and soon she started feeling less ashamed and more proud when her guilty clients walked out of courtrooms. But for some reason, victory from this case, the People vs. Dexter Haven, did not taste like victory from the other ones. She felt more ashamed than proud. Even though she believed Dexter was an innocent man, she still felt as if she had cheated.

An orange–breasted robin skimmed over the green lawn: landing, flying low, and then landing again. It reminded her of the same robin she had seen on Wilma's lawn. That had been less than a month ago, but somehow, it felt like many lifetimes. She walked over to where Julian was loading his briefcase into the trunk of his rental.

"You okay?" he asked her.

She looked at the man she had been married to, a little surprised at the concern in his voice.

"Yes." She folded her arms against the cool of the coming evening. "I'm fine. What about you?"

"Fine. Fine," he shrugged his shoulders. "I can't believe it's finally over." His green eyes pierced her own.

"The trial?" she laughed. "Or the marriage?"

"Only the marriage," he answered while slamming the trunk.

"I can't believe you are ready to do it again." She walked to the weeping willow beyond the car, and stroked the leaves. They felt like velvet beneath her fingers.

"You know me, sweetheart," he told her. "I can't stand being alone."

"Was that why you had so many women, Julian?" She asked him on an impulse, and regretted it immediately, because he leaned against the trunk of the car and regarded her silently for a few minutes, which seemed like an eternity.

"You know, Sidney," he told her, "I've been having affairs for our entire married life, and we never once talked about it."

She set her jaw. "There was nothing really to talk about, Julian." She let go of the branch. It swayed in the wind. "It hurt too much."

He laughed bitterly. "That's a damned lie, and you know it," he answered. "Okay, it may have in the beginning, but you never brought it up. And I know because you were too proud, too private. The more you refused to speak about it, the more determined I became to make you. But all in all, you haven't been in love with me for years, and you know it."

Sidney walked to him. She touched his folded arms. "I never said I didn't love you, Julian."

He jerked away. "Don't get all sentimental on me, Sidney. You didn't have to say it out loud. You made every excuse not to be with me when we were married. And when you felt you had to, you said it with your eyes every time you looked at me."

"If I didn't love you, I would have left you. A long time ago."

"No, you wouldn't have," he answered her. "You felt guilty. Guilty until I gave you an excuse."

She stuck her hands into the pockets of her cutoffs. She felt the uneven cement scraping her bare feet. "Julian, don't you think it's too late to talk about this now? We're divorced. It's over."

"Yes." He smiled with his mouth closed. "That's right, over."

He bent down, and kissed her fleetingly on the mouth before getting into his car. She shielded her eyes from the sinking sun as she watched his car disappear around the corner.

Sidney was so entranced with watching what was left of her marriage disappear around the corner that she didn't hear Jacob until he was right behind her. Before she could turn around, his arm snaked out and grabbed her waist. With his other hand, he grabbed her wrist before she could hit him.

When he spun her around to face him, Sidney felt that same fear she had felt that morning. It was all she could do to keep from screaming.

"What in the hell do you think you're doing?" she hissed at him. "Let go of me."

"Get into the house," he said, his voice stone.

Sidney leaned back to look into his face. She could read nothing there other than anger emanating from every pore. Over his shoulder, she saw the robin she had watched earlier lift into the sky. She forced her body still.

"Jacob, you really need to calm down," she told him.

"Too late," he said. Something in his face gave way as he smiled wryly. "Now get into the house before I drag you."

Sidney jerked away from him and rubbed her wrists. She was about to protest again, but then she noticed some kids across the street leaning on bicycles, watching her and

Jacob as if they were watching the early show. He followed her as she turned and walked into the front door of her mother's house. He closed the door behind him, and leaned against it with his arms folded. Sidney wondered if he was deliberately trying to scare her. If he were, she thought, she wouldn't give him the satisfaction of letting him know how scared she really was.

"What do you want?" she asked him.

"You are a real piece of work."

"Okay," Sidney said, "if you've come here to insult me, just do it and get it over with. I've got packing to do."

Jacob seized her by the elbows and shook her. She heard a picture clatter to the floor. It seemed to calm him down, but only slightly. Sidney closed her eyes briefly against the pain, a little amazed when she realized she was not as afraid as she thought she was.

"You have no idea what you've done, do you?" he asked her.

"You're hurting me," she told him.

"Join the club," he snapped back.

"Look," she said reasonably, "what happened today was nothing personal. Just a case, that's all."

He shook his head slightly. "That's the same thing you said about the other night. Tell me, do you take anything personally?"

"This is coming pretty damn close," she answered him.

He looked at her a moment, then let her go. He ran a large hand over his head. Sidney remained plastered against the wall, wishing he would just leave.

"That's the trouble with you people. Everything's a case," he said. He turned away from her and walked to the center of the living room. "You never consider what you spend in human lives to win your cases."

Sidney peeled herself from the back of the wall, rubbed the back of her neck.

"You know as well as I do that Dexter did not kill Yolonda Brown," she said.

He turned around and looked at her. "That doesn't make one iota of difference to you, though, does it?" he accused.

"If you really cared about that child's death, you would be out trying to find out who really killed her. I have evidence . . ."

"I'm not interested in your evidence, lady," he cut her off.

"What did you come here for, Jacob?" Sidney stuck her hand in the back pocket of her cutoffs. "An apology?"

He walked over to where she stood. "No," he said. "I just wanted to know if you could look me in the eye after what you've done."

Sidney stared at him without flinching. "I did what I had to do to win," she told him. "If you and Grange had done your job in the first place, we wouldn't be standing here today."

"Yes, but you still had my past," he said, his voice a soft whisper, like falling snow.

Sidney looked at the carpeted floor. "I'm sorry about that," she said, and raised her eyes to him. "But I needed that just in case . . ."

"Just in case Judge Harold didn't buy your evidence—tampering story?" he laughed. "But you're wrong there. He's a good ol' boy just like Rupert and Samuel. All he needed was an excuse to dismiss the case against Dexter Haven. He doesn't give a rat's ass about what happened in New York, and neither do you."

"What do you want?" Sidney asked him again, hating having to resist the urge to go to him.

"I want you to know there is more to this than what was on your sterile white pieces of paper. I want you to know what really happened."

Sidney walked over and sat down tiredly on the sofa. She let the silence in the room wash around her for a minute.

"I don't want to know," she finally told him. "I want to be left alone."

"Oh but you're going to," he told her before standing up.

"What difference does it make?" she questioned him. "This has nothing to do with me."

"Yeah right," Jacob said as he headed for the kitchen.

"Where are you going?"

He looked into her face, caught her liquid gray eyes with his. She looked angry, and defiant. Something else was there too, but she hid it behind the gray glass of her eyes. How could eyes so light be so opaque? When he looked in them, he could only see his reflection thrown back at him. The woman gave nothing away.

"I'm thirsty. I'll be back," he answered before turning away.

Jacob felt tightness in his chest as he walked toward the kitchen. He couldn't believe he was here, in this house, after what this woman did to him. But he felt he needed to have her hear the entire story, and he didn't let himself stop to think why this should be necessary.

Light dying with the dusk fought its way through the long window behind the kitchen table. He opened the refrigerator door, and the coolness calmed him, but only for a moment. He returned to the living room with a glass of ice water in his hand, and sat in an armchair opposite her. So they could face each other.

Grange cleaned up the vomit, he told her. *Cleaned it up after Grayson, that dim-headed reporter, spewed vomit all over Yolonda's dead feet. And yes, he covered it up. What difference did it make? They had plenty of evidence in the first place, but he still didn't want that silly man's vomit clouding the issue, and he certainly didn't want to make a big deal about it. Grange.*

He shook his head and walked over to the picture window near the door. He seemed to be fascinated with the coming evening. Sidney began to speak, but he started again before she could get the words out.

Grange, he continued, *I felt sorry for him, didn't want to embarrass him anymore than he had been. The man always wanted to be the perfect cop, always tried to please me. So I let it go, didn't put it in any of the reports. For a brief moment, I didn't think. So sue me,* he laughed without humor.

They sat in silence for a while and when Sidney looked out the picture window, she saw the same fading light Jacob seemed to be so fascinated with.

"Well," he looked at her again.

"Well what?" she asked him. "What do you want me to say?"

"Nothing," he said, and his laugh was bitter. "I guess I don't really want you to say anything at all."

"What about New York?" she asked him and then for a second time that evening, regretted following her impulse.

He stared at her. She dropped her eyes. He walked back over to the armchair, and sighed before starting his story.

"Okay, New York," he finally answered and acknowledged her with a wave of his hand as if he were on the stand in a court of law. "New York seems like another planet from Haven. I mean, you have to know that."

She nodded her head without speaking.

It was dirtier crime, and dirtier defendants. The defendants, he snorted, *disgusted me more and more each day. The more heinous and disgusting the crime, the wealthier the defendants, or so it seemed to me.*

That disgusted me more than anything else, because they usually killed out of greed more than despair. And the wealthier the defen-

*dants, the slicker the lawyers. They always managed some excuse
or a way to wriggle out of a loophole.* He waved his hand at
her again—*everything from battered wife syndrome to the devil
made me do it,* he laughed. *Nothing seemed to keep them where
they belonged: behind bars.*

*Did I bend a few rules? No, I didn't. I didn't even do that,
and I regret it. I grew up with a Catholic mother who instilled a
very limiting integrity in me. But that didn't even help. About a
year before the Heater murder,* he told Sidney, *I arrested a rich
socialite convicted of killing her boyfriend. She beat the poor bastard
to death with a brass-tipped poker. Beat him so bad they had to
use dental records to identify him.*

"Jacob," Sidney interrupted him, "that's enough. I
don't want to hear anymore."

He leaned forward and caught her eyes with his gaze.
"I did everything by the book," he bit out. "But by the
time the thing got to trial, the woman's lawyer had twisted
everything. In the end, if my own mother had been sitting
on the jury, she would have thought I did it. That I set the
woman up," he said as he stood up. "And of course, she
walked. Even though I was cleared by an internal investigation, my superiors insisted I go to therapy. And again, I
told the truth, and look where it landed me. I'm sure you
read the literature," he said, his voice dripping sarcasm.

*When the chance came to come to Haven, I took it willingly,
thinking it would be a clean case I could close easily. A welcome
break from New York. But the Havens, Samuel Haven, epitomized
everything I hated about New York. One of the reasons I stayed
was because I wanted to be around when Samuel caught his. I
not only wanted to see it, I wanted to be the one to dish it out.*

"You were obsessed," Sidney commented.

"Funny, you use the past tense," he answered.

"You can't still believe Dexter killed Yolonda."

"And I still can't believe that he didn't. How do you
sleep at night?" he asked her.

Sidney stood up, and walked past him, trying to follow the air she felt had left the room. He caught her arm as it swung past his face. She stopped, and looked down at him.

"You don't know me," she told him. "I know you think you do, but you don't know a thing about me."

"That's because you won't let me," he countered. "You're hiding." Then he shrugged his broad shoulders before speaking again. "I mean I hope you are hiding. Because if you're not, if you are the cold-hearted bitch you pretend to be, I can understand why your husband left you."

She reached out to slap him with her other hand, but he caught her flinging wrist. He held both her hands and looked up at her. She tried avoiding his gaze by turning her face away from him.

"One of these days," he said softly, as if in warning, "one of these days you're going to care about what's right."

She snatched her hands away from him, and didn't raise her eyes until she heard the front door slam behind him. It was then that she felt more acutely than ever that all the air had been sucked out of the room.

Chapter 18

Sidney woke in the middle of the night to find a man standing over her bed. At first, she thought she was still dreaming, but she could smell the stink of garlic on his breath even from her prone position. Not entirely awake yet, she leaned up on her elbows to get a better look at him. Fear rolled slowly inside her like a gathering wave. She felt bile in her throat.

The man stood at her bedside in a black windbreaker with a stocking cap pulled over his face. The leg of the pantyhose he used to tie the knot bobbed ridiculously at the top of his head. He breathed heavily, and she could smell Bianca covering the garlic on his breath every time he exhaled. The fear Sidney felt collecting inside her made her actually think she could hear him sweating beneath the stocking cap. He stood with his hands at his sides, gazing down at her.

Sidney continued upward, gingerly like a cat. Everything

seemed to move in slow motion. She scooted backward toward the phone on the opposite side of the bed.

The man just stood there, and for a minute again, she almost believed she was imagining things, that he was indeed an apparition. She felt the ivory feel of the phone beneath her fingers. But when she lifted the receiver, he dispelled all illusions that he was not real by suddenly swooping down and knocking the phone out of her hand. Sidney screamed. She scrambled on all fours and jumped off the bed.

Suddenly, she remembered when she was nine years old, and her bicycle hit the lip of a crack in the sidewalk by Johnson's Grocers. She went head–first over the handlebars. The left handlebar caught her in the stomach as she fell to the ground. All of her breath left her on that day. And that's what it felt like now when the man grabbed her by the waist and threw her on the bed—her breath leaving her body in a burst of wind and fear.

She rolled over on her stomach in the bed, gasping for air. She remembered that day on the hot sidewalk. Remembered writhing for air until Mr. Johnson ran outside and shook her upside down until she could breathe again. But the memory dissolved into this new horror as she felt the man's weight press against her back. He put his mouth to her ear.

"Bitch." He slapped her lightly on the behind, but it still stung. "Now you wish you had kept out of it, don't you?"

His hand clawed her head and pressed her face down into the bed. When she opened her mouth to scream, she tasted bedspread. She felt him fumble near her bottom. Fear exploded with her again. She tried to tell herself he didn't mean to kill her, couldn't mean to kill her. If he did, why would he bother to wear a stocking cap? Her mind asked her physical body to remain calm. But it screamed for

attention. And when she heard his zipper open, she almost
went insane with fear. The belt on his pants jingled as he
dropped them to his ankles, while still pressing her face
to the bed.

"I don't care too much for doggie style," he said, while
flipping her over in one fluid motion, laughing.

He shoved the tank top above her breast. The sandy
texture of the stocking cap against her nipple almost made
her vomit. She balled her hand into a fist and punched
him in the side of the head. Before he had a chance to
catch his breath, she drew her knee up and kicked him in
the groin. He rolled from her, clutching himself.

She leapt from the bed and grabbed the Tiffany lamp
from her mother's night stand. She brought it down to
smash over his head. The man saw it coming, and rolled
over to his side, but too slowly. The lamp caught him on
the side of the face. Dark blood gathered under the stocking cap.

Sidney ran barefoot from the room. Each breath she
took stabbed at her chest. She grabbed the cordless from
the living room coffee table and ran outside. The night's
chill did not calm her. For one horrific moment, she
couldn't remember the number to Litttleton's police
department. The town was too small for 9-1-1. Calm down,
Sidney, she told herself.

When she finally dialed the number, it echoed emptily
in the darkened police station, then forwarded to Jacob's
house. When it rang three times, she almost hung up,
thinking she had the wrong number. Then she heard
Jacob's sleepy voice.

"This better be good," he said.

"Sheriff, I mean Jacob, I mean . . ." Sidney's voice almost
sounded calm.

"Oh, it's you," he said. "What do you want?" He put
his palm against his forehead, still not fully awake.

"There's a man . . ." She began sobbing now.

"What?" he said, sitting up in bed. "Where are you?"

"At home," she started again, then took a deep breath. "There is a man . . ."

"Okay, okay," his heart pounded, but he forced his voice to be mild. "Get out of the house," he said.

Sidney opened her mouth to answer him, but then she heard the unmistakable click behind her.

"Put it down," the man said.

She let the phone slide from her ear. Jacob's desperate calling of her name became lost in the clatter of the phone as it made contact with the cement walk.

"Turn around," he told her.

And when she did, she knew it was over. The man stood there with her mother's .357 magnum pointed at her. The barrel of the silver gun was as large as a pig's snout. Her mother bought the gun two days after Carl tried to choke her to death in the middle of the living room.

The man stood there, bareheaded, his face lit by the brightness of the moon and stars. His blond curly hair barely moved in the wind. Blood trickled from the cut on the side of his face and collected in his ear.

"Get in the house," he said. He stepped aside so she could walk through the door. He pushed her over the threshold and clicked the bolt into place behind him.

"It's not loaded," she challenged.

His eyes were blue and very cold. "Now it is, darlin'," he laughed at her. "Someone ought to tell your Mamma not to put the bullets right next to the gun," he said. He walked past her, still laughing. "Liable to be an accident."

"Who are you?" She asked him. But she knew. It was the man in the pictures, the friend of Samuel Haven.

He stood at the bedroom door. "Coming?" he taunted her. "I believe we have some unfinished business."

"You are wasting time," she told him. "I called the police."

He scratched his chin with the gun, pretending to consider her comment. "Now that does present a little bit of a problem. But I know the Sheriff lives about ten minutes from here, and that gives us plenty of time."

"Fuck you," she told him.

He raced over to her and punched her in the face with his free hand. She fell against the glass coffee table, and it shattered like a wafer beneath her. He reached through the glass and pulled her by the back of the neck. She clawed at his wrists. They felt like vices. He tried to stand her on her feet, but she made her body go limp.

"Stand up," he yelled.

"FUCK YOU!" she spat in his face.

He let out a grunting sound, and slapped her with the hand holding the pistol.

"Bitch," he said, letting his anger get in the way of his common sense.

Pain exploded in bright lights all around her. He grabbed the strap of her tank top. When his hand slipped, she realized the back of her tank top was wet with blood. She had obviously been cut when she fell into the table.

He dragged her by the neck to the bedroom. Still holding her, he threw her on the tangled bedspreads, right next to the broken lamp. She felt glass grind into the cut in her back.

Sidney tried to sit up, but he pushed her back down.

"Why don't you just shoot me?" she asked him, then laughed weakly. "That gun was not really loaded, was it?"

The man consciously tried to calm his own breathing. Then he laughed himself. "I guess you are as smart as they say," he said before covering her body with his own.

* * *

Jacob was already stepping into his jeans when he heard Sidney's phone drop. *Dammit! Dammit!* His mind raced as his instinct told him the woman was in trouble. Big trouble. He threw the phone he had been holding, and thrust his arms into a white work shirt. He grabbed his holster and ran out of the front door.

He was halfway to his car when he realized he had left his keys on the kitchen counter. *Please, please let them be there,* he prayed as he slammed back into the house. And they were, all but gleaming like a beacon in the darkened kitchen.

He scooped them up and ran out of the house, leaving the back door standing wide open. He shut the car door as he hurled the red Mustang into reverse. He pressed number four on his cell phone for Grange's number. But the phone just rang and rang, the bell hollow and alone in his ear. Jacob slammed the phone on the dashboard in frustration—slammed it so hard it shattered into two pieces.

Time for Sidney sped up and slowed down at the same time. Sure that this was the beginning of her own death, she felt as if she were watching a time–lapse video of a rose opening. Weeks of precious time crammed into a few tiny minutes. A few minutes which seemed unbearably slow as a rose opened into full red glory.

She watched prone on the bed as the man closed the bedroom door. Her eyes followed him as he ripped the electric cord from the lamp, stretched it tight in his hands. She did not move as he walked toward her.

The rose opening, she thought stupidly. It takes weeks; it takes only a few minutes. She laughed silently to think she would die in Haven after all she had done to get away from this town. She thought about the heat the day she graduated from Ol' Miss, and a picture of Covina's shiny face and her white toothy smile flashed in her mind. And for an instant, she smelled the river she and C.D. Heater sat beside so long ago. And felt Julian's warm hug as he told her good-bye only a few hours ago.

Then she thought about Yolonda, and a sadness filled her as she realized she never even thought about what that young girl must have been thinking when the life drained out of her. She knew it was too late, but now she finally did understand. She understood what Peachy Girl felt as this man, and it had to be this man, kicked the life out of her.

Now he towered over her, twisting the cord round and round in his hands. He tilted his head to the side to get a better look.

"Nah," he said. "I don't want to ruin that pretty neck."

He threw the cord aside, and picked up the pillow next to her. Sidney dodged away weakly, but he firmly pulled her by the arm until she lay flat on her back. White was the last thing she saw as he pressed the pillow over her face.

Jacob left the car running, barely putting it into park as he leapt from the vehicle and ran to where Grange stood.

"Howdy, Sheriff," Grange said. He tilted his hat, and pointed to the black cordless telephone in his hand. "Now what do you make of this thing doing out here?" he said, pursing his pink lips.

"Grange," Jacob said, irritated, "what in the hell are you doing standing out here?"

"Well, one of the neighbors called," he said and

pointed, "from up thatta way. Said they thought they saw
somebody that ain't got no business out this way."

Jacob almost knocked him over as he ran to Sidney's
front door.

". . . a white man in the Bottoms." Grange, nonplussed,
walked behind him. "Then I was driving by, and saw the
porch light on, and this phone in the driveway."

Jacob ignored him, tried the door knob.

"It's locked," Grange told him.

"Did you knock?" he asked.

"I didn't want to wake anybody up," Grange replied.

Jacob looked at Grange as if he had just sprouted another
head as they stood there.

"Stand back," he said grimly.

"Are you going to shoot the lock, Sheriff?" Grange
asked, his pink cheeks flushed with excitement.

Jacob ignored him again as he lifted his leg to kick in
the door.

Sidney fought for air, and tore at the man's hands. Blackness, blacker than the darkness caused by the pillow, over-
whelmed her for a moment. All of a sudden, the pressure
on her face lifted. She rolled onto her stomach, coughing
and gulping at the same time. The man who had been
trying to kill her leapt over her as he bolted out the French
patio doors.

"Sidney?" Jacob questioned, his voice frantic.

"It's about time," Sidney coughed. "What did you do,
take a bus?"

"Go, Sheriff, go," Grange said. "I'll stay with her."

Grange helped Sidney into a sitting position. Her eyes
focused on him for the first time. His blue eyes were wide
and startled. They traveled from her blood–soaked tank
top to her torn bikini panties. He turned as red as a beet.

"Get my robe," she told him hoarsely, and gestured to the chair beside the bed.

"Where you hurt?" he asked her as he draped the robe around her near-naked waist.

"My shoulder's cut," she told him.

She did not look up when she heard the French doors click close.

"Got away?" Grange asked a despondent Jacob.

"Yeah," he answered tiredly. "Are you all right?" He flashed a cautious look at Sidney. She caught his gaze, saw a muscle in his jaw jump.

She paused briefly before answering. "Yeah, fine," she said without volunteering any more information.

"Careful." Grange caught her arm when she stood up.

Sidney turned her back to both of them and shrugged into her robe. She could feel the terry cloth sticking to the open wound on her shoulder, scraping the exposed flesh. She walked past Jacob toward the bathroom.

"Where are you going?" he asked her.

"To take a shower," she told him. "That man's filth is all over me." Her shoulder hurt like hell, and she could feel the side of her face beginning to swell.

"Sheriff." Grange looked questioningly at Jacob. "Do you think she ought to be doing that?"

Jacob took a deep breath, and blocked the door to the bathroom.

"Grange is right," he said without looking at her. "You need to get to a doctor."

Sidney folded her arms. She had to stoop to look into his bent face.

"I wasn't raped," she told him softly. "And all I can smell is Bianca and garlic. So if you will get out of my way, I need to take a shower."

"You still need to get to a doctor." Grange's voice was shrill from the other side of the room. "She got a big ol' cut on her shoulder. And it looks like he knocked her around some."

Jacob reached to touch her face. She knocked his hand away as if it were a welding torch.

"I need a shower," she repeated, making a conscious effort to keep her hoarse voice hard.

He studied her for a moment before answering. "Have it your way," he said, clenching his jaw and moving aside.

Before she turned on the water, she heard him call Doctor Max.

When she stepped from the shower, the bedroom was empty. She didn't know how long she had been there, but every hurt spot the water had touched stung. She heard voices in the kitchen: Jacob, Grange, and Doctor Max.

They all stood up when she walked in. Even though the Mississippi night was warm, she felt cool in her blue satin robe. She had stuffed her mother's red terry robe into the bathroom trash can along with her tank top and torn panties.

"Real smart thing to do taking a shower," Doctor Max said gruffly. "Real smart."

"I've already said . . ." she begin to explain.

"I know you weren't raped," Doctor Max finished for her. "But Grange said you had a cut on your shoulder needing stitches. You should have waited until I got here before you jumped in the shower."

He pointed to the chair beside him, and Sidney sat down. He peeled the satin robe from her until it dropped around her shoulders.

"I'm gonna make some coffee." Grange stood up so fast he almost knocked his chair over. "Anybody want some coffee?"

The room grew smaller in the silence. Finally, Doctor Max answered him.

"Not me," he said absently. Jacob said nothing; he sat and stared at Sidney's bent head.

"Well, I want some coffee." Grange walked in a small circle around the kitchen. His shoes made shuffling sounds on the pink tile floor.

"Everything's by the coffee pot in the corner by the sink, Grange," Sidney answered, her jaw hurting with each word.

"You best be settling down, girl," Doctor Max told her. "Because you've been through enough tonight. You need a rest," he said as he gently touched the cut on her shoulder. "There might be some glass up in here, too."

"Stitches?" Jacob asked, his voice hollow.

"Yep," Doctor Max answered, " 'fraid so, Jacob. At least eight." He tilted his head, considering. "Maybe nine."

"What happened, Sidney?" Jacob asked her.

She avoided the question by sucking in a painful breath as Doctor Max plunged a Novocain–filled syringe near the cut on her shoulder. He stood back to wait a couple of minutes for the medicine to take effect.

"Let me know if you feel anything," he finally said. He picked up some tweezers and begin picking glass out of the cut.

"I can't believe you are not using stapling tape or something. I thought this was the nineties."

"Too deep," Doctor Max said absently.

"Sidney," Jacob cut in impatiently.

"Can't this wait, Jacob?" she asked him.

"No," he said. "It can't. What happened?"

"I don't know," Sidney answered. "I woke up and that asshole was standing over my bed."

"Stop moving around, girl!" Doctor Max warned. "I'm doctoring here."

The room filled with the smell of boiling coffee as Grange sat back down.

"Grange," Jacob said. "You need to put your coffee in a travel mug and start knocking on some doors, scouring the neighborhood to see if anyone heard or saw anything unusual."

"Yessir, Sheriff," Grange said seriously.

"You can't be hoping he'd find anything, do you?" Doctor Max said. His glasses had slipped to the tip of his nose, and he looked over them to thread a needle. "If you did, I know you'd be out there yourself."

"We may get lucky," Jacob replied, his gaze still fixed on Sidney. "Tell him."

Sidney looked back at him. He stared at her as if she were a spider caught on a pin.

"Tell who what?" Sidney asked.

"Tell Grange what he looked like."

"I don't know."

Jacob let the chair he had been leaning back in fall level to the ground.

"He wore a stocking cap pulled over his face," Sidney explained before he could say anything.

"He took it off," Jacob answered her.

"How do you know?" She winced as she felt Doctor Max pull the needle through the cut.

"I found it on the living room floor."

"I didn't see his face clearly," she said, staring at the table top. "But I'm sure it was a white man."

"Grange," Jacob still didn't look at Grange, but gazed at Sidney's bowed head instead. "Start looking around the neighborhood for anyone on foot."

"Jacob," Doctor Max said as he tied off the third stitch in Sidney's shoulder, "stop badgering this girl."

"The *girl*," Jacob said, "is a liar."

Sidney's head snapped up. As Jacob and her eyes caught,

they both knew it was true. She was lying, lying up a blue streak.

"Look," Doctor Max said in a measured voice, "if y'all want to scream at each other, at least wait until I get this needle out of my hand."

Jacob stood up, and threw the stocking cap on the table in disgust. He twirled away from her, and Sidney followed his broad back with her eyes. When he swiveled around again, their eyes caught.

"Why won't you tell me?" he asked her.

"I don't know what you mean," she insisted. She felt Doctor Max gently bend her head out of his way.

"You need to hold your head down, you are in my light," he said softly.

"I can't believe this," Jacob said. "I just can't believe this. What, you think you can handle this yourself? Is that it? Or are you just like everyone else in this town?"

"What do you mean by that, Jacob?" Sidney asked. Doctor Max held the needle in mid-air. He too looked at Jacob, and waited for an answer.

"You think I don't know that there are people in this town who didn't come forward in the past—and won't come forward now—to tell me who murdered C.D. Heater? That they've got some twisted notion about who does and doesn't belong here? Who should and shouldn't know?"

Sidney looked away. Doctor Max just grunted awkwardly, and became intrigued once more in closing the wound on Sidney's shoulder.

Jacob came close, and bent his face down until he was level with Sidney.

"Sidney," he said, "I'm asking you to stop this now. Don't be like them, just tell me what he looked like and who you think he was."

"But I thought you said I was just like the Havens," she spat back at him.

He stood up abruptly, accidentally bumping into Doctor Max.

"Dammit, Jacob," the doctor fumed, "that's it. This is my patient. Get out!"

Instead of leaving, Jacob sighed and ran his hand over his head. He rubbed his eyes before speaking again. This time, instead of sounding angry, he sounded tired.

"You know," he said, "one of the reasons I stayed is because I thought one day, someone would let their guard down and forget who I was and where I was from. Then they would just let slip a tiny piece of information that would help me convict Samuel Haven of C.D.'s murder."

"That's your problem, Jacob," Sidney said, her head still bowed. "That's all you think about, seeing Samuel Haven in jail. You are so obsessed, you can't be trusted. Would it shatter your entire world if you found out he didn't kill the Heater boy?"

"Children," Doctor Max said into the ensuing silence, "children, please."

In Sidney's dream, silence reigned. It was the silence of blackness and emptiness, even though light streamed through each and every curtainless window in the house. It poured through the transparent panes, collected and criss-crossed in places on the floor. She dreamed she walked naked through Rudger's Housing development on 1686 Easterbrook. She twisted the corners of the fully matured carpeted rooms, from one to the other, following a forty-five–year–old Yolonda Brown: Peachy Girl.

She smiled as she took Sidney on the tour. Spittle shone on her false teeth which were white and long and straight as a healthy animal. The wrinkles at the corners of her eyes dimpled with almost every word she spoke. Her words fell from her mouth like glittery multi-colored jewels. Sidney, feeling more naked and cold than she actually was in the dream, folded her arms. Yolanda, ever the hostess, offered to turn up the heat, then wrapped a diaphanous blue chiffon scarf around her as they continued the tour.

And then, in the living room, Yolanda stood in a circle of light, her eyes shining and her false teeth glistening like white fire. The lines around her eyes peeled away to reveal the innocence of youth. The teeth shortened, became yellow, then brown as any real teeth not touched by a dentist on a regular basis.

And her head just separated at the neck. She reached out to Sidney then, reached out as she crumpled onto the floor as if she were performing a grotesque ballet.

Peachy Girl slowly folded herself into the position captured in the autopsy photos, as if this was how it should be. And before her left eye popped out of her head like a ripe grape, she reached out to Sidney. A brown hand with fire engine red Lee Press-On nails thrust out as if making a silent, bloody plea.

Sidney jumped as if someone had punched her in the stomach when Peachy Girl reached out that bloody hand. But instead of the house on 1686 Easterbrook Drive, she found herself sitting up in her own childhood bed. The gossamer pink curtains covering the window didn't block out the chillingly bright sunlight she could hardly believe she had lived to see.

She turned away from the window, and her eyes collided with Jacob's dark ones. He sat sprawled in a ridiculously pink armchair she had had in her room since she was ten years old. His white cotton shirt was open to the waist, and shimmered brightly against the midnight darkness of his skin. The blue jeans he wore molded attractively around his thighs and legs. One bare black foot rested against her

pink bedspread. It was obvious he had been there the
entire night, watching over her as she slept.

"Didn't you have anything better to do last night?" She
fell backward into her bed and immediately regretted it
as pain claimed her upper body.

"Careful," he told her, "you should be in the hospital,
you know."

Sidney let air escape from her mouth in a soft sigh. For
the life of her, she could barely remember last night. What
happened after Doctor Max had left was a purple fog.

"They put sick people in hospitals," she finally answered. "Besides, shouldn't you be out arresting something?"

Jacob's laugh was brittle. "I can't believe you can joke
at a time like this." He sat up in the chair and rested his
elbows on his knees. "What game are you playing?"

"I'm not playing a game," she answered. "I don't know
what you are talking about."

"Yes," he said, and sat back. "Yes you do. Who was he,
Sidney?"

She remained silent while turning the question over in
her mind. She had no intention of answering him. There
was something she had to do first. If she told him who the
man was, there was still a chance the one who was behind
this would get away with murder—once again. She had
no intention of letting that happen. And yet, maybe she
could trust him.

"Dexter didn't kill Yolonda Brown," she started.

He stood up then, and shoved his hands into the back
pocket of his jeans.

"So that's what it's all about?" he said as he walked
closer to the bed. "To salve your guilty conscience? Your
brother's guilty. Nothing you can say or do will change
that."

"He's not my brother."

"You could have fooled me," he shot back.

She knew she couldn't convince him. She needed more evidence—a connection between Samuel Haven and the man in the pictures.

"Me too," a voice said from behind him.

Jacob moved aside to reveal Covina standing in the doorway. Ever since she was little, Sidney thought if eagles could talk, they would sound like Covina. Instead of the plaits she had left for Vicksburg with, shiny finger curls covered her round head. And she wore a sleeveless luminescent yellow sundress with buttons all the way up the front. Sidney had to fight back tears, she was so happy to see her.

"But Mamma," Sidney said, "Marion?"

"Marion?" she countered. "Marion is fine, girl. She has that husband of hers—what's his name. He's okay now all the blood and gore is over with. Besides, you think I'm gonna stay away when my other baby girl is hurt?"

Sidney ached in pain, but still managed to give Covina a hug.

"What's that?" she asked, laughing, pointing to the paper bag Covina held.

"Oh," Covina answered, "these are pictures of Adam." She turned the bag over, and Polaroids fluttered out onto Sidney's legs. Covina had documented the entire birthing experience almost from beginning to end. There were pictures of the masked doctors; pictures of Adam's head crowning; pictures of him with one shoulder out; pictures of his entire body; then parts of his body—an arm, then a foot. Covina had even snapped Polaroids of the placenta and afterbirth.

"Now, that's nasty," Jacob said, staring down at the pictures.

"Mamma, I can't believe they let you do all this," Sidney said.

"They wouldn't at first, but then I promised to stay back out of the way."

"I have to go," Jacob broke in, reminding both of them he was still there.

"Did you call *my mother?*" Sidney stared at Jacob in startled amazement.

"I did." A spark of amusement flashed in his eyes briefly.

"Why?" She could barely speak.

Jacob walked to her dresser and picked up a hand mirror. He handed it to her.

"Doctor Max said you needed observing. And I'll be damned if I'm going to baby-sit while that bastard's on the loose."

Sidney brought her hand to her face, touched the black and blue marks around her left eye and her cheek. The entire left side of her face was as swollen and red as a rotted honeydew melon. The flesh around her left eye squeezed it almost shut. She hadn't felt it when she woke up this morning, but looking at it now, for the first time, she felt a dull, heavy ache in her face.

"You are not doing anything in that condition," Jacob said grimly. "And the doc thinks you may even have a couple of broken ribs. So you might as well tell me who that monster is so I can go and pick him up."

Sidney avoided his eyes, and placed the mirror on the night stand. Covina tsk tsked as she scooped the pictures back into the bag. "He's right, girl," she said. "What do you care about them crazy Havens anyway? See the thanks you get for setting that lunatic Dexter free?"

"I didn't set anyone free, Mamma," Sidney retorted.

"Suit yourself." She bent down and fluffed Sidney's pillows. She then stood upright. She touched the long, feathered earring at her ear before looking at Jacob.

"What now?" she said as if they were co-conspirators.

"If she moves, tell me," he reached under his bed, grabbed his shoes.

"You're on *his* side!" Sidney said, pointing at Jacob.

"Sweetheart, there ain't no sides up in here," Covina told her. "And why should I be on your side anyway? Shit," she said as she continued out the door, "I'm the one who got to live here, not you."

After she left, Jacob gazed at her, his head tilted to one side.

"It could have been worse," he said. "I could have called your husband."

"Ex-husband," she corrected automatically before she could think about it. She wouldn't look at him, just stared out her bedroom window into the backyard, wishing he would go away.

It was only when she could not hear him breathe anymore that she turned her face away from the window, and let the empty room close around her.

Chapter 19

Bittersweet flowers bent the branches on Covina's magnolia trees, almost forcing them to touch the velvet grass. She and Sidney sprawled on white lawn chairs on the patio. It had been three days since the attack, and Sidney's face was still bruised, but not as swollen.

The smell from the honeysuckle and magnolia was so heavy, Sidney imagined she could reach out and touch it if she wanted to. For some reason, the thought reminded her of Jacob. Frowning, she tightened the robe around her.

"I went to Johnson's while you were sleeping," Covina told her as if reading her mind. "And he was still out there."

Sidney's frown grew. For the past three days, it had been Jacob or Grange parked in the police cruiser in front of the house. But she only saw Jacob once, briefly, after that first day. He came to the house to tell her they did not have any leads. And he believed the man who attacked her was no longer in Haven.

"Do you have anything you want to tell me?" he asked

her. They sat on the sofa in her mother's living room. Sidney sat as far away from him as she could get—curled in one corner with her feet tucked beneath her. He sat uncomfortably on the other side rolling a bottle of Pepsi between his hands. Covina had left them alone a minute after he arrived, murmuring something about dinner burning.

"No—no, I don't," she said without looking at him.

They sat in silence for a few more minutes. Then Jacob let out a disgusted sigh and left without saying good-bye.

"He's in love with you, you know," Covina said, breaking Sidney out of the memory.

"What?" she asked Covina, not understanding.

"The Sheriff." Her mother looked at her. Sidney was again surprised at how black her mother's eyes were, like coal. "He's crazy about you."

"Mamma, please." Sidney trained her gaze on the back lawn. She became entranced by a bee flying from one honeysuckle flower to another. "I hardly know him, and vice versa."

"But y'all slept together, didn't you?" Covina was not deterred.

"No," Sidney denied flatly.

"Well," Covina said, crossing her legs, "y'all should have."

Sidney looked at her mother. "Mamma, Covina," she said as she stood up, "I can't talk about this with you." She pushed open the sliding glass door and walked into the air–conditioned cool of the kitchen. Covina followed, her black hair smashed to one side of her head. She had washed it, and now it was back in that low, familiar Afro.

"If not me," Covina said, combing her fingers through her hair to even it out, "then with who? Julian?"

"Mamma, please stop it," Sidney said, folding her arms.

"Look, I've had to live here since you left. And I've seen

plenty of women chase after Jacob, even Wilma, but I ain't never saw him look at them the way he looks at you."

"What has that got to do with anything?" she asked her mother.

But Covina ignored her. Sticking out her butt and putting her hands on her hips, she sacheted around the room on her tiptoes. "This is how they walk by him," she laughed, "and if I was ten years younger, believe me, I'd be doing the same thing."

"Mamma," Sidney said, looking at her incredulously, "did you take your medicine this morning?"

"Yes, I did," Covina said, eyeing her, and still smiling. Her white teeth gleamed against her satin, unlit skin. "Yesterday, and the day 'fo' that too. But I don't need no medicine to tell me that man in love with you."

Sidney shook her head and pushed open the kitchen door.

"You know," Covina said, barely catching the door just before it hit her in the face, "he a lot more man than Julian, ain't he?"

Sidney ignored her, and plopped on the couch.

"And all you got to do is crook your little finger," Covina said. "But be careful, a man like that won't be made a fool of for long."

"How would you know?" she asked her. "You were with Carl for years."

Covina's laugh sounded like church bells. "That's what he thought," she replied. "But I've had enough men to know what end is up." She laughed again.

"Mamma, I really don't want to talk about this." Sidney dropped her face into her hands.

It was the same gesture she made when she and Covina had spoken about Dexter. When Sidney told her mother why she defended him, her mother looked at her wide-eyed, before saying, *Girl, you is a fool.* She then left for a minute,

and when she returned, she had a document signed by
Marion Haven, Carl's wife. It said she would never contest
the will as it related to Covina's house. *May not be legal*, Covina
told her, *but it gave me some peace over the years.*

Covina walked over to her daughter and stroked the back
of her bent head.

"You know darlin'," she said. "You don't have to make
everything so complicated." She opened her mouth to speak
again, when the phone rang. She handed it to Sidney.

"It's Julian," she said dryly.

Sidney pressed the receiver to her ear. "Julian," she
said, "What did you find out?"

She had phoned him the day before, asking him to see
if he could find Wilma, and if he could find anything else
suspicious in the Haven's account.

"What's Covina doing there?" he asked her. She had
told him nothing of the past few days. "I thought she was
in Vicksburg."

"She lives here, Julian," she said, trying to sound exasperated.

She could almost see him shrug his shoulders. "Aren't
you even going to congratulate me?" he asked her. "And
I didn't even get a card."

"Congratulations," she replied. "I hope you treat her
the same way you treated me. Now, what did you find out?
Did you find Wilma?"

He laughed. "For someone who's come a–beggin', disturbing my honeymoon, you sure are a smart ass."

"Julian." Sidney's voice was tired, and her jaw began to
hurt.

"Okay, okay." He turned solemn. "You are not going
to believe this, but here goes . . ."

Chapter 20

The river. That was where Sidney ended up the morning after she talked to Julian. The river, wearing nothing but a thin, tight T-shirt, flip-flops, and cut-off blue jeans. She sat near the river's edge with her knees drawn up and her feet in the water. Her arms rested on her knees.

And for the first time, the gavel wasn't in her book bag, but rested against her thigh. It felt like a mallet in her hands. She never knew how damnably heavy the thing was.

The morning sun fell through the trees, sparkling and shining like raining diamonds. Pointed rocks pierced the clear, trickling water. She could see the slick backs of silver fish threading through the water. A breeze lifted her hair around her face slightly. She took a deep breath, felt it stab at her bruised ribs, and then let it out, thinking about the conversation she had had with Julian the previous night.

Now she knew who killed both C.D. Heater and Peachy Girl. She knew it as sure as she was sitting there, as sure as the sun falling through the trees and the fish swimming in the river. She supposed she could go to Jacob, but she felt she had been trusted with this knowledge for a reason.

She thought about her father's funeral, how badly both she and her sister wanted to be accepted there. How she had clung to that gavel all of her life, trying to prove something to them and everyone else around her. Now, she stood up and dusted the dirt and leaves from her backside, still holding the gavel.

She stood for a long time looking at the river. *Now is the time,* she thought, *now is the time the Havens will get everything that is coming to them.* And her heart leapt when she realized she would be the one delivering the bill.

She took a step backward and threw the gavel far and high into the air. It twirled and then arced for a brief second, high in the air before falling with the sunlight into the clear river. Sidney was halfway to her car before she heard the splash.

Jacob sat at his desk in Haven's police station, turning a pencil over and over against the wooden surface of his desk, which was already pocked with pencil and pen marks. He tried all he could to hate Sidney McCalaster without much success. But he knew she had lied to him about not knowing who attacked her, and he had been trying to figure it out ever since. The phone cut into his thoughts like a knife. He snatched it from the receiver.

"Haven Police," he said, his voice terse.

There was a brief silence on the other end of the line, then "Sheriff Conrad? This is Julian. Julian McCalaster."

"Yes?" Jacob questioned while ignoring the thin stream of anger piercing through his body.

"It's about my wife." When Jacob did not respond, he added, "I mean my ex-wife."

"What about her?" Jacob asked him coldly.

"She's in trouble," Julian said.

"I could have told you that," Jacob laughed bitterly.

"No," Julian said, annoyed, "I mean real trouble."

"Mr. McCalaster." Jacob leaned back in his chair and put his feet on his desk. "Your *ex-wife* is currently at her mother's house, probably curled up watching a movie. We've been keeping an eye on her ever since the attack."

"The attack?" Julian asked, and listened, horrified, as Jacob explained everything to him.

"You mean you didn't know?" Jacob said after he finished.

"No," Julian said, audibly phased, "I didn't."

"Well, now you do. But as I was saying, she's at home."

"You don't know her very well, do you?" Julian's voice dripped with sarcasm.

"Get to the point, Mr. McCalaster." Jacob's voice was a low growl.

It was then Julian's turn to update Jacob. He told him about the phone call, and what Sidney had asked him to find out. He had found Wilma, and she confessed that she had been blackmailing Samuel for years. She knew the man he had hired to kill C.D. Heater, because they had worked together at the Haven mansion. And he also found a money trail.

When he told Sidney, he begged her to go to the police. But as usual, she wouldn't listen. Jacob hung up the phone before Julian stopped speaking. He dialed Sidney's number by heart. His blood ran cold when Covina answered.

"Sidney," he commanded.

"Why, hello Sheriff," Covina said. "Ain't I still young and pretty enough to warrant a hello from you?"

"Where is your daughter, Covina?" he asked her.

"Hmmm," Covina stalled, "she's lying down. Asleep."

"Get her."

"You mean you want me to wake her up?"

"Get her."

Covina paused for a minute. "Okay. Okay. I will."

He heard the receiver being placed on the table. He felt a twinge of relief, but he also felt uneasy. He heard Covina pick up the phone again.

"She's in the shower," she explained. "All soaped up and dripping wet. I'll have her call you later."

The feeling of uneasiness canceled out any relief he had felt. Eight minutes later, he parked his red Mustang behind the police cruiser.

"Grange," he said and banged on the driver's side door.

"Yes." Grange sat up, and pushed the hat off his face.

"You're sleeping?" Jacob asked him.

Grange sat up. His hat fell to the floor of the car. "Yes," he said. He looked up like he did not know where he was. "I mean no," he contradicted himself, clearly confused.

Jacob turned away from him in disgust. Grange pushed open the police car door. When he tried to get out, he stumbled and Jacob had to pull him by his elbows to keep him from falling.

"Grange," he asked, "what in the hell's the matter with you?"

"Don't know, Sheriff," he said. "I guess that tea made me sleepy." He rubbed his hand over his face.

"Tea?" Jacob asked. "You went for tea?"

"No, Sheriff," Grange said, insulted. "I stayed right here just like you tol' me. Miss Covina knew I might be thirsty, it being so hot, so she came out here with some iced tea."

Jacob looked at him. "You telling me you took tea from them?"

"What's wrong with that?" The words tumbled out of his mouth. "I was very thirsty," he said seriously.

Jacob threw his hands up.

"This ain't New York, Sheriff," Grange said.

"It doesn't have to be," Jacob yelled over his shoulder as he stepped up to the front door. When Covina opened it, he pushed past her and walked into Sidney's room.

"Where is she?" he said as he turned away from the empty room.

"I don't know," she said. "She wouldn't tell me."

"Do you have any ideas?" he asked her.

"No, but I heard her talking to someone before she left," Covina said. "I think it was Samuel Haven."

Jacob's blood ran cold. He felt like he had just stepped into a nightmare.

Sidney parked her car across the street from the Haven mansion. She stepped out and looked up at the darkening skies. Evening was coming. The pillars on the front of the mansion glinted a warning in the half darkness. The house reminded Sidney of a fortress.

As she watched the mansion from across the street, she thought of Peachy Girl, Yolonda Brown, playing house in the skeletal frame of the half–finished house where she was murdered. She imagined her standing inside the two-by-fours and bare pipes of what would someday be a kitchen, pretending to cook dinner. She could see the moonlight highlighting the cinnamon freckles on her even lighter brown skin.

Sidney jumped when her imagination told her of a light, lilting voice telling everyone dinner was ready. She touched the bruises on her own face and thought about that life cut short. The girl did not deserve to have her throat slit from ear to ear on a cold cement floor, at fourteen.

Sidney crossed her arms in front of her and walked over to the mansion. She stepped slowly up the fluid marble stairs, lifted the heavy lion's head knocker, and let the cool metal fall from her fingers. It thudded heavily against the door. She heard steps, and the door opened. Jason stood looking at her, his wrinkled face gray and greasy in the dusk.

"May I help you?" he asked as if he had never seen her before.

"I need to talk to Samuel Haven," she replied.

This time, he didn't protest. He just turned back and left the door open for her to follow him. Samuel was in the study with Rupert. The glass doors to the garden opened to reveal red and purple flowers, which looked black in the darkness. A glass table in the corner was filled with white china plates and Waterford crystal goblets. Rupert stood up immediately when she entered, but Samuel remained seated. He looked up at Jason and Sidney with a chicken leg inches from his greasy mouth.

"What do you want?" he grunted.

"Hello, Counselor," Rupert bowed sarcastically from the waist. "I guess congratulations are in order."

Sidney strode into the room without being invited. Jason continued to stand there for a minute, opened his mouth as if to speak, then changed his mind and abruptly left the room. Samuel jerked the white linen napkin from the neck of his shirt. He threw the napkin on the table after wiping his hands. The legs of the chair scraped against the floor as he stood up.

"Can't you see we are eating dinner?" he asked her. He gulped wine from his goblet and regarded her above the rim. "Besides, you look like shit. You are spoiling my appetite. Good thing Marion and Dexter don't have to look at that face."

"Where are they, anyway?" Sidney asked.

"Sent there asses to Vicksburg to visit some friends of mine out there," Samuel said. "I didn't want Dexter feeling all guilty, and fucking things up."

"Samuel," Rupert said, disgusted. He turned to Sidney. "What may we do for you, Sidney?"

Sidney folded her arms without taking her eyes from Samuel. "You killed her, didn't you," she said, the question sounding more like a statement. She barely heard Rupert's gasp over Samuel's strangled laughter. Sidney continued, ignoring his laughter. "Dexter didn't kill her. And you didn't pay anyone to kill her like you did the Heater boy, either. *You* did it." Sidney took a step toward him. "You did it with your own two hands."

"Sidney, please," Rupert said, standing up from the table. "This is ludicrous."

Sidney turned her gaze to Rupert in surprise. "You really don't know, do you? How can you be so stupid? Go ahead, ask him."

All three of them stood paralyzed. Neither of them moved even when the phone rang hollowly on Samuel's desk. A delicate breeze blew the doors slightly inward.

"Samuel." Rupert's voice was hoarse. "What is she talking about?"

Samuel ignored him. He walked toward Sidney. He stood so close to her, the sweet spicy scent of his cologne stung her nose.

"You can't prove a thing," he said.

"I can't believe you were willing to let your nephew take the wrap," she said, staring at him until he blinked. "You're an animal."

"Samuel," Rupert asked, "is it true?"

Samuel walked behind his desk. "I don't know what she's talking about."

"Don't lie," she said. "Wilma has been blackmailing you for years, hasn't she? About the Heater murder. We traced the money back to a Haven account. You paid to have C.D. killed, didn't you?"

"Samuel?" Rupert questioned.

"The man in the photograph." She turned to Rupert. "I didn't put it together until he tried to kill me, too. Samuel, he's your hired gun, isn't he? His name is Billy Shepard. We have the phone records."

"What picture?" Samuel challenged. "I don't know what the hell you are talking about."

"Oh, come on, Samuel," Sidney answered. "The photo I showed you and Rupert at his house. If I remember correctly, that's when you became so upset."

"I don't understand," Rupert leaned tiredly against the back of his chair. He looked like a man whose entire world had just crashed around him.

"Don't you get it?" she asked him. "He had been paying Wilma off for years. She knew he killed C.D. just like the rest of the town. But she is the only one who had enough proof or guts to blackmail him."

"You talked to Wilma?" Rupert said. "I heard she left."

"I didn't talk to her personally," Sidney explained, "but we have her, and she's safe. She's also willing to testify that she saw the man who killed C.D. in this very house with Samuel."

Samuel laughed then. "Who is going to believe that lying slut?" he asked.

"Don't be a fool, Samuel," she said. "They're already looking for the man who broke into my mother's house. It won't be long before they catch him, with Wilma's help. And whose skin do you think he will be worrying about when he's arrested. Yours? There's a question of the money you paid Wilma, too. We can trace it back to this family, if not directly to you."

"Shut up." Samuel's eyes blazed hatred. He opened the drawer on his desk.

"But why kill the girl?" Rupert asked, beginning to believe Sidney.

"Because," she answered for Samuel, without taking her

eyes away from his florid face. "She threatened him, too. Not for murdering C.D., though. She threatened to tell the entire town they were sleeping together."

Not knowing for sure if this were true, Sidney held her breath, waiting for a response, wearing the poker face she usually reserved for the courtroom. But Rupert answered before Samuel could speak.

"Samuel," Rupert exploded, "not that young girl! She was only fourteen."

"And you wanted to kill me because you found out I had been tracing the money, looking into your bank accounts. You knew I would make the connection." Sidney finished.

Samuel laughed again, a sound containing no humor. Beads of perspiration broke out on his forehead. "You give yourself too much credit," he admitted. "I wanted you dead because I wanted to wipe out the little piece of filth my brother made." He walked from behind his desk holding a stubby pistol—the barrel a black rose blooming from his white hand.

Sidney laughed disbelieving, and shook her head. "What are you going to do, shoot me? You'll never get away with it. Besides, you are already caught, Samuel."

"For a lawyer," he answered, "you are pretty naïve. If I'm already caught, what have I got to lose? And I'll deny everything—Heater, that slut—everything. All I need is a good lawyer, right?"

"Then why shoot me?" Sidney asked.

"Because, little girl, you are getting on my nerves. It will give me great satisfaction of getting at least one of you out of my sight."

He waved the gun at Rupert. "I will say you came into my house uninvited, throwing wild accusations about. You tried to kill me. This whole town knows how you feel about the Havens. I was defending myself. I even have a witness."

"No. Samuel. No," Rupert said. "This has got to stop."

"And it will, my friend, right here and now," Samuel answered.

He pointed the gun at Sidney. Fear prevented her from moving. Suddenly, Rupert ran in front of Samuel and grabbed the wrist holding the gun. They struggled. Sidney watched the men in horror; then she heard the gun go off. Rupert eyes widened in surprise as he crumpled to the floor in a heap.

With a horrendous effort, Sidney took a step backward without taking her eyes from Samuel Haven. She turned and ran for the open garden doors which flopped almost closed behind her. Samuel fired another shot, and Sidney heard one of the glass doors shatter.

She tripped over a rose bush. Her hands and the left side of her cheek burned as she slid against the gravel strips separating the flowers. She tried to rise, but realized her legs had somehow become tangled in the long vines of the rose bush. Sitting back on her hands, she frantically kicked her legs free. She saw Samuel run toward her from the house.

She sprang upward and sprinted toward the woods at the back of the mansion. The branches whipped her face, and Samuel crashed after her like a stampeding elephant. All of a sudden, she stood in a clearing. She heard Samuel stop behind her, and the clicking sound of a gun being cocked.

She covered her face when she heard a sound like a tire backfiring. She waited for the sting of the bullet. When it did not come, she looked up. Samuel lay on the ground holding a wound in his fleshy gut. Blood spurted from his fingers. She looked past him to see Jacob standing about ten feet away. A bit of smoke curled from the barrel of his own .357 Magnum. His eyes were like flint.

Epilogue

The half-finished house where Yolonda was murdered stood barren. Not a piece of equipment to finish the house occupied the gravel yard. Not a wheelbarrow, not a ladder. Even the piles of lumber had been cleaned up. This house would never be 1686 Easterbrook Drive.

After Samuel's arrest, the builders had decided to level the entire house and build a small playground for the neighborhood children. Reverend Robinson's church had even raised enough money to have a small memorial placed there for Yolonda.

As Sidney walked from would-be room to would-be room, she was glad the place would be torn down. She could almost feel Yolonda's ghost wisping around the beams. This was *her* house. And it was only fitting that Yolonda should take it with her. Sidney stood in the living room, looking down at the place that once held Yolonda's body.

"I hope you are at peace, Peachy Girl," she whispered to the cool cement floor.

Both Rupert and Samuel lived. The accidental bullet passed harmlessly through Rupert's shoulder. Samuel was protected by his fleshy gut from the bullet Jacob fired to save her life. She had tried to see Rupert in the hospital, to thank him, but the man would not take any visitors. And Samuel. Samuel was going to prison, and if the state did not kill him, he would surely die there of old age.

She walked out into the light, trying not to think of the other man she did not have the courage to thank. When she had decided to leave Haven, she did not want anything to get in her way. So she kissed her mother good-bye, *until next time,* she told her.

Then she went to Miss Johnie Mae, who greeted her with a hug and a peace in her eyes that Sidney knew she would never forget. The man who had murdered her grandson was safely stored away in a Vicksburg jail, waiting to be moved to Haven for trial. Sidney hoped like hell that this time, the prosecutor would get a change of venue.

Sidney sat on the curb, and rested her chin on her hands. She watched a piece of plastic tumble down the quiet street in the warm wind. Just as she was about to rise, she saw Jacob drive up in his Mustang.

It seemed an eternity before he turned off the ignition and strode over to her.

"How did you know I was here?" she asked him without looking up.

"I'm a detective, remember?" he asked, then sat down beside her.

"My mother told you," Sidney said, understanding.

"No, your mother said you had gone to the airport," he said as he reached over and gently turned her face toward him. "I figured you would be here. Don't I even rate a good-bye?'' he asked as she pulled away, and stood up.

"Good-bye," Sidney answered, still not looking at him. It felt as if there were leg weights on her ankles as she walked slowly over to her car. Jacob's large black hand covered hers as she placed it on the door handle. Only the chatter of crickets heralding the approaching night broke the silence. He put his other hand around her waist, and bent until his lips were just touching her ear.

"You are just going to run away?" he whispered.

"I didn't know I was running," she responded. "Now, if you don't mind, I have a plane to catch."

"And if I ask you to stay?"

"I'll still have a plane to catch," she answered.

He dropped his hands away from her as if he had been burned. He stepped back to stare at her, and put both hands in his pockets. Sidney turned to face him and raised her eyes to meet his.

"I need some time," she told him softly.

His own eyes remained unreadable.

"You could stay with me tonight, and still leave tomorrow," he finally ventured.

Sidney let out a short, breathless laugh. "If I do that," she said, "I won't want to leave."

He reached out, touched her arm, and guided her gently to him.

"That may not be so bad," he answered.

"I need some time," she repeated.

She heard him sigh. He let her go, and stepped back so she could get into her car. He closed the door for her, and leaned in the open window.

"You know, if this is the big kiss-off," he said, "I don't give up that easy."

Sidney squinted at him in the dying sunlight, "I know," she said simply. Jacob smiled.

"But I'm not waiting forever," he warned.

She started the ignition, still looking at him. She put her foot on the brake, and the car in drive. There was the slightest glimmer of a smile on her face.

"I know," she finally said. She let her foot off the brake, and slowly began to roll forward into the street. Jacob took his hands off the car and watched as it sped away. He continued watching as nightfall spread gently over the half-finished house that would someday be a memorial for a young girl who had once dared to dream.

ABOUT THE AUTHOR

Faye Snowden grew up in the south, but left after high school to join the United States Navy. She traveled extensively in the Navy and had the opportunity to live in Italy for two years. After returning to the States, she left the Navy and went to work as a computer professional for a large retail grocery and drugstore chain. Throughout her career, she continued to pursue writing and has published several poems as well as a short story. She currently lives in northern California with her husband and two young sons, where she is writing full-time.

A World of Eerie Suspense
Awaits in Novels by Noel Hynd

__Cemetery of Angels   0-7860-0261-1 $5.99US/$6.99CAN
Starting a new life in Southern California, Bill and Rebecca Moore
believe they've found a modern paradise. The bizarre old tale about
their house doesn't bother them, nor does their proximity to a graveyard
filled with Hollywood legends. Life is idyllic…until their beloved son
and daughter vanish without a trace.

__Rage of Spirits   0-7860-0470-3 $5.99US/$7.50CAN
A mind-bending terrorist has the power to change the course of world
history. With the President in a coma, it's fallen to hardboiled White
House press aide William Cochrane to unearth the old secrets that can
prevent catastrophe. After an encounter with a New England psychic,
he finds himself descending deeper into the shadowy world between
this life and the next…

__A Room for the Dead   0-7860-0089-9 $5.99US/$6.99CAN
With only a few months to go before his retirement, Detective Sgt. Frank
O'Hara faces the most impossible challenge of his career: tracking
down a killer who can't possibly exist—not in this world, anyway. Could
it be the murderous psychopath he sent to the chair years before? But
how? A hair-raising journey into the darkest recesses of the soul.

Call toll free **1-888-345-BOOK** to order by phone or use this
coupon to order by mail.

Name _____

Address _____

City _____ State _____ Zip _____

Please send me the books I have checked above.

I am enclosing	$_____
Plus postage and handling*	$_____
Sales tax (in New York and Tennessee only)	$_____
Total amount enclosed	$_____

*Add $2.50 for the first book and $.50 for each additional book.
Send check or money order (no cash or CODs) to:
Kensington Publishing Corp., 850 Third Avenue, New York, NY 10022
Prices and Numbers subject to change without notice.
All orders subject to availability.
Check out our website at **www.kensingtonbooks.com**